NICE WEREWOLVES DON'T BITE VAMPIRES

A HALF-MOON HOLLOW NOVEL

MOLLY HARPER

Nice Werewolves Don't Bite Vampires
Copyright © 2020 by Molly Harper
Ebook ISBN: 9781641971560
KDP POD ISBN: 9798689274263
IS POD ISBN: 9781641972079

NYLA Publishing
121 W 27th St., Suite 1201, New York, NY 10001
http://www.nyliterary.com

ACKNOWLEDGMENTS

My sincerest appreciation to the readers who continue to offer their support to this series. Thank you to my children, who were so patient and cooperative while we were all stuck at home together – homeschooling, Mom working, Dad working. It could have been a mess. But you worked hard and I am very proud of you. Thank you to all of the writer friends who have supported me and kept me sane over text while we all tried to navigate this weird new reality – Jeanette, Lish, Jenn, Anna, Kathleen, Jaye, Nicole, Melissa, Kristen, Robyn. I appreciate you all so much. And thanks, as always, to Natanya Wheeler, who is an amazing agent and human being.

"Find a way to honor the trappings of your youth without clinging to them. This is especially true if you grew up in an era of the ruff collar or parachute pants."
—*A Gentleman in Any Era: An Ancient Vampire's Guide to Modern Relationships*

*P*eople who said libraries were a useless and outdated relic of the pre-Internet age had never spent time around the McClaine pack.

The Half-Moon Hollow Public Library might have been a dinosaur. But it was a silent dinosaur. A "keep-me-from-losing-from-my-freaking-mind-due-to-my-loud-ass-family-osaurus."

Maybe calling it a "dinosaur" was unfair. The place certainly hadn't seen new public funding in a few years. The most recent addition was the Jane Jameson-Nightengale Youth Reading Room, which was marked with a rather showy brass plaque very close to the head librarian's office. But the computers in the lab were less than five years old. The gray industrial carpet was worn, but not shabby, the dust pilling ever so slightly around the edges of the floor-to-ceiling walnut shelving. And I did recognize some of the titles from the last few years' best-seller lists, probably also donated by Jane Jameson-Nightengale. Her name seemed to be on a lot of plaques around the building, most of them within the direct eyeline of the head librarian's office.

Something about that seemed to be a little vindictive. But having met Mrs. Stubblefield, the head librarian with the inexplicably aggressive eyebrows, that made sense.

Mrs. Stubblefield seemed to think the library was her kingdom to rule. She'd reminded me multiple times that the library didn't allow "loitering" at the private study carrels— despite the fact that I had a laptop with me and was very clearly working. As a werewolf, I respected her need to protect her territory. As someone who depended on the library for a quiet workspace to earn their living, it was deeply annoying.

Living on the pack compound, surrounded by the constant noise and interruptions of my large extended family, going to the library was the only peace I got all day. I tried working from a café, using a secure wi-fi hotspot to protect my clients' privacy while I designed their social media, email campaigns, and other digital promotional materials. But the constant motion from other customers, plus needing to pack up my stuff every time I left for the restroom, was a non-starter. It was just easier to work in the library, where there was less "traffic." The locking study carrels—another contribution from Jane Jameson-Night-engale—were quiet and clean and comfortable. My productivity had skyrocketed when I started sneaking to the library in the afternoons several times a week.

My phone grumbled inside my precious backpack, a sturdy blue camouflage model I'd carried since high school. I'd set it up to sound like a growl when the text was from my family. I was sure it was a message from my mama, asking where I was. I glanced at the clock on my computer screen. It was after eight. Where had my time gone? It felt like I'd just gotten here! I rolled my shoulders. Nope, apparently, I'd been in this position for far too long.

The project I was working on—social media headers for a small bed-and-breakfast in upstate New York that themed itself around a Medieval Celtic romantic imagery—needed help. The owners kept insisting on using a specific stock photo of a sword, but it simply didn't look right to me. The carvings on the hilt just didn't have the sort of patterns I'd seen in Celtic weapons. It looked more like Viking swords I'd seen on TV shows, all pointy runes and triangles. But knowing these diffi-cult-but-always-prompt-with-payments clients as I did, I was going to have to have evidence on my side if I was going to convince them that they were wrong.

I stood from the comfortable desk chair, cracking my spine back into place. I rarely ventured into the stacks unless it was for reference material. Sometimes clients wanted to center their promotional messages around some strange detail that was not accurate. I liked being able to check actual physical books written by experts—as opposed to online image searches—to prevent that embarrassment for them…and for me.

While they may not have liked being told when they were wrong (and sometimes "super-wrong"), it was my attention to that sort of thing that kept my clients coming back for repeat business. I'd developed a solid reputation for engaging, afford-able, and *correct* work. Sure, there were plenty of platforms out there that helped not quite computer-literate people design their own graphics and such. But for small business owners who already had enough on their plate, it was easier to just pay my very reasonable rates to bring clients to their doors.

I slipped my phone into my back pocket, just as it growled a second time. I wouldn't respond to my mother's text, because that would only mean pointless arguing until I left earlier than planned. My time would be better spent wrapping up for the day and then texting her on my run home. I closed the small study carrel door behind me and punched in my temporary code to protect my stuff, silently blessing the name of Jane Jameson-Nightengale—even though she wasn't exactly a favorite around my household.

Jane, who I'd only met in passing when I was a kid, was a close friend of my cousin. Jolene had been the pack's pride and joy until she'd married a human, had his adorable children, and moved a whole ten miles away from the packlands. Well, Jolene was still pretty much the pack's pride and joy, but my relatives grumbled under their breath about her a lot more often— usually involving the phrase "such a shame." Jane was (unfairly) blamed for this.

Turning out of the study carrels, I narrowly missed bumping into a guy around my age, wearing a hoodie and jeans.

"Sorry," I murmured, brushing past him without looking up. I had to move with purpose if I was going to finish this assignment and get home on time.

As I passed the European History section, I saw two teenage boys wrestling around, bumping against the bookshelf while they fought to look at woodcuttings of nude women from the Dark Ages.

This was one of many reasons why I'd rarely dated in high school.

What were so many teenage boys even doing at the library on a Friday night? That was suspicious in itself. Shouldn't they be in a nearby field somewhere with an illegally-obtained keg, shouting "wooooo?" I knew why *I* was at a library on a Friday night. I was avoiding my house and pursuing cash. I liked cash. It was silent, dependable, and never judged you for not having a social life.

Rolling my eyes, I turned my back on the disruptive goofballs and walked into the weapons section. I crouched, scanning the bottom shelf for an illustrated guidebook to swords throughout history. I'd used it for a report on warfare in the Renaissance period when I attended Half-Moon Hollow High. There was a comforting sort of consistency to that book still being there seven years later. Being able to count on the little things was one of the perks of living in the Hollow. It almost outweighed the many, many drawbacks.

The teenage tussle behind me continued and I blocked it out to focus on the book in front of me. It was a skill I'd developed as a teenager, very useful when trying to ignore about a dozen people all trying to tell you how you should be running your life over Sunday dinner.

Opening the thick reference guide, I studied the illustration diagramming the various parts of Celtic swords versus Viking swords. The photo my clients wanted to use was definitely Viking. And even if it was a beautiful image, they couldn't use it. People delighted in calling companies out on inaccuracies like this—especially history enthusiasts, who were very quick to pick up on social media gaffes, no matter what era. Sometimes, those gaffes made you famous for the wrong reasons.

I took my phone out of my pocket and took a picture of the pages showing examples of both swords. I sent an email to the client, explaining that we couldn't use their preferred stock photo, but I would find a historically accurate image they would love just as much by tomorrow. Still concentrating on careful email phrasing, I heard a grunt behind me and what sounded like an appendage—an elbow?—thumping against book spines. My head whipped toward the noise.

Several things happened all at once. The bookshelf behind me wobbled, despite being almost floor-to-ceiling. A literal ton of wood and paper was clearly no match against the adolescent desire to see block-printed boobs. Several extremely heavy books on the last legal duels in Kentucky—I could see the titles on the spines as if they were frozen in time

—tumbled towards me. All I could think to do was drop the sword guide, cover my head and hope I didn't get knocked out. My ears detected lightning quick steps against the worn carpet just to my right. The soft, woodsy scent of cedar with the crisp edge of some sort of resin filled my nose and I felt my heart *squeeze*—though honestly, I wasn't sure if it was the lovely smell or if I was having some sort of book-related cardiac event.

From under my arm, I saw a tall, dark-haired man dashing toward me, hands outstretched. I waited for the impact of the books against my skull, but despite the rain of reference material hitting the carpet all around me, the weight never landed on me. Dropping my arms hesitantly, I looked up and saw the man crouched over me. In his large hands, he held the books that should have been scattered on top of my unconscious body.

While sheets of music were littered around our feet like fallen snow, he held the books in a neat stack on his palms. He looked so calm, as if it was no big deal that he'd plucked falling hardbacks from mid-air. His eyes, a light shade of hazel surrounded by a darker ring, met mine and his generous mouth parted to say something. Because my brain seemed to be fixating on weird little details, I got completely absorbed in the thin, dark moustache on his upper lip. Normally, I automatically assigned men with moustaches in the creeper category, but on him…it worked. He was older than me, again, not to creeper levels, but enough for me to appreciate it.

I reached up to touch his face, to trace the sharp curve of his cheek and the soft flesh of his lip with my thumb. I wanted to wallow in the sweet woodsy scent of him, to roll around with him, until I could smell nothing else for the rest of my life. This was the way a person was *supposed* to smell, all complex warmth sending rippling energy along my nerves. And the pulse of that energy spelled out the word *"WANT"* like Morse Code in my belly. For the first time, I wanted to take advantage of the seclusion of the library stacks, drag him to the farthest corner and see what was hidden under those maddeningly practical clothes.

He spoke, but I had no idea what he was saying. I was too distracted by the roar of blood in my ears and the flash of his supernaturally white fangs. Well, everything made a lot more sense now. It was easy to defy the laws of physics when you were a vampire.

The idiot teens were now fighting over who was responsible for knocking into the books, meaning more bumping against the shelf. Over the vampire's shoulder—wow, those were some broad shoulders—the bookshelf continued to sway back and forth, picking up momentum as it pitched forward. I shot to my feet and planted my shoulder against the shelf with an "oof," easing it back up as yet more books fell to the floor. Miraculously, those books didn't hit us, either.

It took all of my considerable upper body strength to push the shelves back into position. He grinned at me as I gripped the shelving, preventing it from overcorrecting and knocking into the shelf behind it. The last thing I needed was for Mrs. Stubblefield to find me in a mess of Three Stooges-style domino-ed bookshelves. That would not help my whole workplace situation.

This time I was able to hear the vampire say, "You're rather fast on your feet, aren't you?"

"Well, you saved me from a concussion first. It's only neighborly that I return the favor." I smiled, surprising even myself. I was not the kind of girl that came up with clever lines on the fly.

Usually, in an awkward situation like this, I froze up and let one of my louder family members take over the conversation. But I was able to pronounce all of my words clearly and smoothly, like I talked to attractive strangers every day. In a tone that was downright cheeky, I added, "Us supernaturals should stick together."

His smile widened, his eyes becoming warmer. "I've noticed that sort of hospitality since I relocated here. It's very refreshing. I've lived in many places that...weren't as friendly, particularly to vampires."

"Well, just be careful around other weres. We're not all hot dishes and welcome wagons. I'm sort of the exception to the rule," I said with a weird-sounding giggle. With growing dread, I realized I'd just exhausted my supplies of smoothness. It would all be downhill from here. I cleared my throat. "Not that you're probably into hot dishes that much, what with vampire digestion...or lack of it. Also, I've heard not-great things about the vampire welcome wagon situation here in town. Be wary of vampires bearing gift baskets."

I pressed my lips together because that was an awful lot of words. But in another unexpected turn, rather than looking disturbed by my verbal disgorgement, he threw his head back and laughed. Not in a "laughing at me" way, but "laughing with me." I'd made him laugh! Simple pleasure, bright and warm, bloomed in my chest.

Damn, he was pretty. And he hung out at libraries. Who did that?

Besides me, that is.

Meanwhile, the boys were still fighting. The shelf I'd just corrected trembled as the taller one threw his friend against the Asian History section.

The vampire rolled his eyes. "Oh, for pity's sake."

I snorted. He sounded like a hero in one of those historical BBC movies I had to hide in my room like porn, to keep my parents from mocking my "fancy" choices. He held up his hand, not quite touching my shoulder. "Excuse me for a moment, miss. Please don't go anywhere, I'd like to continue—"

The shelf rattled hard. I held up a hand to steady it.

He huffed out an unnecessary breath and ducked around the bookshelf. I took out my phone and checked the time. I needed to go. As if my mama could hear my thoughts, my cell phone vibrated to life in my hand. At the sight of my mother's photo on my screen, I shook my head and hit the "deny" button. "Nope."

I tiptoed through the minefield of fallen books and sheet music, careful not to step on any of the fragile covers. As much as I would have liked to score points with Mrs. Stubblefield and help clean them up, I should have been home already. My parents started asking intrusive questions if I put off going home too much. They had no idea what I did with my time outside of the house. If I didn't go to a brick-and-mortar building—preferably one owned by family members, where I could be closely supervised—I didn't have a real job, as far they were concerned. And any time I tried to explain I had an Internet-based job, they immediately jumped to thinking I was doing something inappropriate or that I was just goofing off. My daddy made a lot of comments about "those dumb dragon games" I played online. I didn't actually play online games. No judgements - they just weren't my thing. But if that's what he wanted to believe, fine. I made a pretty good living and with no rent to pay, I had a considerable nest egg and could afford little extras like my laptop. And it was a lot more fun than working at my Uncle Hank's butcher shop. It was certainly less bloody.

As I scurried away to the study carrel, I heard scuffling from the other side of the bookshelf. I unlocked the door and stuffed all of my belongings into my backpack. When I came out, the vampire was standing by the front desk, holding both boys by the collar, immobile as they tried to squirm away. He was speaking to Mrs. Stubblefield, giving the boys a gentle (by vampire standards) shake occasionally to make a point. I tried to catch his attention to at least wave goodbyes, but he was wholly focused on Mrs. Stubblefield...or maybe her eyebrows. They were like two gray, hairy exclamation points on her forehead. I knew I had trouble looking away when I talked to her.

My phone buzzed again. Another impatient text from
Mama. *"Where are you?! You better answer this phone now!!!"*

I winced. Mama was not one for text speak, but she was one
for excessive punctuation.

I glanced back toward the checkout desk and the handsome
stranger with the velvety voice. Who was I kidding? Why would
I need to stay to talk to him? It wasn't like this attractive
stranger was going to ask me out for...did vampires drink
coffee? It didn't matter. I doubted I would see him again. My life
was too complicated for that sort of connection. I needed to get
home, and *quickly.*

With one last look at the vampire's back, I hurried out of the
library and into the street. It would take me about twenty
minutes to jog home—ten if I ran at full speed.

My pocket buzzed and somehow, it sounded angrier.

Full speed it was, then.

I ducked between the library and the courthouse, into the
less desirable area of the Hollow's town proper. It was shocking,
really, how close the woods edged the more vital areas of town.
I wasn't the toughest member of the pack, or the fiercest, but I
was the fastest.

When I reached the tree line, I slipped out of my clothes and
stuffed them into my backpack with my phone and laptop. I
secured the straps around my shoulders and clipped the belt
around my chest so it would stay on my back when I changed
into my other form.

I rolled my shoulders, glancing up at the moon. Just another
Friday night, running naked in the woods.

I tried buying a car when I was nineteen, scrupulously
saving my earnings at the butcher shop until I had enough for a
used Ford sedan the color of spilled beer. I sold it within a year.
Every time I turned around, my aunts and cousins had
borrowed the keys without asking or my daddy had insisted
that someone should use the car for some random errand

because "pack shares with pack." Eventually, it was just easier to sell the car to a distant cousin to avoid the frustration, and save my gas and insurance money.

As usual, shifting into a wolf felt far more comfortable than my human skin, like shedding an itchy wool sweater. I shook out my sleek chestnut fur, stretching the muscles I would need on a run over land I knew as well as the back of my human hand. My phone buzzed insistently in my backpack, reminding me that I didn't have time to relish just how *good* this felt.

Scanning the area one last time for people or predators, I bounded through the trees and followed the scent of *home.* My paws slipped over the soft grass silently and the wind tickled at my sensitive ears. Scent and sound and sight blended into one sense, channeling information into my hind brain—the rustling of potential prey under the brush, the light of the moon against the leaves, exhaust from cars on the faraway interstate. It was like trying to read a dozen books simultaneously, all at once distracted and laser-focused. *Home* was the only thing that could keep me from following the myriad of prey scents that flared across my nose.

As I loped over what my cousins called the "wrassling hill," the McClaine pack compound came into view. The McClaines were among the first to settle in Half-Moon Hollow, choosing to stay far away from the early human settlements and stick to our own. Though my family was sinfully proud of it, the compound was nothing fancy, an ancient farmhouse surrounded by a neat array of trailers on nearly seventy acres that stretched all the way to the Ohio River. The trailers stood in varying states of repair and the pickup trucks had seen better days, but as my Uncle Lonnie liked to say, "They're paid for, and that's what counts."

Still, we were better off than some packs, who had to sell off their territories as the wilds of the world shrunk and poverty was an ever-looming threat. People talked about the disappearing middle class without realizing exactly how bad things were getting for were-creatures in this new modern world. While there were a precious few werewolves who could stand to live in crowded cities, to attend college and become doctors and lawyers, most of us remained pretty blue collar. The sort of jobs werewolves could do without losing our damn minds—mechanic work, farming, anything that kept us outdoors and out of an office—were changing so fast that we couldn't keep up. And so, some packs were forced to sell their land to developers to keep the *metaphorical* wolves from the door.

All you had to get my old Uncle Creed cussing was say the words "gated community."

Werewolves were the most highly evolved were species and underwent the most complete, dependable changes. We also had the most stable social hierarchy, so our lives were a bit easier to balance between the two forms. Each pack had an Alpha male mated to an Alpha female, who controlled their packs through a combination of biological imperative and social conditioning. While their "subjects"—like my parents—had all of the property rights and general free will of any regular person, all major decisions had to be approved by the Alpha couple. Everything from mate selection to major (or sometimes, minor) purchases had to be deemed for the good of the pack to be acceptable.

Our Alpha couple, my Uncle Lonnie and his wife, Mimi, lived in the trailer closest to the old farmhouse, which had mostly been used as a communal meeting space since the family outgrew it decades before. My daddy technically should have been Alpha as eldest son of the previous Alpha and Lonnie's older brother, but he'd been overlooked after he'd left the pack-lands to wander. By some strange instinctive magic, leaving had stripped Daddy of his authority and transferred it to Uncle Lonnie. Personally, I'd always thought Lonnie did a much better job than my father would have done. He was fair, but firm, with a kindness in manner that made you *want* to do as he asked. And yes, he bothered to ask, which could not be said of all Alphas.

Of course, I never voiced these thoughts in front of my parents. That would lead nowhere good.

After years of his wandering, Daddy came back mated to my mama, who was carrying me. While Lonnie accepted Daddy back, it was just "understood" that Daddy's place in the pack was tenuous. My whole life, I'd heard Daddy rail about being given a spot on the far end of the land, how he'd been edged out, rejected. Our placement may have allowed Daddy his privacy, but in his eyes, it was also a daily reminder that he'd never be fully accepted back into the pack.

So, the situation had soured long before I was born into it. I was an only child, an anomaly in werewolf society, and not the much-desired son – which only added to Daddy's list of perceived slaps from the universe. We were an alarmingly fertile bunch, which was why there were so many trailers on the compound. Our three-person family unit was just another thing that made us "odd."

Secretly, I'd always been grateful for it. Crowding more people into our house definitely wouldn't have made it a happier home.

I whuffed off the calls of the uncles and aunts who were out on their front decks, enjoying the soft spring air. Uncle Eagan commented on how I was out late, with that tone that managed to express disapproval, along with genuine concern. Aunt Paulene asked if I'd eaten yet with the same fretting anxiety she always had: that any member of the younger generation would drop dead if she didn't cram them full of carbs every three hours.

I stopped just in front of my family's trailer. White and laminate paneling, it certainly wasn't the nicest one on the compound, but it wasn't the worst-off. (That particular honor belonged to my cousin Vance, whose moldy "bachelor pad" would be condemned by any health inspector with eyes and sense.) But Mama made an effort to spruce it up, planting bulb flowers around the stoop and hanging a pretty windchime she'd made from tumbled bits of old glass Coke bottles.

I ducked around the corner of the trailer to shift back to two legs and put on my clothes. Generally speaking, nudity was no big deal for a werewolf. Clothes just got in the way when you were trying to shift back and forth between two forms. But I didn't enjoy seeing my family members naked, so I was a little more careful of where and when I was dressed. Fortunately, my parents felt pretty much the same, at least, if we were in the house.

Though the windows were lit, the trailer was silent aside from the screech of the front door. Normally, the TV would be blasting some sort of sports channel or one of Mama's game shows. Maybe they'd decided I warranted the cold shoulder and decided to go to bed early? No—the last time they'd done that, they'd shut the trailer door with one of those anti-theft Club things and I'd had to sleep in my car.

"Tylene McClaine!"

Shit.

Like a lot of female McClaines over the last two generations, my name ended in some form of "lene." Because my daddy was Tyler, I was Tylene. Still, I was better off than my poor cousin, Eugenelene.

"Where have you been?" my father thundered from where my parents were seated at the dinette set with two of my aunties, Lurlene and Braylene. Oh, hell.

Petite and cherubic with meticulously dyed auburn curls, Braylene had had three cubs by the time she was my age. She included that little factoid in almost every conversation we had. She even wrote it in my birthday card once. Lurlene had been a great beauty in her time, blessed with what she called an "hour-glass figure." She'd had her pick of mates from the best packs and never let anyone forget it. Of all my aunts, Lurlene and Braylene were the most "involved." They didn't like how I dressed, how I spoke, how I refused their constant advice. (I much preferred Aunt Paulene and her endless carbs.)

When I was younger, I'd learned how to quietly fade into background of the pack, easy enough to do when everybody else was so damn *loud*. My parents were lucky I was a good kid who was more interested in my schoolwork than the bad choices available to me as a teenager in a rural area. But once I graduated, it was if I popped back up on the pack's radar and they started questioning what I was going to do with my life, when I was going to settle down, get serious about my role in the pack. My aunts and uncles, for the most part, weren't content with my plans for community college and a job I enjoyed.

In general, werewolf attitudes towards social justice may have evolved over the last century or so, but it took much longer for my relatives to adjust to the idea that I might want something more from life than marriage to a big strong male who could provide for me and the children I would bear for him.

When I didn't immediately change this attitude, they'd taken to ambushing me with makeovers and "sons of friends" visiting from nearby territories. I tensed, scanning the trailer for the sight or scent of an unknown male.

When I didn't see a stranger, or a set of hot rollers , I relaxed ever so slightly and smiled, like I didn't have a care in the world.

I hadn't done anything wrong tonight, not even by werewolf standards. Okay, sure, I was about to lie...but that hadn't happened yet. My whole life was spent dancing on the edge of this sort of subtle distinction. "I was out with some friends from school."

"What friends? You haven't talked about friends in months," Daddy scoffed, rising from his seat. Like most McClaine men, he was huge, well over six feet tall and still fairly muscled for a man in his early fifties. Deep, unhappy lines bracketed his mouth, the roadmap of his unsatisfying life. My mother sat, quietly working through a crossword puzzle book, as if her husband wasn't hollering to wake up the whole pack just a few feet from her face. I'd watched over the years as she'd perfected her little bubble of concentration, impervious to noise or tension or the verbal barbs from my aunts. Unfortunately, the bubble had also hardened against her daughter's discontent a long time ago.

"Where were you?" Daddy demanded.

"I was at the library with *friends*," I told him.

He burst out laughing. "What the hell would you be doing at the library on a Friday night?"

"Reading?" I suggested.

"A girl your age should be on a date," Aunt Braylene said, shelling peas into an old stoneware bowl. "What happened with that Scottie? Darla's boy? I gave him your phone number. Or do you kids just talk over the texting now?"

I clamped my lips together to keep my expression neutral. I'd agreed to *one* date with Scottie Briggs. He'd been so handsy, I'd barely escaped the movie theatre without popcorn butter-flavored handprints on my ass. I would not subject myself or my jeans to that again.

A headache started to bloom behind my eyes.

"It didn't work out," I said vaguely.

"You know, when I was your age, girls didn't hide in their rooms behind computer screens. If you want to catch a man, you're going to have to work for it," Braylene told me.

I shrugged. "I'm good. Really."

Lurlene looked sincerely offended. "You need to think about your future. You know, your daddy isn't gonna put a roof over your head forever."

I had a lot of opinions on this topic. I'd been willing to move out for years. I'd even tried a few times, only to cancel my plans when my parents claimed it would somehow make their position in the pack even worse. So, my secret savings account grew right along with my frustrations. Daddy glared at me hard enough not to bring those opinions up.

"Why don't you come on over to my place tomorrow? We can freshen up your hairstyle a little bit, make you over," Braylene pressed, with a significant look towards Mama and her dishwater blond hair. "You were lucky enough to get the McClaine coloring, honey, but you gotta take full advantage."

"I'll think about it," I promised, angling my body towards my room, so I could make my escape as soon as possible. I would not submit to another torture session in the chair Lurlene's oldest son had ripped out of a defunct hair salon. Last time, she'd damn near given me a perm.

"Well, what else do you have goin?" Lurlene asked. "Hank said that you're not signed up for a shift at the butcher shop. Or the bait shop. Or the towing business. What are you gonna do with yourself all weekend?"

"I have homework," I lied again smoothly. Community college coursework had been my go-to excuse for years. And while I did have a few associates degrees under my belt, including computer science and marketing, I hadn't taken actual classes in about six months. My parents didn't need to know that.

"Oh, honey, community college isn't gonna get you anywhere you want to go," Braylene said. "If working for family is good enough for your cousins, it's good enough for you. You know how busy the butcher shop is on weekends."

"Angelene met her husband while she was working at the butcher shop," Lurlene added.

"Angelene's husband thinks he's gonna make money off of selling homemade batteries!" I retorted.

"He says it's all about who you know," Braylene said, shaking her head.

"Pardon me if that isn't exactly what I'm looking for in a mate," I huffed.

"Well, you're never gonna find one if you're so all-fired picky," Lurlene shot back.

I objected, "It's not 'picky' to—"

Daddy cut me off with a gesture. "All right, all right, enough. I'm sure Tylene will come to her senses soon enough."

Braylene stood, picking up her bowl of peas. "You need to talk to that girl, Tyler."

She pulled Lurlene up by her elbow. Lurlene was trying to pull away, whispering to me, "Just some layers around your face maybe. Or some bangs! We could tease 'em real high!"

"With all due respect, Aunt Lurlene, I would rather be bald," I said quietly, shaking my head.

With the front door slamming behind my aunties, Daddy whirled on me. "I've had enough of that library bullshit, Tylene. I know when you're lying to me. Where were you? Were you with some boy we don't know? Go ahead and tell me. You know I could smell him on you if I wanted to."

Pointing out that at twenty-four, I should be spending time with *men*, not boys, was a point that would have been completely lost on my whole family. Instead, I chose to focus on the idea of my father literally trying to sniff out my sins.

"Oh, gross, that is a huge violation of privacy," I said, backing away from him.

"You live under my roof, so you follow my rules."

"Well, then maybe I shouldn't to be under your roof."

"Don't start that again, Tylene," Mama said quietly. "Until you're grown, your place is in our home. If you leave sooner, the whole pack will ask why. You'll put our place at risk."

"I am grown! I'm twenty-four years old! I have savings. I can pay my own bills, my own rent."

Mama rolled her eyes. "You know what we mean by 'grown!'"

"'Married' does not mean grown!"

"How do you all the sudden have all this money?" My father's eyes narrowed. "Who's been giving you money?"

I gritted my teeth and took a big breath through my nose. These arguments were always so circular, not to mention pointless, because they never listened to a word I said anyway. "I don't suddenly have money. I've been saving it for years! I have more than enough to support myself. I could get out of your hair. You don't even like having me around. You think I can't tell when I'm not wanted? Trust me, I've picked up on the signs."

"What do you mean 'not wanted?'" Mama exclaimed. "We're your parents!"

"Okay, but most people move out from their parents' home by the time they're twenty!"

"Most *humans,* you mean," Daddy countered.

"I knew this was going to happen," Mama murmured. "I told you, when Jolene married that human, that she'd bring the whole pack down with her."

"This has nothing to do with Jolene," I groaned.

"Just look at this." Mama tossed a copy of the local newspaper onto the table. The headline read, *Beeline Abuzz: Hollow-based vampire concierge service expanding to five new cities.* When I failed to react—because I couldn't figure out what that had to do with us or Jolene—Mama rolled her eyes and flipped the paper over to show a photo of an event celebrating Beeline's "statewide launch." Mama stabbed a long finger into the background of the photo, where Jolene and Zeb seemed to be happily wrapped in a sort of group hug with the vampires.

"Your cousin's out there *in public*, huggin' a bunch of vampires like she doesn't have a care in the world," Mama huffed. "Like vampires haven't looked down their nose at us since before time began. Like everything is just rainbows and roses. And now she's corrupted you along with her."

"Mama, honestly, this has nothing do with Jolene."

"Y'all be careful when you talk about the Alpha's daughter," Daddy stepped between us and growled in a low voice. "She's still everybody's favorite, even if my brother should have disowned her the minute she moved off the packlands."

Considering Daddy's own wanderings, this seemed more than a little hypocritical. This was definitely not the time to bring that up.

"Tylene's always careful to stay on Jolene's good side," Mama said, her eyes begging me to help her change the subject. "She's watching the twins on Monday night for her. Aren't you, hon?"

I nodded. "They need a ride to some music class. Jolene's got a meeting she has to go to."

"See? That's the sort of thing we *want* to see you doing with your time. Helping out the pack," Daddy said, nodding, his mood suddenly lifted. "But when you're out, you answer your mama's calls, no matter what. And her texts. Otherwise, we come looking for you. And you know we can track you if we want to."

When I opened my mouth to argue, he cut me off with a sharp gesture. "End of discussion. Now, why don't you go on to bed? I'll ask Hank to come by to talk about your shift tomorrow morning."

"But—" He leveled me with a look and I clamped my lips shut. "Goodnight."

I turned on my heel and walked to my room. I was careful not to slam the door. I sank onto the bed and rubbed my hand over my face. I'd been having such a nice, quiet night. How had so much gone so wrong so quickly? I hated arguing with my parents. It was always so pointless and frustrating. And I knew, just like I knew that I'd accomplished nothing talking to them, that I would end up working that damn butcher shop shift the next morning. Because I would feel too guilty to tell my sweet Uncle Hank "no" to his face.

Robotically, I changed into my pajamas and got ready for bed. As I pulled the blankets up to my chin, I realized I hadn't looked for that replacement stock image for the sword. I would have to get up early to look for one in the morning.

I closed my eyes and the vampire's face floated to the surface of my mind. Never mind the fact that he was a gorgeous specimen of man...vampire...manpire? He'd been so *polite*—just unfailingly appropriate and considerate. How sad was it that I was so impressed by basic manners that was what I remembered about him?

It didn't matter. I doubted I would see him again.

2

"A stagnant vampire is a vampire who loses their will to live. Be open to new experiences. Otherwise, you're just wasting your eternity. Nobody likes an eternity waster."
—*A Gentleman in Any Era: An Ancient Vampire's Guide to Modern Relationships*

A vampire named Dick Cheney made me the best cappuccino I'd ever had.

My life was very strange.

I sat at the shiny maple bar at Specialty Books, scanning the shelves as I sipped my frothy coffee drink. After seeing Jane Jameson-Nightengale's name on library plaques over the years, it was sort of shocking to find myself inside her shop, with its comfortable purple chairs, restful purplish-blue walls and twinkling fairy lights. The air smelled of coffee and old paper and dried herbs inside the pots lining the back wall. I could also smell the tang of blood in the air, which was a little off-putting, but I found I didn't mind it all that much. It wasn't that different than hanging out at Hank's butcher shop.

Western Kentucky harbored a secret supernatural world that was downright magical that I never even knew about, and I was a freaking werewolf. How had I never visited this store in my twenty-four years? Of course, I knew that vampires were a thing. Vampires had even been part of human daily life for almost twenty years now, since a vampire accountant from Milwaukee decided to launch his species out of the coffin with a lawsuit.

Were-creatures were more reluctant, preferring to watch how the vampire Coming Out played for a few...decades. It turned out to be one of our more prudent decisions as a species, considering how immediately after finding out that they'd lived alongside the blood-sucking undead for centuries unawares, humans ran out to buy silver and stakes by the ton. If humans knew how many people around them could shift into any number of animals—bears, wolves, big cats, even skunks—I shuddered to imagine what they would do. Of course, no were wanted to admit that the vampires were braver than us. We chose to think of it as being "cautious."

But even with my more "liberal" supernatural education, I had no idea there was a treasure trove of supernatural literature guarded by the undead right in the middle of town. I'd heard Cousin Jolene talk about "the shop" before, but being so removed from that part of her life, I'd never connected it to the little store-front I'd driven past probably a million times. Even with the bright blue-violet awning, I'd sort of assumed it was a sketchy adult bookstore...Come to think of it, there *had* been an adult bookstore next door at one point. But I'd never imagined what a cozy, cheerful space was inside, lined with more books than even I could read.

Of course, I didn't spend a lot of time in this neighborhood. There were a lot of vampire-owned businesses here, not to mention its proximity to the local headquarters of the Council for the Equal Treatment for the Undead. And while I didn't have a problem with vampires, sometimes the older ones didn't much like my kind...except for that one vampire...who'd I thought about pretty much constantly since Friday. I hadn't returned to the library. I'd spent the weekend behind the counter at the butcher shop, taking customer orders and cleaning out the fridge cases. I liked to think I did enough cleaning to justify working so few days there.

In order to finish the Celtic email campaign, I ended up staying up past midnight, searching stock art sites over the weekend. I didn't hide under my covers with a flashlight and my laptop, but it was a near thing. The clients were happy. That was all that mattered.

"You need a warm-up?" Dick Cheney—the vampire, not the vice president—asked from behind the bar. He was definitely a different sort of vampire than "my" library vampire, handsome in a roguish way that I didn't quite trust, even though I wanted to snatch his *"In need of supervision"* t-shirt. And it felt like he didn't trust me, either. He'd watched me carefully for the past twenty minutes, as I'd waited for Jolene to show up with the twins for their Monday night class. I didn't know if it was because I was a werewolf in a vampire shop or because I was the first member of Jolene's family he'd met since her wedding all those years ago.

"I'm fine, thank you. It's delicious, just the right amount of milk." I drained the cup, carefully swiping my top lip for errant foam.

"Well, if you need anything, just let me know," Dick said, smiling awkwardly. Brow raised, I bent my head over my phone, scrolling through my Fiverr account for job offers. I had enough to keep me busy for the next few months, which was gratifying. I glanced up and caught him staring again, his expression concerned.

"Is everything all right?" I asked. "I'm not gonna steal anything, I swear. Jolene's told me all about you, and the rest of her friends here. I would never do anything to hurt friends of the pack."

"Oh, sweetheart, no!" He burst out laughing and patted my hand. It was curiously cool against my naturally warm skin, making me think of the library vampire again. Is this how his hands would have felt?

Nope, nope. Stop those thoughts right now.

"I know you wouldn't steal anything!" Dick exclaimed. "But I'm trying to find a way to say this without offending you."

"It's nice that you're concerned about that, but I'd rather you just come out with it."

"You smell like blood," he said. "Old blood, new blood, just lots of different kinds of blood, from different creatures. It's not all that unpleasant for me, but I just want to make sure—are you okay? Are you safe? Do I need to call someone?"

Now, it was my turn to laugh. "Oh, no! I worked in my family butcher shop this weekend and the smell kind of gets into your hair, your skin. I don't even notice it anymore."

"Oh, it's just butcher shop blood, that's good...which is a sentence I never thought I'd hear coming out of my mouth. I had this image in my head of trying to explain to Jolene that something was going on with her cousin and then she'd wolf out in the store. The cleanup involved." He paused and shuddered.

A pretty brunette woman stuck her head out of the office, a confused expression on her face. "What about butcher shop blood?"

"Oh, like that's the weirdest thing you've ever heard me say," Dick shot back.

"True enough." The woman walked out of her office, carrying a box of books on her hip.

"Jane, this is Jolene's cousin, Ty. Ty, this is—"

I stuck my hand out with what was probably too much enthusiasm. "Jane Jameson-Nightengale. I know. I spend a lot of time at the library. Thank you so much for everything you've donated. I get this weird feeling you only did it to mess with Mrs. Stubblefield, but it's made my life easier."

Jane grinned. "You're welcome...and you're very perceptive."

"I knew it!" I whispered, holding up my fist in triumph and making Jane giggle.

Behind me, the little cowbell over the door jangled and the shop was filled with what could only be described as "thundering chaos." Jolene McClaine-Lavelle herded two unnaturally tall eight-year-olds through the door as they chattered and bounced off of each other, the shelves, the stools. Joe, a serious boy with his father's sandy hair, was wheeling a cello case nearly as tall as he was. He was wearing a t-shirt that read, *"They told me I could be anything and I chose 'kid who plays a musical instrument the size of a car."* Janelyn's case fit under her arm. Her t-shirt read, *"Will trade sibling for a Stradivarius."*

They were beautiful children and just smart enough to be worrisome. And Uncle Lonnie and Aunt Mimi absolutely doted on them, meaning that no one in the pack dared do anything else.

"Hey, Twin Terrors!" Dick crowed as the children launched themselves over the counter with an agility that would have been impossible for entirely human children. They threw themselves at "Uncle Dick," and only his super-human strength kept him from toppling over into the scary copper espresso machine.

While I wasn't insecure about my looks, Jolene was widely acknowledged as the family beauty—the McClaine auburn hair, high cheekbones, wide green eyes and a figure only made lusher by bearing two babies. It was probably why my family was so embittered by Jolene's marriage. The McClaines could have forged a bond with some well-to-do pack with Jolene "on offer."

But instead, they saw her as being wasted on a goofy, affable human.

Secretly, I thought Zeb was a far better partner than any girl in my pack landed. He was funny and kind and didn't feel the need to prove that he was in charge all of the time. But I would never ever say that to my parents. I didn't want to know whether they believed they could ground me.

"It's all right," Jolene whispered out of the side of her mouth, picking up on my alarm as the kids crawled on the vampire like he was a jungle gym. "I know I don't bring the vampires around you much, but Dick and Andrea and the rest have spent just as much time with the kids, if not more, than the pack. They just love their Uncle Dick to death. Hell, they have sleepovers at Jane's every other weekend so Zeb and I can have a date night."

I suddenly remembered a very loud argument just after the twins were born, where the whole pack spent Thanksgiving unanimously freaking out because Zeb and Jolene asked Jane and Gabriel to babysit the kids. It had seemed very sensible to me, to leave your newborns with someone with super-sensitive hearing who didn't need to sleep at night. My relatives had not agreed.

Like this charming little nook of supernatural wonder, her relationship with these vampires was a whole piece of Jolene's life I didn't know about. And in our family, that was a damn miracle.

"I can't believe you went on the Internet specifically to get smartass string instrument t-shirts," Jolene muttered. She turned to Jane. "I told you to delete his Etsy account."

"Andrea says he keeps finding ways to set up new accounts. He's surprisingly tech savvy for a senior citizen."

"There's no limit to the number of email accounts you can open!" Dick said, while the kids hung off of his arms.

Jolene handed me a small musical case, while lugging a larger wheeled case up to the bar. "I really appreciate this, Ty. Zeb got elected to some sort of important staff committee for the school, poor soul, and I promised Jane I would attend this meeting for local supernatural muckity-mucks. Represent the pack, you know?"

You would never know it looking at them, but Dick and Jane *were* the big muckity-mucks with the local office of the Council for the Equal Treatment of the Undead. They were sort of like the Alphas of the local vampires, regulating their behavior, communicating with the human community and helping other supernatural species maintain their cover. According to Jolene, vampires were way less bite-y and way more socially responsible under their recent leadership.

"It won't be fun, but it *will* involve a really tedious and lengthy agenda," Jane chirped.

"Stretch, you've gotta stop trying to sell it with words like, 'tedious,'" Dick told her.

"I know," Jane admitted. "But Jolene's family. I don't like lying to her."

Hearing someone else calling Jolene "family" left me with an odd sensation in my chest—empty and sour. And to my surprise, I didn't feel possessive insult at the very idea that someone was trying to claim my cousin. It was a different sort of jealousy. Jolene had found a place here in the outside world, independent of the pack—hell, almost in spite of the pack. She had a life and people who loved her for herself. I hated to imagine what I would trade for that.

"Uncle Lonnie didn't want to go to the meeting?" I asked, clearing my throat. "Did Jane use the word 'tedious' on him, too?"

"Wow, we reached the mockery stage of our relationship really quickly," Jane told me, throwing up her hands.

Jolene shook her head. "You know Daddy. He accepts the idea that working with the vampires is better for us, but he just doesn't like the idea of doing it himself. Besides. I've been friends with Jane for years. If anybody's going to be cooperative, it's me. Daddy, not so much."

"That's a really good point," I conceded.

"And when I tell anybody in the pack that the kids are getting special lessons for cello and violin, they act like I'm getting all snooty. 'What's next? You gonna put them in private school? You gonna start taking vacations in *Europe*?'" she huffed, mimicking what I thought maybe was Aunt Lurlene's voice. "It's not like I can sign them up for team sports. They're faster than all of the other kids—like, *obviously* faster. And Janelyn is so competitive, she doesn't know how to hold back. They'd boot werewolves out in the open before the end of their first practice."

"Jolene, I get it," I assured her. "We weren't able to play sports, and it's not like we were able to afford extra music lessons. You're trying to do something good for your kids."

"And not get mocked for it," Jane added.

"Exactly. It's what good parents do," I agreed. "I'm really impressed."

Jolene took a deep breath. "Thank you. It's good to hear that from someone who grew up like we did. Here are the keys to the van. I'll ride with Jane and Dick to the meeting. I texted you the address for the music studio. Just make sure they eat their jerky snacks on the way to class. It's two hours long and the last thing you want to do is to hand wooden sticks to a couple of hangry werewolf cubs."

"Mu-ohm, they're called *bows*," Janelyn sighed in that derisive tone only tweens could manage toward their parents. "And it's not like you can hurt anybody *that bad* with them."

"Watch the sass, Janelyn, or there will be no triple cheeseburgers after class," Jolene informed her daughter in her nasal twang.

Having a voice that could peel paint was Jolene's only real

flaw. Janelyn seemed to sense she'd gone too far and mimed zipping her lip.

Jolene told me, "I left cash in the glove box. Our drive-thru bills can get really ugly. Just tell the cashier it's the Lavelle twins. They'll know what to do."

"Which fast food place?" I asked.

Jolene jerked her shoulder. "Any of them. We're known pretty much everywhere."

Thinking of the amount of food my own family could put away at any given meal, I nodded. "That makes sense."

"Okay, kids, have a great time," my cousin said, kissing each of them on the top of their heads. As the twins trooped out of the door, Jolene handed me a pair of packaged, high-end foam earplugs.

"Why?"

Andrea winced. "Trust me, you're going to need them."

"What have I agreed to?" I asked Dick.

Jane sniffed, smirking at me. "Suddenly 'tedious' doesn't sound so bad, now does it?"

I HAD to add "special violin studio" to the list of things I didn't realize existed in the Hollow. The nondescript, beige cement block warehouse was on the industrial side of town, painted with a stately sign reading Half-Moon Hollow Music Academy. If I hadn't seen a parking lot full of cars, I probably wouldn't have stopped there with children. But the twins ran in with a confidence that spoke of familiarity—or at least, the reckless-ness of being eight.

I had no idea there was enough local interest in string instruments to merit a whole studio devoted to them. Local kids could sign up for piano lessons or even guitar fairly easily. Or if they couldn't afford private instruction, they usually joined their school bands for woodwinds and brass. Those bands rarely included a string section. I'd known a girl in high school who had been considered a violin prodigy, thanks to her well-off parents' early intervention. And she'd had to travel to a youth orchestra in Nashville just for the opportunity to play. But this room was packed with at least twenty kids and their parents, holding everything from a tiny violin to an enormous contrabass. (I could only identify it because of a previous work project involving a regional orchestra.)

The school was basically an open rehearsal space with chairs and music stands arranged on risers in the center. It smelled familiar, a warm woodsy scent that immediately calmed me. Maybe it was the instruments? The owner had painted the walls a crisp white and hung carefully-placed acoustic panels. The floor was an immaculate maple that shone in the bright over-head lights. The only decorations were photos of students performing in various concert halls, interspersed with portraits of famous composers. Little brass nameplates labeled Brahms, Bach, and Beethoven, with a little sign underneath that read, "Learn Your Three B's!"

Immediately, the space seemed very professional and focused, which was reflected in the kids' behavior. Yes, they were still kids, talkative and loud, but they weren't running around or roughhousing. I hoped this was a demonstration of how much they valued the lessons, and not the music teacher being some sort of super-strict ogre.

Most of the students were around the twins' age, with a few teens who seemed to be in charge of getting the youngest kids into their seats with their instruments intact. It struck me that the crowd here was much more diverse than the average gath-ering in the Hollow. While most of the region's occupants were Caucasian, the students here represented a healthy blend of Asian, Latino, Indian, and African American. I couldn't help but think that was good for the twins, too. Growing up on the

McClaine compound, where everybody was exactly like you, could leave you unprepared to deal with the outside world and all its differences. Jolene's kids wouldn't have to struggle with that and it made me all the more proud of her as a mom.

Janelyn, always the more social of the two, was greeted with hugs from several of the girls in class, while Joe seemed to have two or three "core friends" who separated from the class to talk very intensely about the instruments they were unpacking.

"Okay, I'll just wait over here then," I said awkwardly, joining a row of parents sitting along the wall. Some of them were knitting or reading. I guessed sideline coaching wasn't a big thing in youth classical music classes—another point for Jolene and her ability to choose activities for her kids. I pulled out my phone to check my emails and two older boys led the twins' group through breathing exercises and arm stretches.

The older boys, who continued to glance towards a closed office door near the front, stood in front of the seated group and raised their arms. Watching each other carefully to keep time, they lifted their arms and the children raised their bows in response. A chaotic clash of noise—the likes of which I'd only heard that one time a raccoon dared to infiltrate my uncle Eagan's trailer—knocked me back against my chair. At first, it was just an assault on my eardrums, but eventually, I could hear that some of the notes were perfectly played—the tone whole and soothing. Others sounded like a hacksaw drawn across a chalkboard.

Suddenly, the earplugs made so much sense.

I wondered how Jolene could stand this at all. With our supernatural hearing, sitting through these sessions had to be torture for her. And the kids had private lessons on top of these weekly classes! Never underestimate the tenacity of a devoted werewolf mama.

It took a few moments for my nerves to adjust to the aural anarchy, but eventually, it became background noise. I couldn't tell whether it was because the students were getting warmed up or I was simply able to block it out. I'd spent years tuning out my relatives nonstop droning. By comparison, the screeching scales were far less annoying.

The noise stopped and the "assistant teachers" called out advice for the kids who were making errors. Joe was asked to demonstrate a proper finger position for a B flat. The sound that filled the room was warm and rich, like honey flooding over a sweet, dense cake.

I chewed my bottom lip. I had food on the brain. Maybe I should have had some of the beef jerky in the car.

"Are you with the twins tonight?" a nearby mom asked kindly. When I nodded, she added, "They're very talented."

"Like, suspiciously talented?" I asked, my brow raised.

She stared at me for a long beat because I'd just said something very weird. "No. Some kids are just a little more musically inclined than others."

I smiled awkwardly. "Oh, well, thank you, that's very nice of you to say. I'm their cousin, Ty. I'm filling in for Jolene tonight."

"Namita Singh," the lady said, shaking my offered hand.

"Which one is yours?"

"Amelia." She nodded to a tiny form almost entirely hidden behind a youth cello. She didn't seem to be struggling with its size or playing scales. While not quite as smooth as Joe's playing, she clearly knew what she was doing.

"Wow," I marveled. "How old is she?"

"Six. Joe has been helping her since she started here. He's such a sweet boy, and very patient with the younger kids."

"That's our Joe," I said, grinning proudly. On the other side of the room, Janelyn demonstrated a scale, the notes rippling off of her bow at a hummingbird's pace.

"Janie's a little more intense," I added, making Namita laugh.

"It's good for the kids to get together like this," she said. "The private lessons are essential, for the kids to get the individual attention they need to grow. But they really need this time together to see how the other students play, the little tricks they use and how they cope with frustration if they're not getting it right. And of course, it's good for them to socialize and learn how to play as a group. Mr. Bonfils says music can be lonely pursuit and that can be very bad for the musician."

"Mr. Bonfils is the teacher?"

Namita blushed, glancing down at her book. "He's very good."

In the risers, a boy tried to copy Janelyn's speed on the scale and failed. Repeatedly. Janelyn tried to calm him down and tell him that she'd worked for weeks to get it right, and he just needed to slow down. But he stood up suddenly, red-faced and frustrated, knocking over a music stand and nearly smacking the boy seated in front of him.

Suddenly, the office door opened, and a blurred blue shape sped toward the falling stand. A tall, dark-haired man caught the stand before it fell. None of the other parents reacted, so I assumed they were used to this sort of vampire speed displayed in class. The kids' music teacher was a vampire. Interesting.

The teacher knelt in front of the frustrated kid and spoke to him, so quietly that no one else could hear what was said—not even with my hearing. The boy's shoulders relaxed, and he took deep breaths. The vampire showed him how to place his fingers around the violin's neck and handed him the bow. The student played through the scale slowly and the notes were far less jarring on the ears. The tension in the classroom immediately eased.

"Welcome, class, sorry about the late start," he said as he turned. "But what do we know about responsibilities?"

"Responsibilities, like school and chores, are just as impor-tant as music," the kids chorused together as if they'd heard it many times before.

The vampire crossed to the conductor's stand and I got a

good look at his face. Only my werewolf speed kept me from fumbling my phone to the floor. He wasn't just any vampire. He was the library vampire.

All around me, the moms seemed to straighten in their chairs and suck in their stomachs simultaneously. I couldn't even blame them for the unified hair fluffing. If I'd had any idea I was going to see him again, I would worn something besides a t-shirt and jeans tonight... even if he had seen me in t-shirt and jeans before. But I would have at least worn a tinted lip balm or something.

I ran a hand through my thick auburn hair. Yep, it was frizzy; there was nothing I could do about it.

For a moment, it was like a scene from one of those movies, two people making eye contact across a crowded room while time slows and sound makes way to the dramatic swell of a hundred violins...more advanced violins than the ones I was currently hearing. I could see the moment he recognized me, and his face filled with a delight that made me dizzy.

And now that he wasn't looking directly at me, that dreamy movie feeling faded away and I was full-on panicking. I'd never thought I would see him again. I had no idea what to do. What would I even say to him after class was over? Should I say anything at all? The tone of our last conversation had been decidedly flirty, and I don't think I'd ever had more than one flirty conversation with a man. At least not one I was interested in, as opposed to some poor blind date I'd been corralled into by my pack—and on the rare occasions I flirted with those guys, I was generally trying to make them uncomfortable enough that they would find a reason to end the date early.

The ease with which I had spoken to him in the library was a fluke brought on by adrenaline and gratitude that I wasn't suffering a book-related concussion. And was it even worth the risk of talking to him? The kids would be sure to mention to their parents—or God forbid, their grandparents, *my Alphas*—

that I was having flirty conversations with their vampire music instructor.

I slumped back in the uncomfortable plastic chair. What if I was making entirely too much of this? What if I was just imagining this whole thing on my side and he was just a gregarious personality who treated everybody like they were interesting and delightful? What if this was some weird vampire thing where he was just trying to bite me so he could brag to his friends about this time he fed from this gullible, back-country werewolf?

As if he could hear my thoughts, the vampire turned and smiled, like he was relieved to find me still sitting there.

I couldn't just run away again, right? That was technically child abandonment. Jolene would definitely notice if I dropped her car off at her house without her kids in it.

"Wow, um, I've never seen Mr. Bonfils smile at anyone like that before," Namita said.

"He's usually pretty reserved,"

"Do you know him?" another mom asked to my left. I glanced around and saw

that several of the mothers were watching me with interest...and resentment. Great, because I needed to level up the difficulty in getting to the car after class.

"Oh, I just met him once at the library," I said, shaking my head. "No big deal. We barely spoke."

"He was at the library?" a third mom murmured, chewing her lip. Somehow, I got the feeling she was planning her own excursion to the local book depository.

I hummed in a non-committal tone. It was official. I could never go back to the library. I'd just infested it with aggressive music moms. I checked my phone again and pretended to stare at the screen for the next hour, instead of the library vampire and the way his jeans clung to his rear.

The class ended and Mr. Bonfils spoke to the students about

an upcoming performance at a community meeting. I hurriedly packed my belongings into my backpack. I wondered if I could get away with scooting across the floor to the kids' cases and packing their stuff up as quickly as possible. But none of the other parents moved, so I just sat there, watching. He was so… careful with the kids. He spoke to them gently, never getting too close. I understood the instinct. I tended to be overcautious about contact with humans, even the ones I liked. With super-strength, all it would take would be an ill-timed movement of my hand to result in broken bones. And he had bloodlust and insane noise levels to deal with on top of that. Why would he put himself through all this?

He either truly loved teaching, or he was charging a lot more for these lessons than Jolene would admit. The kids clapped, marking the end of the teacher's speech. I tried to bolt towards their bags as subtly as possible, but I was sure it still looked like bolting. The twins scampered across the floor to me, their hair plastered across their foreheads.

"Okay, kids, let's go get in the car," I said, handing their cases to each of them. I eyed the vampire from across the room as he talked to students, glancing up at me every few seconds.

"We have to pack up our instruments carefully," Joe told me, his expression solemn. "Dad says if they get damaged, he'll have to sell a kidney to replace them."

"I still say he could get more for a lobe of his liver," Janelyn said, sliding her bow into its compartment.

"Janelyn, that is creepy," Joe told her. Janelyn shrugged.

"Okay, great, be responsible and respectful of your belong-ings, but let's get out of here as quickly as possible. All right?" I said. "First one back gets extra fries!"

I looked back over my shoulder, but couldn't see the vampire. I'd lost him in the shifting sea of parents and kids.

"Hello, you must be the McClaine twins' cousin," that same smooth voice sounded over my other shoulder and it was all I could do to not shriek. It pricked my pride as a predator that he'd been able to sneak up on me. I was having a *really* off night. "They were very excited you were coming to see them tonight."

"Tylene McClaine. Just call me Ty. Everybody does," I said, laughing in a breathless way that made me want to facepalm.

"Alexandre Bonfils," he said, glancing down at my hand. I remembered something from an old movie my aunt Maybelline loved, some corseted historical romance where the heroine was highly offended that a man reached for her hand, instead of waiting for her to extend it for a kiss across the knuckles. "But you should call me 'Alex.'"

"Nice to meet you." Smiling, I extended my right hand and was grateful that he stuck with shaking it. If he'd kissed my knuckles, I'd probably get tackled by a jealous mom in the parking lot. Parking lots could be very dangerous places in the Hollow.

"Truly, I'm glad to see you again," he said. "I was afraid I might never have the opportunity."

If he was this charming towards everyone...he was really good at it. I probably deserved to be bitten at this point and I didn't even care. I was so used to guys my age behaving like, well, guys my age. He didn't accuse me of running off on him or trying to dodge him. And then, *that* put me on edge, because that was just not what I was used to from guys I'd interacted with.

"I had to get home, and you seemed determined to finish your conversation with Mrs. Stubblefield," I said.

He pressed those full lips together into a frown. "Yes, those boys didn't seem to understand that they'd done anything wrong, or that they should apologize...or at least try not to do it again."

I scoffed. "Kids today. I blame the video games that should be parenting them."

He didn't laugh. Oh, no. How was I making this situation

more awkward with stupid dad jokes? That shouldn't be possible!

"How old are you?" he asked. I lifted an eyebrow and he winced. "That sounded less sinister in my head. I'm asking for ethical reasons, not legal. I can't tell human ages anymore."

"Does it matter?" I asked, tilting my head.

He nodded emphatically. "Well, yes, if you're a teenager, I'm going to have to change the way I speak to you and look at you, not to mention my thoughts around you. I don't want to be… what do my students call it? A creepster."

"I can appreciate that, I think. But it's "creeper," if you don't want the kids to make fun of you," I told him. "And I'm twenty-four. How old are you?"

"Much older than twenty-four," he said. "Hmmm, still sounds sinister. Maybe we should avoid age, as a topic?"

"I could do that." I snickered. "So, what were you doing in the library? It's not exactly a hot spot for the vampire underworld."

"The library has a remarkable selection of classical sheet music, believe it or not. Some donation from a music enthusiast's estate. I like reading them over in person." He shrugged. "I have to maintain an online presence for my business, but in all other ways, I try to live life as what you might call a 'beta-version.'"

"How dare you!" I mock-gasped, making his eyes widen in alarm.

"I'm sorry," he said, his brow furrowed.

"No, that was a bad joke. *I'm* sorry. I meant it as 'how dare you reject the Internet' in an over-the-top, meant-to-be-funny way. I spend a lot of time on the Internet," I said. "Wait, that sounds sad—why is this conversation going so badly? I can't even tell if it's your fault or mine! I work in digital promotions for clients I meet over the Internet…there are no explicit images involved. I should stop talking."

"I would be very sad if you did," he replied, his lips quirked into a smile that made my stomach do this weird flippy-thing.

Over his shoulder, I could see the twins packed and ready to go...and about a dozen music moms giving me the evil eye. "I should get my cousins home. It was nice to see you again, without the books raining down from the sky."

"Would you like to meet me sometime for...coffee?" he asked, as if searching for a food group that might appeal to both of us.

"You paused before coffee," I noted.

"I almost said drinks, but I don't know if you drink," he said, nodding.

"Is 'drinks' some sort of euphemism?" I asked.

"Why? Do beverages make you uncomfortable?" he replied.

"No, it's just...you're a vampire and I'm a werewolf and we're not supposed to date. I think it's a rule."

"Did you sign something agreeing to these rules?"

My lips twitched and his eyes flicked town. It felt like he was staring at my mouth. With intent. "No."

"So have coffee with me. I've heard of a place in town, Specialty Books. They make vampire-friendly drinks. It's a nice public place, lots of witnesses, should you feel unsafe. Maybe I'm the one who should stop talking, because I don't think I'm making this sound appealing."

I giggled. I actually giggled. Because he was not *quite* as awkward as me, but he was still a little awkward. And it was adorable that I was able to chip under the smooth exterior enough to make him appear to be anything but suave and courtly.

I grinned at him, prompting him to smile at me just as warmly. "Dick Cheney does make a magical cappuccino."

OUR DEVASTATING RAID on the local Burger Shed left the back seat of Jolene's car littered with cheese-covered wrappers and ripped fry containers. It was fast food carnage as far as the rearview mirror could see. I felt bad feeding the kids a mess of non-organic, corporate-fueled empty calories, but I also knew how expensive and difficult it was to feed growing werewolves. Jolene tended to cook pretty healthy when the kids were home —another marked difference from the ranch dressing-soaked, deep-fried cuisine that our mothers embraced. So, I figured it all balanced out eventually.

The Lavelle house was a tidy little ranch, unremarkable in any way beyond the fact that a werewolf lived there, away from her pack. The instinct to run back to the packlands must have driven Jolene insane, but she did it so she could raise her kids on her own terms. And well, for Zeb's safety, because if they'd tried to live on the compound, he would have lost a lot more than a toe. (There was an "accident" involving a chainsaw.)

I carefully parked the car in the garage and herded the kids inside. Without having to be told, they hung up their backpacks and took their instruments upstairs, instead of just dropping everything by the door. It was a minor miracle, as far as were-wolf child behavior was concerned. I heard keys jangle in the front door and Jolene stepped through. I could practically see the maternal tension bleed out of her face when she saw her cubs. I didn't take it personally. It wasn't that Jolene didn't trust me. She just didn't trust the rest of the world. It was a common attitude among most werewolf parents.

Jolene threw her arms wide. "Hey, guys! How was practice!"

"Great! And we made the kid at the drive-thru cry again!" Joe informed her, throwing himself against Jolene's side and nuzzling his face against her ribs.

"Joe ordered everything with no onions, so they had to make them fresh," Janelyn said.

"Onions taste like that stuff that grows on the bottom of the toothbrush rack," Joe insisted.

"Why would you taste stuff at the bottom of the toothbrush rack?" Janelyn asked.

"Kids, please spare cousin Ty your thoughts on what weird things taste like." Jolene flashed a brilliant smile at me. "Thanks, Ty. You're a lifesaver."

"No problem, it was really interesting to watch," I assured her. "How was your meeting?"

"Productive," she said. "But I got roped into serving on a committee."

"Sucker."

"I know," she sighed.

I dug into my backpack and handed her the package of earplugs. "Here, I didn't use these. I know they're the good ones."

Jolene frowned. "You didn't need them?"

"It wasn't that bad," I told her, making her jaw drop. "What? I've spent years tuning out the aunties and they're way louder."

"That's what the twins say," Jolene said, chewing her lip.

"It's all about *focus*, Mama," Janelyn told her solemnly before following her brother down the hall. "I call first shower, Joe! You never clean your nasty hair out of the drain! Joe!"

Before Janelyn managed to reach the closed bathroom door, the shower started.

"Well, that will be a fun fight to referee," Jolene sighed. "So it looks like these meetings might be taking up a lot of my Monday nights. Would you mind taking them to the music classes on those nights? I didn't know if you were usually working then."

I shrugged. "I think I would like that. I get out of the house and I get points for being helpful to family. You know how that goes."

Of course, this arrangement would only work if the date I'd

scheduled with Alex didn't go terribly awry. But I wasn't about to mention that in front of Jolene. If things went wrong, I would just make some excuse about not being able to take the kids to class.

From down the hallway, I heard what sounded like the shower curtain being ripped off its hooks.

"I'm just gonna run home, and let you deal with that," I said, nodding.

Jolene cringed as something crashed and the twins yelled simultaneously for their mom. "Thanks."

3

"Understand that the courting manners of other generations will be different than your own. However, no matter when or how you were raised, back-handed compliments are always bad."
—*A Gentleman in Any Era: An Ancient Vampire's Guide to Modern Relationships*

*S*pecialty Books very quickly became my new "office space," though the change came more out of necessity than the charms of Dick Cheney.

Mrs. Stubblefield seemed to blame me for the ruckus the previous week and was decidedly cold to me on the one night I'd returned. Suddenly, there were no study carrels available to me, despite the fact that they were all empty. I took the hint and made myself scarce. Also, there were at least three moms from the music class sitting "casually" at the reading tables, dressed to the nines. The library was now infested.

Jane had almost as many books as the library anyway. And I

knew I could depend on the vampires to defend my stuff if I stepped away. They'd been so incredibly welcoming since I started showing up, occupying one of their tables for hours at a time. Jane and Dick tried to switch nights in the shop as they were also expected to work at the Council office. But I could tell the shop was where they preferred to spend their time, along with their partners. They were comfortable there in a way I tried not to envy. This was their home and I had the feeling they'd worked hard for it.

Dick kept me in caffeine, letting me try experimental "human coffee drinks" before adding to them to the permanent menu. I ingested more bottled caramel sauce than any human would be able to metabolize. Jane's husband, Gabriel, found the writing for media process to be fascinating and would spend my breaks discussing obscure typography rules with me. Dick's wife, Andrea, hovered like a mother hen, making sure I had water, pens, a coaster for my coffee.

And the location included one hundred percent fewer disturbing eyebrows, which couldn't be discounted, in terms of a perk.

Other that their usual complaints about me not being home, my parents didn't really notice the difference. Well, they did ask if I was drinking unhealthy amounts of coffee, and then we had to have another discussion about sniffing me.

"Can you come give this a try?" Dick asked on the night I was supposed to meet Alex at the bookshop for our date. I'd taken a little more care with my appearance than normal, wearing a pair of jeans so dark they were practically navy slacks and a new shade of lipstick that I would have to wipe off before I went home.

Reluctantly, I abandoned the special anniversary edition of *The Princess Bride* I'd been ogling ever since I'd spotted it on the shelf days ago. I knew that most people preferred the movie to the book, with its ambiguous and potentially gloomy ending, but that story had gotten me through some very unhappy times as a preteen. I'd devoted many hours to imagining that I'd be whisked away by some handsome man in a mask. Hell, at several points, I would have settled for an angry Sicilian genius. This was a gorgeous leather-bound tome that I couldn't bring myself to splurge on. I was sort of a tightwad when it came to buying things just for me, just for fun.

Dick slid a purple Specialty Books mug across the bar. It smelled...funny.

"Is there blood in this?" I asked him. "I think, legally, you have to tell me before I drink it."

"No blood, just a sample of some flavoring syrups," he said as I took a tentative sip. "But they're made by a new vampire-run company and sometimes I wonder if it's a good idea for us to produce food products. Human food tastes like garbage to us, so vampires making human food products seems like a not-great idea."

I smacked my lips, trying to clear my mouth of the weird, synthetic raspberry cough syrup taste combined with nicely brewed coffee. "Well..."

"Well, what?"

I pressed my lips together before whispering, "My mama always told me if I couldn't say anything nice, don't say anything at all."

Dick cringed.

"So I'm trying to figure out a way to go back in time so I can take some words back from my lifetime total, to make up for how bad this is," I said, making him draw the mug back across the bar. "I mean, when was the last time these people ate fruit?!"

"I'm guessing a long time."

"It tastes like a cough drop that's been left in an old lady's sweater pocket for like a year, and then she digs it out and you take it because you don't want to be rude, but then you're just left with this awful pocket fuzz taste in your mouth," I said, shuddering. "But then add a weird synthetic chemical taste afterwards."

"For someone who doesn't want to say anything mean, this is a very specific old lady-based scenario," he deadpanned.

"I do what I can," I said.

"So…don't buy the line of syrups."

I shook my head vehemently. "Don't buy the syrups."

The bell over the door rang and a vampire in a floral peasant top came in, carrying a large shipping box labeled "SPECIALTY BOOKS—TEA ORDER" in a haphazard hand.

"Hey Meadow, how'd the move go?" With Dick's accent, the name came out as "Medda" but the lady didn't seem to mind. She smiled brightly at him.

"As well as you could expect when the people moving are one person with what you might call a lax attitude towards organization and the other one is Erik," she said, jerking her shoulder. "You and Andrea have been really good to us and we appreciate it. So, to thank you, I brought you this."

She reached into the shipping box and pulled out a package wrapped in brightly patterned cloth.

"Is it slippery elm bark tea?" Dick asked, his expression caught between affection and dread.

"It's slippery elm bark tea!" she chirped, relentlessly cheerful despite Dick's clear lack of enthusiasm.

"I know you say this stuff is good for me, Hippy Dippy, but by comparison, Ty's old lady cough drop description sounds tempting."

Meadow blinked at him, confused. I snickered.

"Drink the tea, Dick!" Andrea called from the stacks.

"It's good for you!" Jane added.

"This is a vast conspiracy among the women in my life to drive me nuts, isn't it?" he asked Meadow.

I laughed, clapping my hand over my mouth.

"You got something to add there, Little Red?" he asked.

I shook my head. "Is that my nickname?"

"You have to admit it's better than Hippy Dippy," Meadow said.

"We're still working on it." Dick looked at me, his lips pursed in contemplation. "Cough Drop Hater?"

I shook my head again. "We'll figure it out."

"I'm Meadow Schwartz," Meadow said, offering her hand. "I own the tea shop down the street, Everlasting Health. Stop by anytime."

"Thanks, but I'm more of a coffee drinker. Or at least, I was before Dick and his cough drop syrup ruined the drink forever," I said as Jane and Andrea joined her at the bar. Jane gave her a quick hug before setting an electric kettle to boil. Andrea took the box and began emptying bags of loose tea into enormous glass apothecary jars.

"Everybody says that at first," Meadow assured me. "Except for the cough drop thing. I'm hearing way more about cough drops than I thought I would today."

"This is Ty McClaine," Jane said. "Jolene's cousin."

"Nice to meet you," she said, tilting her head as she looked at me. If I wasn't a werewolf, I probably wouldn't have picked up on the almost imperceptible flaring of her nostrils. It wasn't personal. She was a predator, taking stock of another predator. I was doing the same. She seemed like a gentle thing, too kind to do what was needed to survive as a vampire, but I also knew better than to underestimate her. I'd heard enough stories through Jolene to know that Jane and her little chosen pack had been through hell and high water over the years. Vampirism in Half-Moon Hollow wasn't for the ill-prepared.

"You're uncertain about almost everything, huh?" Meadow said, patting my hand. "Well, don't be. Once you get a nickname, you're basically adopted in."

All right, I hadn't been expecting that. Because Jane and her friends seemed so normal, I sort of forgot that every vampire had *some* sort of special ability beyond their already unfair predatory advantages of super-strength, super-speed, and forever preserved more-than-above-average good looks. (Yeah, I was a little bitter.) At some point, after turning, every vampire developed a special talent—being able to persuade someone to do their bidding or find hidden objects.

Werewolves didn't get that. (Still bitter.)

I wondered what Alex's special ability could be … maybe it was just looking really, really good in jeans? Could that be considered a super-power?

My eyes must have gone wide at that because Jane elbowed Meadow lightly. "Sweetie, we've talked about the emotion-sniffing thing. It's rude to do it without permission."

"You know I can't help what I *smell,* Jane. Besides, you've dipped into my brain on occasion without a password," Meadow replied, shooting me an apologetic glance. "Sorry. It's a gift and a curse."

I'd completely forgotten Jane was telepathic. Shit.

Jane told me. "Don't worry, I'm getting much better at keeping my shield up. As long as you're not thinking loud, panicky thoughts, we should be fine. Also, to my knowledge, looking really, really good in jeans isn't considered a super-power. But I think it should be."

"I say this as someone who grew up with a bunch of were-wolves, but this is the weirdest conversation I've ever heard," I told her.

"Well, I have a hard time believing that," Dick said. "I've hung out with Jolene for too long."

I chuckled, turning to Meadow. "So do you work here, too? I just started visiting."

"I'm usually here for book club nights, but I'm pretty busy with my own shop," she said. "And I used to be Dick and Andrea's tenant, but my boyfriend and I just bought a house together." She preened as she dropped a set of keys into Dick's hand.

"I'm so pleased for you," Andrea said, hugging her. "That's a huge step."

"Especially for me and my trust issues," Meadow admitted.

"You own an apartment building?" I lifted a brow. Dick didn't seem like the landlord type. Owning a building that people lived in was a *lot* of responsibility and upkeep and dealing with people and their complaints. And while Dick was a super nice person, that seemed like a lot for him. Then again, he had Andrea, and I once saw her defuse a fifteen-minute customer meltdown over the absence of cashew milk at the coffee bar—with a smile on her face.

Cashew milk. At a vampire coffee bar. In Kentucky.

"Yeah, are you looking for a place?" Dick asked. "We were going to advertise it, but we'd rather rent to people we know. You're way less likely to try to grow hallucinogenic mushrooms in the laundry room or something."

"But you barely know me!" I scoffed.

"You've been in here every night this week, working steadily for hours at a time," Andrea said. "Clearly, you have a job to which you're very dedicated. You're pleasant, responsible and you haven't once tried to stick gum under the table, which means you respect other people's property."

"The gum thing drives her crazy," Jane added.

I was frozen like a—well, werewolves never got caught in headlights, but it was close. Just thinking about the offer almost made me dizzy—living alone, in my own space that I controlled. It was enough to make me nearly tear up right there in front of everybody. It was so tantalizing. I could almost taste it, the freedom, the control. My own life.

My parents had always told me that landlords would never rent to me. My work history was spread out across several family-owned businesses simultaneously, making my resume a nightmare. My references were limited to family members. I had *no* rental history. And it was just too hard for werewolves to try to assimilate into town, they'd insisted. I'd never even considered looking at apartment listings. No one my age had ever moved off of the compound unless it was to get married and move onto some other pack's lands. What I wanted had always seemed impossible, until now.

"How much is the rent?" I squeaked. I took a quick sip of coffee to wet my throat and then immediately regretted it because cough drop syrup.

Dick checked under the coffee bar and pulled out a piece of paper with all of the specs for the apartment. One bedroom, one bath, kitchen, breakfast nook, a balcony overlooking Millard Street. It wasn't exactly huge, but it would be more space than I was used to having on my own. And I had more than enough in my savings to cover rent for the first *year* on my own, plus utilities and Internet. It was pretty reasonable considering it was right in the middle of town. I could work from home! I could take on jobs I had been turning down because I would have hours of uninterrupted time! Which would mean I could afford things like furniture and sheets and toothpaste!

Was this real?

Andrea seemed unnerved by my losing the ability to speak. "Do you want an application? We'll waive the references."

My mouth opened to say 'yes, please!' but then Jane's cell phone jangled in her back pocket. She pulled it out, grinning at the screen. "Iris? What's up?"

I could only hear a distressed jumble of words, muffled by Jane's ear being pressed to the phone. Jane gasped. "Oh, honey, I'm so sorry. I'll come on by right now. No, it's no trouble. Does Cal think I need to send the UERT guys? No, that's not an overreaction! Okay, okay, I'll see you in a few minutes."

"Why would Iris need the Undead Emergency Response Team?" Dick demanded.

Jane blew out a long breath as she hung up. "Meadow, I'm going to need a bunch of that Calm Your Ass Down Blend to go. Iris will appreciate it."

"What's going on?" Andrea asked as Meadow started frantically looking through her box of teas.

"Somebody threw bricks through all of the windows at Cal and Iris's place. Spray painted some nasty stuff on the porch. Threw bleach on her rose beds. She's beside herself," Jane said. "That was her parents' house. You know how she feels about it. I'm going to head over there and talk to her with my Council hat on, take a report. Which means a meeting with the local sheriff, Lord help me."

"I thought people had pretty much accepted vampires around here!" I exclaimed. "I haven't seen any sort anti-vampire stuff since the first few years after the Coming Out."

Except for the anti-vampire stuff my family said on occasion. But I didn't think that would be a helpful contribution to the conversation right now.

Jane nodded. "That's what Dick and I have been working toward during our whole tenure. We've worked to encourage vampires to pay taxes at unprecedented rates, recycle, participate in Neighborhood Watch programs, volunteer. Hell, Libby's an officer in the PTA, now. People are comfortable with us being here. Why would that suddenly change?"

I thought about my parents, and the way they muttered angrily under their breath any time they saw positive vampire news on TV. But I didn't think it was a good idea to bring that up here and now.

"I thought Cal and Iris had all those fancy security systems," Dick mused.

"She said it must have happened just after dark. They only keep the steel shutters down during the day," Jane said as Meadow handed her a package containing a *lot* of dried tea. "They woke up at sundown. Everything was normal. Cal went into his home office. Iris was down in the basement, something about seedlings and grow lights. She was talking super-fast and it was about gardening, and you know I don't do well with that particular subject. Anyway, they're settling into their day and bam, broken glass and anti-vampire slurs painted on their porch."

"Poor Iris," Dick murmured. "How's Cal handling it?"

"Also, beside himself," Jane said as she grabbed her purse. "He's talking about building some sort of secret underground lair to protect Iris. Again."

"Well, good luck with that," Dick said. "But if Cal is serious about the secret underground lair, I know a guy."

Jane shot an alarmed look at Andrea, who said, "He hasn't built one for us because I threatened to burn all of his t-shirts."

"Of course, you know a guy," Jane sighed. "And no, I will not encourage secret underground lair-building. Next thing you know, Gabriel will be shoving me into one, whenever he thinks I'm in danger."

"Maybe stop being in danger so much," Dick suggested.

"Stop saying ridiculous things," Jane told him, kissing his cheek. "I'll see y'all later."

Jane dashed out the door, leaving us in her wake.

"I take it that you don't have that sort of thing happen very often around here?" I asked.

Andrea shook her head. "Not since Jane and Dick took over the Council office. They've devoted so much time to getting humans and vampires on the same page, the humans tend to write grumpy letters to them instead of outright vandalism."

"It's the first report we've had like this all year," Dick mused. "And it just happens to be one of our friends."

"You're getting that look in your eye," Andrea warned him. "That 'Danger approaching, build a secret underground lair' look."

"Please don't tell Erik," Meadow pleaded.

"I'm just saying that it helps to get ahead of the curve on these things," he protested.

"All of your t-shirts, Dick," Andrea said sternly. "Even the ones without writing."

The bell jangled over the door. I turned, sure that somehow, my parents had psychically sensed me thinking about moving out earlier and had stormed into Specialty Books to put a stop to it.

But it was just Alex was walking through the door, that warm smile on his face. In his hands, he held a flat package wrapped in purple paper with a silver bow. In fact, it was the exact purple of the upholstery, mugs and walls. That seemed...odd.

"Hello," he said, his expression confused, as I appeared to be surrounded by vampires. "Is everything all right?"

"Oh, I was just talking to Dick and Andrea Cheney, who run the shop. And this is Meadow Schwartz. She owns Everlasting Health down the street. Everybody, this is Alex Bonfils. He owns a music school here in town. He's the twins' coach."

"Nice to see you again," Alex said, offering his hand to Dick. He waited for Andrea to extend hers.

"Oh, you've met?" I asked.

"When I moved into the region, I made it a point to stop by the Council office and introduce myself," Alex said.

My cheeks flushed warm. Of course, he'd met them. You didn't just move into the Council's territory without so much as a by-your-leave. I was reminded all over again how different my life was, compared to Alex and these other people who seemed to want to be my friends. Not for the first time, I wondered if we were making a big mistake even meeting here tonight. I thought it was smart to meet a vampire in a place he would be comfortable in, but members of my family wouldn't be—other than Jolene, that is. But while Jane and Dick and the rest were super nice, they were also very loyal to my cousin. What if they told Jolene about this? And despite the fact that logically, I knew I wasn't really doing anything wrong, the possibility of Jolene telling my parents seemed very real. And that was terrifying.

What was I thinking? I'd been so caught up in the moment, the excitement of Alex being interested in me that I hadn't considered the very real consequences until he was right in front of me. It had seemed like some pleasant dream, a distraction from the drudgery I went through every day at home. But now it was real, and I was having second, third and fourth thoughts.

Vampires and werewolves didn't date. In fact, generally speaking, we didn't get along all that well. On our side, there was too much hostility—probably barely-repressed envy that they got to live out in the open. Vampires, particularly older ones, could be, well, snotty. We only enjoyed solid diplomacy here in the Hollow because of Jane's efforts and her friendship with Jolene.

And I was processing all of these thoughts while standing in front of him. And Dick Cheney, whose eyes were tracking between the two of us as he frowned. "What is happening here?"

Alex pressed the wrapped package into my hand. "I thought you might like this. I'm told that flowers and chocolates are outdated."

"What is happening here?" Dick asked again.

"Thank you." I opened the package and burst out laughing. He'd given me the illustrated sword guide I'd been holding at the library when the bookshelf tried to murder me.

"Now you don't have to take the risk of going into the history section," he said.

"Thank you, that was very sweet, and I think I was unofficially banned from the history section, so it's extra thoughtful. Did you get this here?" I asked, holding up the purple paper.

"I ordered it over the phone earlier this week," he said. "It seemed rude to bring a book into someone's bookstore."

"Like bringing a cake into a restaurant," I suggested.

"I haven't ever done that, but I'm assuming it's…very bad?" he guessed.

"It's not good," Andrea told him.

"What is happening here?" Dick asked again, much louder this time. "Are you here on a *date* with Ty? Was that book a courting gift?"

My heart sank at Dick's angry tone. I thought he liked me, but I guess that was easier when I didn't want to mix in with his kind. I shrunk away from the group ever so slightly, back toward my table, just in case I needed to pack up and get out quickly.

For his part, Alex seemed caught off-guard by Dick's vehemence. "Is there a problem?"

"Only in that Dick never thinks any man is good enough for the women in his life," Andrea said as Dick drew me against his side, his arm around my shoulders.

"Damn straight," Dick muttered. "As someone who's not good enough for his wife, I know what I'm talking about."

"He offered to keep a getaway car warm for Jane at her wedding," Andrea said. "And he was the best man."

"He gave Erik the shovel speech. In German," Meadow added. "He paid someone on the Internet to translate a threatening speech into my boyfriend's native language just so it would come across as more intimidating."

"I sure the hell did," Dick agreed. "You're a nice girl, just like Ty here. Someone needs to look out for you, make sure that anybody who wants to have any sort of connection to you knows that you're not alone in the world. That you have people who would be very *responsive* if you were upset or mistreated or even irritated a little bit."

I gritted my teeth and inhaled deeply through my nose. I

would not cry. I had more eye make up on than usual and I did not want to spend half of our first date in the bathroom scraping it off of my cheeks. I was used the pack having my back, but lately, that felt more like having a whole platoon of people who wanted to tell me what I was doing wrong with my life. The support, the assurance that the pack was supposed to give me, had been missing for a long time. I didn't *get* this sort of reaction from people. Granted, most of my interactions were with other werewolves, but even within my own pack, I was considered weird. Too bookish, too stubborn, too mouthy, and overall off-putting. I'd only known these people for a short time, and they'd given me more acceptance than I'd had since I was a child.

"Half of that German speech was grammatically incorrect, by the way," Meadow told him. "But thank you, for trying."

"Got the point across, didn't it?" Dick asked, leveling a long, meaningful look at Alex. "So don't make me learn French, Bonfils. You be a gentleman. Or else."

"I wouldn't dream of making you give another 'shovel speech,'" swore Alex, who seemed to be taking this all very seriously.

Dick squinted at him for a long moment and crossed the store to the self-help section. He came back to the counter and slapped a copy of a softcover book on the counter. It was called *A Gentleman in Any Era: An Ancient Vampire's Guide to Modern Relationships* and had a bright blue cover featuring a man in a sharp suit, standing inside an hourglass. "Just in case you have any questions on how to stay a gentleman. Consider it a gift, and a warning."

"Sorry, hon, he'll lighten up after a few...years," Andrea promised me.

"All right then, why don't you two go sit down, and we'll make you some drinks. And we'll be watching, from over here," Dick said, while Meadow and Andrea rolled their eyes fondly.

"It's really okay," I told her, my voice suspiciously raspy.

"I'll make your drinks, so Dick isn't tempted to tamper with anything," she offered. "What would you like?"

"I'll try a mocha this time," I said.

"Just a filter coffee with a little B-positive, please, if you have it," Alex asked, keeping his tone very polite as he pulled my chair out from the table.

"Is that like ordering a plain drip coffee at Starbucks?" I asked Andrea.

She nodded. "Essentially, but we'll do it, no problem."

Alex slid into the chair across from me.

"This is a little more awkward than I expected," he said. "I can't remember the last time I went on a date. I'm not sure I've ever really dated, to be honest. I certainly never had to deal with my lady friend's disapproving friends and family."

"What do you normally do?"

He tugged at his collar, as if he hadn't meant to venture into this conversational territory. "Most of my partners have been vampires. We tend to stay to our own places, only venture out to gatherings hosted by other vampire gatherings. It's more of a private situation."

"Oh, well, this is what we do now. We meet in public and let our friends harass our dates to the point of embarrassment," I told him.

"It wasn't that bad," he assured me. "There was no actual shovel involved. And it's nice that you have so many people who care for you. I will put up with the questions and the concealed threats, even if it's not entirely in my nature."

"Are you sure it's a good idea to try to want something that isn't really in your character?" I asked.

"No, but that's half of the fun."

"You're a very strange man." I smiled as Andrea brought our drinks to the table. Alex thanked her politely. Dick made the "watching you" gesture, pointing two fingers at his eyes and then at us.

"We agreed to stay away from age as a topic, right?"

"Yes, we did," he said. "But just in case you start making pop culture references, I suppose I should tell you I'm around six hundred years old. So, I probably will not get those references. It's not personal."

I tried to keep my jaw from going slack. I really did. But he was older than anything I knew. He was older than my *country*. I was just able to drink *legally* a few years before. I had so many questions—what country was he from, how was he turned, what had he seen? But all I could squeak was, "And the music school. How do you get into something like that?"

"Practice?" he suggested, grinning when I gave him a glare with no real heat in it. "I'm afraid I have led what you might have considered a dissolute life. I was disowned, ran away from home to study music, caught the attention of the wrong vampire while performing at a concert. He didn't ask me, he just drank from me and told me that if I wanted to live, I would have to drink from him. He said he wanted to give me time to perfect my talent for centuries. I did not respond well. There was crying. And some whining. My sire was immediately sorry he turned me, but he was stuck with me until I was ready to go out on my own."

"I'll bet he didn't do that again."

"As far as I know, he did not," he said, shaking his head.

"So you've just wandered around the last six hundred years, playing your instrument?" I asked, immediately wanting to suck the words back into my mouth. "Yeah, I heard it."

Alex just suppressed a little smirk and said, "I've had plenty of time to master all of the strings. I learned from some of the best musicians on the continent. I taught students of my own and discovered how much I enjoyed working with young musicians, polishing their talents. I performed in grand concert halls and tiny salons and country dances, wherever I could earn coin and shelter over my head. And when I couldn't find work playing, I did lots of things to survive. I fought for causes I didn't particularly believe in, which is how I met my friends who live nearby. The friendships outlasted the battles by a long shot. I worked aboard vampire-owned ships. I worked on archeological digs in environments where breathing would have been a problem. But I always come back to music. It's what I love doing."

As his words wove a tapestry of images in my head, I pictured him standing on stage in front of an adoring crowd, as a soldier running across a battlefield, wearing the full Indiana Jones outfit *and* the whip.

I would file the Indiana Jones image away for later.

He'd been to so many places, had so many adventures. By comparison, my life felt small and half-lived. How was I possibly going to keep him interested when he'd seen so much?

"Did you meet anyone famous? Like Mozart?"

He grinned.

"What?"

"It's just so interesting that you would ask the same sort of question a human would. It's a common misconception. Just because we've lived longer than the average person doesn't mean we're more likely to meet famous people."

"Well, you're more likely to meet famous people than I would be!" I objected.

"I saw Mozart play once," he confessed. "From the nosebleed section in a concert hall in Amsterdam. He was only a child, but he was a genius. It was obvious, even then. In a way, I suppose that was what inspired me to teach, seeing such potential in a musician so young. I knew I would never reach that level myself, but maybe I could help someone else find it."

"So how did you end up here in the Hollow?"

"Those local friends I mentioned," he said. "In all that 'wandering' as you put it, I've never had a home. I've never really wanted one. I enjoyed chasing one adventure to the next. To put a vulgar point on it, over the years I have built considerable wealth—certainly not from music, just solid investments and a lot of time to let them build up—but not much else. I have no home, no family, not even nestmates. If I were to be dusted, I would leave no mark on the world. And I find myself longing for...permanence."

"And yet, you seem to be resisting the very idea," I said, snickering.

"I talked to Cal and Nik over the last few years. They seem so contented, having found their place with people they love. And I wanted it for myself, that security, the feeling of belonging somewhere," he said. "Maybe that sounds a little strange, but one can only face near-death so many times before it's no longer thrilling. I wanted to wake up in the same place every night and know that I didn't have to be ready to pack up and leave at any moment. I wanted to know people. Other than Cal and Nik, I didn't have friends. I could go months without speaking to anyone and that seemed wrong."

I thought that I would love going months without speaking to anyone, but I thought it would come across as anti-social if I said so. "If I ask more questions about music, can we come back to that?"

He chuckled. "Sure, but I would like to talk about you."

"I've had twenty-four years and I have never worked on a ship, fought in a war, or dug up anything interesting. My life is pretty quiet, boring really."

"You're a werewolf," he countered.

I burst out laughing, and Dick seemed to relax ever so slightly.

"Not a very good one, ask anybody," I snorted. "So, is it difficult, getting students here? We don't exactly have a symphony orchestra in the Hollow."

"It took some time for the parents to get used to the idea of a vampire teaching their children," Alex said. "But it helps that there are so few instructors in the area for string instruments. They don't have many options. If they have the interest and they don't want to travel to Nashville or Louisville just for lessons, they come to me."

He pronounced Louisville all wrong, calling it "Lewisville," in a way that would make most locals mock him. But he was so earnest about it, I just didn't have the heart to correct him.

"Music teaches focus, discipline, patience, cooperation. Not to mention the studies that show how involvement in the arts improves a child's academic performance. I wish those had been around when I was a child. Children need that and I think their parents recognize it. And I'm told it's much more interesting to put on your college applications than the recorder."

"Having attended a few recorder concerts for my younger cousins, I can confirm," I said, shuddering. "Did you realize my niece and nephew were werewolves?"

He shot me a confused smile. "Of course, I did."

"And you still taught them?" I asked.

"Why wouldn't I? They're eager to learn, well-behaved, and they have talent. That's what I set out to do, to teach children who want to learn."

I smiled, reaching out to press my fingertips to his hand. I didn't know why of all the things he'd said, that touched me the most. Maybe it was that if he could be so open with the kids, that he would accept me, too. Or maybe it was just nice to meet someone who was kind for no reason other than they wanted to be.

He cleared his throat. "So, enough about me. You work in social media for people you've never met? That seems as foreign to me as a music school must seem to you."

"I was a little bit of a grammar stickler in high school," I said.

"And after high school. Most of my life, really. Combine that with computer nerdery and you get this job."

"This is going to sound somewhat rude, but when you speak…"

"I sound like an extra on *Justified*?" I suggested.

"I'm not sure what that is," he admitted.

"I'm only strict about grammar for the written word. Verbally, I'm a little closer to my roots," I said. "It's one of those 'do as I write, not as I speak' things?"

"Oh, one of those," he said, nodding before grinning widely.

I nodded solemnly. "It's a classic conundrum. Anyway, I can't imagine starting something like a music school or a restaurant, but I love being able to help someone find the right words to help them market their business."

"But you're also growing your own business, which is just as important," he noted.

"That's a good point."

And on and on it went. It felt like I spent hours talking about myself, the books I'd read, the places I wanted to travel, non-traumatic childhood memories. I hadn't been on a date that hadn't been arranged by one of my relatives in so long that I'd forgotten what real "date conversation" sounded like. Alex didn't care about my family or who they were or what they could offer him. He didn't ask me what I could cook—which was good, because the answer was "not a lot." I had serious doubts that he cared about my pack or my bloodline. He wanted to talk about *me*, what I liked, what I read, what I thought about interspecies politics. It was almost exhausting talking about myself that much, but a) no one ever asked me about those things and b) he was very good at dodging questions—in a way that could have been suspicious if he wasn't so good at appearing engaged and curious.

My phone buzzed. I glanced at my laptop screen. It was almost midnight. Nearly three hours had gone by and I hadn't even noticed! Dick and the other vampires were quietly tending to shop chores, acting like they *weren't* watching our every move.

I didn't have to look at the phone screen to know the text was from my mama. I hadn't mentioned staying out late tonight. I'd really counted on them being distracted by the NCAA basketball tournament. Usually, when University of Kentucky was playing, they didn't register that I was in the same hemisphere, much less not present in the same house. The Wildcats must have lost...which meant my dad would be in an even worse mood when I got home.

Shit.

"Are you all right?"

"I'm so sorry. I have to go."

"But are you all right?" he asked again. "You seem upset."

I hesitated before finally admitting. "I live with my parents."

He had no reaction. I sort of squinted at his face, as if I could read micro-expressions that would tell me whether he felt sorry for me. But nothing happened, and that was almost worse. Had I shocked him into total immobility?

"Is that unusual for unmarried women of your age to still live with their parents?" he asked. "Keep in mind that when I was your age, women stayed with their families until they were married. Of course, most of them were married by the time they were sixteen."

"Well, that's not the case now. Most people my age live on their own, but with my parents and pack dynamics...I think I'm just embarrassed. I'm having a nice time and I don't really want to leave."

"And I'm assuming that you didn't tell them that you're out with me," he said, the corner of his lips lifting.

"No, I did not." I shook my head, my cheeks flushing.

"Surprisingly daring and rebellious," he noted, wiggling his eyebrows.

"This is as about as rebellious as it gets for me."

He stood and held out his hand. "I'll walk you to your car."

I packed my things away in my backpack and slung it on my back. "Oh, I don't have one. I usually run to and from town."

His mouth dropped open. "How far do you live from here?"

"Just a few miles. In my wolf form, I can run it in fifteen minutes." When the appalled expression didn't move from his face, I added, "It's good exercise!"

"That's insanity," he exclaimed. "I'll drive you home."

"Damn right, you will!" Dick exclaimed from the back of the shop. "Like a gentleman!"

"I think a vampire dropping me off at the werewolf compound I call home will cause a lot of questions," I replied. "Questions I probably shouldn't answer."

"That is a good point," Dick conceded. "I'm still watching you, Bonfils."

"I wouldn't expect anything less," Alex conceded.

"Goodnight, Dick! You adorable menace!"

"Goodnight, Cough Drop Hater!"

"Still gotta work on the nickname!" I called back as we walked out. "Goodnight, everybody!"

The various vampires called their goodnights as the door shut behind us. I gestured towards my usual "exit point" into the woods. He kept a respectful distance, and I felt grateful for it. I'd been on too many blind dates where the moment I stepped into a secluded space, my companion basically attacked my face. Respectful distance was a pleasant contrast.

"So, when you say you run to your home from town, do you mean in your human form? Or your wolf form?"

"My wolf form, usually. I'm faster on four feet," I said as we reached a wooded area where it would be safe for me to strip down.

"Will you show me your wolf form?" he asked, frowning when I threw my head back and laughed.

"It's the first date! We're not in the 'transforming into supernatural creatures in front of each other' stage yet!" I exclaimed, only half-kidding.

"I've just never had the opportunity to see a werewolf in an interaction that didn't involve me getting bitten, clawed or otherwise injured. I didn't realize I was asking anything untoward. I'm sorry."

I giggled. "Okay, but you don't just *ask* someone for that. It's like saying 'send nudes' two messages in."

He shook his head. "I have no idea what that means."

"That's for the best, trust me," I assured him.

It dawned on me that he had no way to inappropriately ask for nudes because he had no idea how to contact me. "This is a weird conversational transition, but would you like my phone number? We could text instead of waiting for both of us to end up at the same place at the same time."

"I would very much like to have your phone number, but I don't text that often," he admitted. "Cal and Nik mock me constantly for it."

"Well, I will help you catch up to modern dating conveniences," I told him, holding my hand out for his phone. He handed it to me and I programmed my number into his contacts under "Tylene, Terribly Interesting Werewolf Girl" and then texted to my phone so I could have his info.

"Did you just save me in your contacts as *Aunt Myrtle?*" he asked.

"If an unfamiliar male name pops up on my screen while my family is around, you will be on the receiving end of a lot of harassing calls," I told him as I tapped on my phone screen. "It's better to save you as a fictional aunt."

"Won't your parents realize that you don't have an Aunt Myrtle?" he asked.

"I have so many aunts, it's pretty unlikely." I grinned up at him as I hit send on a text.

He paused to look at his screen. "Heart, winking face, grey German shepherd."

"That's a wolf," I told him. "Our first step towards modern communication is getting you comfortable with emojis."

He frowned. "I don't know if I want to be comfortable with emojis."

"I promise not to use frustrating and abbreviated text speak."

He looked down at his screen and hit a button.

"Cowboy hat, cardboard box?" I asked.

"It's going to take some time," he told me, nodding.

I burst out laughing. There was this moment of silence, where I wondered whether he was going to kiss me. A strange sensation of dread rippled down my spine. This part of the date could be so, well, freaking awful, when you were dating an alpha male werewolf type. You're just standing there, minding your business, and suddenly they lunge at you, like they're going to eat your face.

What if it was worse with vampires? Would there be fangs involved? I didn't know a lot for sure about this…whatever it was. But I knew I was not ready for that.

But like everything else I'd observed about Alex, he was a gentleman. He wasn't timid. He just didn't push. And like everything else about him, I appreciated that. I'd had more than enough of alpha types wanting to take my choices away from me. Alex seemed to care about what I wanted. That was sexy in a way I didn't expect.

Deciding to seize the moment, I stood on my tiptoes and kissed his cheek. He smiled, bumping his forehead against mine. Another girl might miss that gesture, but among wolves, a forehead bump was a significant expression of affection. It was practically a non-verbal "would you like to go steady?" proposal.

The question was, did Alex know that? Probably not.

I inhaled deeply, enjoying that woodsy smell of him. "Do you smell like the instruments? Or do they smell like you?"

He startled. "What?"

"You smell like cedar and resin," I said, nosing at this shoulder.

"You know, I've never thought about it," he said. "But it makes sense. I've spent more time with them, than anything else in my life. Do you know what you smell like to me?"

"I don't think so. Jolene mentioned that she and Jane had some 'scent incompatibility issues' when they met. Turn around, please," I told him. Though he looked more than a little disappointed, he turned. I dropped my clothes and stuffed them into my backpack, watching him for any sign of turning or craning his neck. But he all but whistled innocently while contemplating the moon.

I rolled my shoulders and concentrated on the change, shaking my fur free and stretching my long lupine back. I was grateful that I was in full command of my mind when I changed. Some weres who left long gaps between changes or tried to live too "normal" could lose track of their time during the change. They could do unspeakable things, under the influence of their other forms—mostly involving the slaughter of chickens—and not remember a thing. Suddenly, my family's insistence on weekly runs through the woods together seemed very wise, instead of a pain in my furry ass.

I chuffed lightly. My keen eyes detected the delight on his features, even in the dim light. In werewolf terms, I was a fine specimen—silky russet fur, long lines, sharp teeth. Alex knelt in front of me and rubbed his hand over my ears, pressing the tips a bit between his fingers. "Just look at you!"

I nuzzled my nose against his chest, making him scratch behind my ears. "Who's a pretty girl?"

I growled in a way that I hoped implied, *I will bite you.*

He chuckled and nudged his nose against mine. Again. Maybe he had read something of our mating rituals. There was a book written years before, about the love customs of the were, though most people wrote it off as some sort of joke. Thank goodness.

"Goodnight, Ty."

I yipped and dashed off, only glancing over my shoulder once to see that he him waving. He didn't follow me, and for that I was grateful. I was going to have enough to deal with when I got home.

4

"Approach younger partners' families with caution, like you would a ballista loaded with flaming pitch, or the nuclear option of your day."
—*A Gentleman in Any Era: An Ancient Vampire's Guide to Modern Relationships*

*I*t is very unwise to wake a sleeping werewolf by ripping the covers off of her head.

And yet, my aunts chose to do this, practically blinding me with early morning sunlight and shouts of "Wakey-wakey!"

This made me transform as I rolled over, resulting in a snapping wolf, circling on my bed. I was not a morning werewolf.

Aunt Lurlene and Braylene stood over me, with my mother standing by the door, her arms crossed over her thin chest. Lurlene and Braylene's lips curled back simultaneously in distaste at my display. You just didn't snap at your elders, particularly these aunts. It just wasn't done.

Daddy was at the door in a flash, all teeth and snarling. He didn't even have to change. I quieted down almost immediately, slipping back under the covers so I could shift back to human.

I sighed, throwing the scraps of my favorite sleep shirt to the floor. I'd shredded my pajamas to rags. Again.

"Apologize to your aunts!" Daddy shouted.

"I'm sorry, Aunt Lurlene and Aunt Braylene," I mumbled, rubbing a hand over my face, "that you woke an apex predator up from a sound sleep."

"You must be tired from your *late* night," Lurlene sniffed as Daddy strolled off, having proven that he was still in control of his household.

I groaned and wanted more than anything to pull the pillow over my head. I should have known I'd gotten off too easy the night before, walking into the house under my parents' glares and brazening my way into bed, pretending that I didn't smell like aggressively floral moist towelettes I'd wiped down with right before I walked in. But hiding under bedding would just give my family the impression than I'd done something to hide from—which I hadn't.

The trick to not giving away incriminating information to one's nosey relatives was to make a lot of eye contact and keep your expression neutral. This was sort of difficult to do when your still-adjusting eyes were all squinted from the sunlight pouring through your windows.

"We have good news," Lurlene announced.

"That seems unlikely," I muttered, grabbing a spare shirt from the floor, next to my bed for just such an occasion. Mama tossed me a pair of sweatpants, which was more than she'd intervened on my behalf in years. I slipped into my clothes under the blankets.

"Braylene has called in every favor she had and gotten you a dinner date with Donnie Ansen," Lurlene told me.

"What kind of favors?" I asked, squinting up at them.

"I'm gonna have to curl and set every woman in the Ansen

family, and do an ungodly amount of plucking," Braylene muttered.

For just a moment, I felt an unfamiliar flash of warm affection for Braylene. While Braylene loved to ply her trade as a not-quite-licensed beautician, it would be a blow to her pride to work on the Ansens, who were a couple of tax brackets higher than our pack. I could only imagine their wealth (something to do with fertilizer) had a lot to do with why my aunts were pushing me to make a match with Donnie. I'd met him a few times. Young werewolves tended to mix together when the packs gathered. He was tall, dark and handsome, the cliché Alpha male package, but we just weren't compatible . He didn't understand why people made fun of the *Cats* movie. He thought "that Shakespeare dude" was still alive somewhere. But my approved werewolf dating pool was so small, he was probably considered the best I could get.

"We thought you might like to meet at that nice restaurant in town, Southern Comfort. Donnie's going to call and set up a time," Lurlene told me.

"He has my number?" I asked, carefully refusing to mention that Southern Comfort was well-regarded in undead circles for its vampire-friendly options.

"No, he's going to call your daddy and set it up with him," Mama said softly.

"Of course. Why would he call me to ask *me* out?" I muttered, swinging my legs out of bed.

"He's not asking you out, you're going. That's it. We've let you do things your own way long enough," Lurlene informed me.

"When?" I giggled. I couldn't help it. The very idea was just freaking preposterous. "When have I ever 'done things my own way?'"

Lurlene ignored me. "And that ends now."

"Mama, thoughts?" I asked.

"I'm sure your aunts know what's best," Mama murmured. She rubbed the sleeves of her worn gray cardigan before backing out of the room.

"You stop by my place, when Donnie and your daddy set up a time," Lurlene told me, thumbing through my limited closet options. "We'll go over what you should wear."

"And what to do with your hair," Braylene added as she and Lurlene bustled out of my room. "Now, get yourself up. It's too late to be lazing around. My Annaleese has already done three loads of laundry and butchered a hog this morning."

I groaned, rubbing my face with my hands. "That explains the laundry."

SINCE I WOKE TOO late to start a shift at the butcher shop, Daddy sent me to the enormous vegetable patch the pack kept just over the hill from the trailers. Yes, we did eat mostly meat, but even we knew better than to go completely without roughage. McClaines had figured out a lot of tricks to grow the cheapest bumper crops possible. Which was why I was on my knees in the dirt, transferring tomato plants that would result in the stewed tomatoes that I despised.

Several of my cousins, plus a few aunts and uncles who preferred the garden to the other family ventures, were working the rows around me. The Kentucky growing season started relatively early in the spring, as long as the weather held, and it took quite a bit of work to get the ground ready for the endless rows of strawberries, sweet corn and who knew what else.

Personally, I thought stewed tomatoes tasted like mushy sour dirt. Every year, I considered sabotaging the crop so I wouldn't have aunties trying to shove them onto my plate.

I shuddered at the thought, even with the pleasant warmth of the sun on my shoulders.

I didn't mind working in the garden. It was nice out here, and when I was alone, it was quiet enough that I could think. As it was, my cousins were chatting loudly about sports and town gossip and whatever else could fill the silence, but I could mostly tune them out as I moved down my row. I would have worn earbuds, but on previous gardening excursions, I'd been told it was rude.

I wondered what it said about me, that I was supposed to be a pack creature but clearly preferred my own company. Well, that wasn't true. I preferred the company of the vampires I'd met, and that was probably even weirder. Why was it so easy for me to be accepted by creatures who were supposed to loathe me, but my own blood, the people who were genetically disposed to like me, seemed to find so much wrong with me?

"So how's school going, Ty?" Eugenelene asked from two rows over.

Eugenelene, for whom we'd never come up with a decent nickname, was one of the closest cousins to my age. My parents considered her damn near perfect, what with her recent engagement and persuading her husband to move on to our packlands instead of taking her to his own. I'd resented her quite a bit when we were kids. *Eugenelene always did what she was told. Eugenelene ate every bit of venison on her plate. Eugenelene always took care of her baby brothers and sisters without complaining.* But as I got older, I realized that Eugenelene gave up a lot for those compliments. By comparison, I wasn't as well-liked, but I was happier.

"Oh, just fine," I lied. "Classes are interesting. Professors are really cool. Nothing crazy."

Eugenelene, who had dreamed of opening her own café when we were kids, gave me a soft smile. "Sounds nice."

"You know, the technical school has culinary classes."

She shook her head, even though I could see longing in her eyes. "Oh, I couldn't, not with the wedding coming up."

"You never know until you try," I told her. "You could start classes next semester, maybe finish a certificate before you start having kids. It's not selfish to do something for yourself. It's your life."

Eugenelene stood, ripping off her work gloves. "Not everybody's like you, Ty. Some of us put a priority on the pack."

She stomped down the row and started working next to her sister, Shaylene.

"Three minutes and I managed to piss her off enough to storm off," I muttered. "That's got to be a record."

Interactions like this were what kept me so isolated from the family, while still living within ten freaking feet of them. And even bigger fights were coming. I didn't want this date that my aunts were setting up for me. I didn't want to marry some nice werewolf boy and settle for a life where happy kids and a clean house were the most I would hope to achieve. But at the same time, I knew – as sure as the sun would rise and fall —I would go on the date because otherwise the constant pressure, the snide remarks, the scenes like this morning would become so much worse. I was only delaying the inevitable, but it felt like my only power lived in that delay. I didn't want to give that up any more than I wanted to give up the work I loved.

I was drawn out of these gloomy thoughts by the sounds of footsteps through the grass to my left. I scented pipe tobacco on the wind.

"It's real nice of you to plant the tomatoes, even when you hate them."

I glanced up to see my Uncle Lonnie standing at the end of the row I was working. He was wearing an old work shirt and battered jeans with his muck boots. The garage advertised on his hat—McClaine Auto Repair—had closed when I was a child, but I'd never seen him wearing another.

I stood up, taking off my UK cap. I swiped my forehead, ignoring the dirt it left smeared across my skin. Uncle Lonnie and I had never been close, but I admired him. I'd seen too many Alphas use fists and fangs to bully their packs and run their packlands like dictatorships. So I appreciated Lonnie's tendency toward good sense and a stern, quiet voice. Mimi was much the same. She didn't swan around like my aunts, shouldering an ax to grind. Aside from the brief period of losing her damn mind around the time of Jolene's marriage and childbirth, Aunt Mimi tended to just give orders and then stared at whoever was giving her trouble until they relented.

My parents tended to keep me out of both of their reach. I'd always assumed that it was because they didn't want me to embarrass them, but now I wondered whether they didn't want the Alpha couple to know what was happening in our house. The money problems, the desperate unhappiness of my parents' marriage, the constant conflicts with me—my father didn't want Lonnie or Mimi sniffing out any of those issues.

"It's all an elaborate ruse," I told him. "If I flood the barn with tomatoes, the aunties will be so overwhelmed by supply that their canning might not turn out."

Uncle Lonnie just squinted at me and shook his head, all amusement. "Well, it can't be any crazier than your cousin Waylan's plan to build a tractor that runs on expired mayonnaise."

Cousin Waylan was either a genius or completely freaking crazy. Nobody had ever been able to figure out which, no matter how many tests they ran.

"I actually liked that plan," I said.

Lonnie jerked his shoulder. "Waylan's a dreamer. How's the job search coming?"

I dropped my garden knife, nearly impaling my foot. "Beg pardon?"

"Your daddy said you're looking for a job. That you're not much for working at the butcher shop." He kept his lips pursed. I imagined he was trying to find a way to avoid saying, "because you think you're too good for the butcher shop," which I'm sure my father had added.

I flushed red, which had nothing to do with the sun.

"If you don't want to work at the butcher shop, you don't have to," Lonnie told me. "A smart girl like you has plenty of options, especially in this family. Your cousin Vern is getting busier and busier with his construction business. He needs someone to take care of the billing and the scheduling and such. And Vonnie could always use some help at the Bridal Barn."

I shuddered. Nearly all of the McClaine brides got their formalwear from my aunt's shop. Aunt Vonnie made all of the dresses herself, based on a circa 1982 pattern called "Ruffles and Dreams." It looked just as awful as the title implied, and Vonnie usually used the shiniest sateen polyester she could find. Despite steadily dwindling business, she insisted that eyesore was the height of elegance.

I would not submit. I might humor the aunties with their dating machinations, but I would not connive unwitting brides-maids into wearing the Ruffles and Dreams. Every person had their ethical limits, and this was mine.

"I have a job, Uncle Lonnie," I told him carefully. "I help people with social media...um, it's like advertising for their businesses on the Internet."

He tilted his head. "You can make money at that?"

Well, that was a more interested response than I expected. Unlike my parents, Lonnie seemed to be waiting for me to explain, instead of just huffing dismissals about what they were *sure* I was doing. "I make enough. I would make more if I could get a bit more peace and quiet."

"Don't get enough of that at home, huh?"

I shook my head and pinned my lips together, because any words I said would just be destructive and disastrous.

"You happy doing that?"

"Sure." I managed to say that without adding "so much more than cutting up animals and wrapping them in butcher paper."

"Well, then, I don't see why you shouldn't go on doing it. I'll tell your daddy to give you some, uh, breathing room," he offered.

I grinned at him, grateful to the point that it was sort of sad. Suddenly the vacancy in Dick and Andrea's apartment building came to mind. If I asked Uncle Lonnie for permission to move off the compound, would he give it? The very idea made me dizzy with the possibilities. Bathroom privacy. Sleeping, working, and *living* on my own schedule. Kitchen privacy. Being a grown ass woman without a curfew. Garage privacy.

I opened my mouth to say the words, but I seemed to run out of air. I'd scored a victory for my independence, getting Lonnie on board with my self-employment and his offering to get my father off my back. It felt like pushing too far to ask for more. It might have seemed like sad baby steps for a human, but these were giant furry leaps for werewolf kind.

I RAN through the woods on four feet, scenting the wind, leaping over fallen trees. My prey was only a few hundred yards away, taunting me with the promise of a belly full of my favorite kill.

I paused at the edge of the tree-line, listening, waiting as my brain processed the flood of sensory information from the hunting grounds. The flat terrain. The number of targets. The dim light of the starlit sky. The scent of hot dogs frying in the grill.

I'd seriously missed Marv's Drive-In Picture Show.

I shifted to my human form, pulling a pair of jeans and one of my nicer tops from my backpack. Fully dressed, I used the faint light from the drive-in's streetlights to put my hair up in some semblance of a ponytail. I'd thought about make-up, but even with my keen eyesight, I didn't think applying eyeliner in the dark would be a good idea. The bravest I got was applying some raspberry-colored lip gloss. Alex met me without a lick of make-up on and he'd been attracted to me then. What was the point of putting up layers of illusion between us on a date? He knew what my face looked like. It was sort of the point of vampire super-vision.

I'd told my parents that I was watching the twins for Jolene. And she had (reluctantly) agreed to confirm my story if they checked up on me. I didn't feel great about it...but I also didn't feel great about the prospect of telling my parents I was out on a date with a vampire they'd never met.

I walked out of the woods with my backpack slung over my shoulder, as if it was totally normal for a girl to walk alone for miles through the trees toward a drive-in. Carrying yourself with confidence, that was the key.

Marv's was something of an institution in Half-Moon Hollow, built in the 1950s when drive-in theaters were all the rage. Even as the passion for outdoor cinema waned, Marv's endured, with the same ancient window-clip speakers, the same old cement block concession stand and the same weirdly outdated playground equipment in front of the screen. The movies were also incredibly outdated because Marv couldn't pay the distributors for recent releases.

Once upon a time, my parents had loved bringing me here. It was one of the few things we did just for our family, just for us. My daddy would buy enough food to make the back gate of his truck dip as we sat on it, watching 1980s classics. It was a place where I'd felt loved and *normal*. I was accepted by my parents, good enough for just one night at a time.

And suddenly, we'd stopped. Sometime around my turning twelve, Daddy was "too tired" to sit all night in an uncomfortable lawn chair getting bit by mosquitoes, and Mama didn't like

old movies. She said she never had, though some of my fondest
memories involved her laughing so hard at that Steve Gutten-
berg robot movie, she had tears rolling down her cheeks. Based
on what I heard, eavesdropping from the hallway, drive-in
nights became another thing we gave up in order to keep the
pack happy.

Towards the back of the parking lot, I spotted the music
school's black SUV among the neat rows of cars. I took the long
way around, avoiding the foot traffic areas. I didn't know if I
would be recognized, but I figured the fewer people who saw
me, the better. Alex was hopping out of the car before I was
anywhere near it. "You look lovely."

"Thanks for coming," I told him.

He grinned, taking my hand in his. "How could I resist the
invitation? 'Would you like to go sit in a dark car with me and
watch a weird old movie you've probably never seen?'"

"Yeah, I haven't asked a lot of guys out on dates," I told him,
shaking my head.

"I find that comforting in a way that is probably outdated
and unhealthy," he admitted.

"The windows of your car are super tinted," I noted, realizing I could barely make out the outline of his seats from
outside the SUV.

"Well, it comes in handy, if you have to leave your house
before the sun has entirely set," he replied. "Why, what are you
planning for the two of us to get up to inside this car?"

"Nothing like that," I scoffed, nudging at his shoulders as he
chuckled. "I just mean, it's a good thing. It will keep us off of the
kitchen gossip circuit...unless we stand out here all night."

He sighed, opening the passenger side door. "I could have
picked you up. I believe Dick mentioned that as part of the
'rules for gentlemen who don't want to have their asses handed
to them.'"

"No, you really couldn't have," I assured him. "My family

wouldn't have understood and answering the questions would have been…difficult."

"You could have just said I was a friend," he said as he handed me into the car.

"Werewolves don't have vampire friends," I told him. He closed the door, but not before I saw the injured expression on his face. When he returned to the driver's seat, I added, "I'm sorry. It has nothing to do with you. You're…I don't want to use the word 'perfect' because that seems like a little much. But it wouldn't matter that you're kind or smart or you treat me well or that Jolene trusts her children to you. My family just wouldn't understand. And they would make life really difficult for me at home. I would never be allowed to forget 'that time you brought home a vampire.' And this is so new…"

"That you don't want to risk that sort of repercussion without knowing whether this is going to work long term." He took my hand and I leaned across the front seat, my forehead almost touching his.

I wanted to object, but honestly, he was right. I didn't want to risk that sort of estrangement from my family if this relationship wasn't going anywhere. "Thank you."

"I'll try not to push," he promised, his lips hovering over my skin, just over my cheek. My fingers stroked over his jaw, tracing the sharp lines of it. All I would have to do was move my head up just the tiniest bit and my mouth would connect with his. And the closeness, the knowledge that kissing him would be so effortless, made butterflies the size of condors fistfight in my belly. "But that's going to be difficult…I want you, Tylene. And not just with the aggressive and slightly creepy implications of the way I just said that. I want all of you. I want to be able to take you out on my arm, without you looking over your shoulder like we're doing something wrong. I want you in my home, relaxed, knowing you belong there. I'd like to be able to meet members of your family beyond Jolene and the twins. I just want to be part of this strange, colorful life you live. I haven't been a part of the light in a long time. I hope to borrow a bit of yours, for as long as you'll let me."

I breathed him in. I wasn't sure if he closed the distance between us or I did. All I knew was the cool, sweet press of his mouth against mine. He let me lead, only opening to me when I slid my tongue tentatively across the soft line of his bottom lip. He moaned softly as I licked into his mouth, tasting mint and the copper-bright tang of blood.

His hands slid down my back, not quite pulling me closer, but keeping me right where I wanted to be. His skin was so cool against mine, smelling of cedar. I wanted to wallow in it, to carry that scent on my skin forever so I would never forget this moment and how it felt to kiss someone I wanted so much. Someone who wanted me in return. I slid my hands under his jaw, my thumbs brushing his earlobes.

I guess they were pretty sensitive because something seemed to shift in the kiss. The console of the car kept us apart, and that was probably for the best, considering that my instincts were commanding me to climb into his lap and test how far back his seats reclined. I could feel his teeth moving and a sharp point drew across the sensitive flesh of my bottom lip. I gasped at the sting, though it wasn't enough to draw blood.

"Sorry!" he exclaimed, cradling my jaw so he could examine my mouth. "Are you all right?"

His fangs had come out, which, from what I understood from the books I'd skimmed at the shop, usually happened when vampires were thirsty, angry or…excited. My blood rushed to my cheeks and I was weirdly proud that I'd managed to get that reaction out of him. I felt…powerful. Which was probably wrong, but I was willing to go with it.

"I can't always control them," he said, gesturing to his mouth and clearing his throat awkward. "Though, uh, it's been a long time since that's happened."

"I'm fine," I promised him. "And not to be a buzzkill, but no matter how well things work between us, we may never be able to have all those nice things you mentioned."

"I'd still like to try," he mumbled, kissing me again. "And a proper first date—without your contingent of vampire chaperones—is a good way to start, I think."

"Dick doesn't mean half of those threatening gestures," I swore as we settled back into our seats.

"I would like to believe you, but somehow..." Alex shuddered.

"I can't believe you've never seen this movie," I said. "I figured *Amadeus* would be right up your alley."

He shrugged. "I don't spend much time on television or movies. It's always seemed so loud to me. Too much."

"That seems so outside of my experience," I laughed, thinking of how often I would come home to not only the living room TV blasting, but my parents' unit blasting in their room. No wonder I was so good at tuning out noise at the music school. "But I think you'll like this. It involves Mozart...though I can't guarantee historical accuracy...or that you won't be insulted by the way the era's hairstyle was portrayed."

"Impossible, the era's hairstyles were horrifying," he informed me, making me giggle.

As the last pink fingers of sunset faded from the sky, the screen lit up with the same old WELCOME TO MARV'S slide. As usual, the classic dancing concessions commercial played, encouraging the audience to "go to the lobby." Which didn't exist, because we were outside.

Alex glanced towards the concession stand, grimacing at the sight of a line that stretched all the way across the parking lot and around the corner towards the screen. "The line has barely moved since I got here. Is there service really that slow?"

I grinned. "No, that is the magical draw of the pizza bacon dog on a stick."

Alex froze. "I'm sorry, what now?"

"It's a hot dog wrapped in bacon with cheese, pepperoni, and chopped onions sort of secured inside that porky cocoon, then dipped in corndog batter and deep fried."

Alex gagged and held up a finger. "Pardon me for a moment."

"No, I get it, if solid food tastes like garbage to you, that would basically be a nightmare on a stick."

Local legend had it that Marv invented the pizza bacon dog on a stick late one night when there was a rush on the concession stand and he had hot dogs, but no buns; pepperoni, but no pizza dough. He'd combined them in desperation and created a snack food that captured local tastes and imagination. (It wasn't that hard to do, considering that Marv had used cheese food product, processed meats and deep-frying...and this was Kentucky.)

Despite the increasingly mediocre movie selections, customers still showed up for the pizza bacon dogs on a stick. Sometimes, they just ate pizza bacon dogs and then left before the movie started—even after paying admission! That culinary marvel kept Marv's open through recessions and heat waves and the IMAX craze.

"Did *you* want something to eat?" he asked. "It's considered a cornerstone of any modern date, yes?"

"You're sweet to offer, but I wouldn't do that to you." I snickered. "I ate before I left the house. I don't want to trap you in a car with food that smells disgusting to you."

"Your sacrifice is very considerate," he said, smiling at me. "Jane told me how important food is to werewolves, what with your fast metabolism."

I didn't mention the devastating effects of a pizza bacon dog on a stick on one's breath. The one natural ingredient in the pizza bacon dogs on a stick—the onions—were homegrown in Marv's garden and were legendarily potent. I was doing us both a favor.

"That is one of the few things werewolves have over on the vampires. The ability to eat multiple pizzas in a single bound without suffering the consequences," I conceded. "But you all get super-secret extra powers and I am very jealous."

"Some of those powers aren't very useful," he assured me. "I met a vampire in Munich whose special vampire skill was knowing when sun was about to rise."

"But isn't that important information for people who burst into flames when they come into contact with the sun?" I asked.

"Yes, but generally, the best indicator that the sun is rising is a big ball of fire in the sky."

"Fair enough." I nodded. "Is it considered rude to ask about a vampire's special power?"

"Not at all. I can hear the true emotions in a person's voice, which I know sounds like I'm just listening to their tone. But I can hear hidden love, I can hear hidden hate. When we met, I could tell that you weren't just annoyed with those boys knocking into the bookshelf. I could hear your desperation to get away. I could hear how nervous you were to talk to me. I could hear that you wanted me."

"Well, that sounds…I really wish I had known that before I talked to you,"

"It's not an exact gift, like mind-reading and I try not to use it to my advantage," he said, rubbing his hand on the back of his neck. "And when you think about it, it makes sense. My hearing was highly attuned in life, and music has always affected my emotions profoundly. My gift just combined the two."

"Well, it's definitely more helpful than the sunrise thing."

The movie started and we stopped speaking, leaning towards each other as the story sprang to life on the screen. For the first time since we'd met, we managed to be alone and still, without people watching or my having to rush away. It was so nice, to sit there together in the quiet dark and just be.

LATER THAT NIGHT, as I settled into bed, having showered and changed into PJs and thrown my drive-in clothes in the washer while my parents dozed in their recliners, there was a knock at my window. It was so soft, it was almost unnoticeable. I cringed, wondering if one of my relatives had followed the smell of popcorn to my window from the perimeter. I'd changed into fresh clothes after I ran home, and then used the floral-scented wet wipes to clean my skin before I walked through the door. But you could only do so much to get rid of movie snack-smell.

In my dark bedroom, I crept to my window and saw nothing but tree branches swaying, as if they'd just been swept aside. I opened the window, a narrow horizontal affair I couldn't hope to slide out of…which in terms of parenting, was pretty diabolical. I turned the crank to vent it outward and picked up on the warm scent of cedar…and onions and pepperoni.

Which was *not* a great combination.

I sniffed, glancing down to a shiny object placed just under my window. Winking in the moonlight was a pizza bacon dog on a stick, carefully wrapped in aluminum foil.

A silly, stupid grin broke out on my face.

My phone pinged. Under Aunt Myrtle's screen name, Alex had texted me, *"It didn't seem right to me, that you missed out on your favorite treat because you're such a considerate person."*

"Thank you, you're very sweet," I replied. *"How did you get one? The line was still crazy when I left"*

Alex had not been thrilled about not driving me home, but his protests were minimal after I laid what I considered to be an impressive second goodnight kiss on him and then ran away. Had he really stayed behind and shelled out cash to get me a stinky processed food treat and sneak it across supernatural enemy lines? Somehow, it was the most romantic thing anyone had ever done for me.

That was sort of sad.

"If you offer enough people bribes, they'll let you skip ahead in the pizza-bacon-dog-on-a-stick line."

I laughed, typing back. *"Your chivalry is very impressive. But please don't sneak onto the compound again. It's very dangerous. If my family caught you."* I paused, trying to think of the most appropriate and not-insulting way to phrase "werewolf ass-whooping." But I just went with, *"It would be very bad."*

But then I added several emojis—a cursing angry face, a wolf, a fist, flames, an ambulance. He did not respond to these images, only sending, *"It was worth it, to see you smile like that."*

I gasped. If he saw me smile, did that mean he was standing in the woods, watching? It already denied logic that my family hadn't smelled him. *"You're still here? Go!"*

The trees rustled just a bit more and I imagined him running through the woods—I hoped to get far, far away from here. I snuck through the living room, past my sleeping parents and the blaring TV and out the door.

I opened the door as quietly as I could and tiptoed around the side of the trailer. The foil package was waiting there for me and I took it to the garden plot to sit among natural, healthy plants...and eat the most unnatural and unhealthy thing possible. I was a creature of contradictions.

That man had risked nausea and limb to get me something he knew I would like, something I'd given up to make him more comfortable. When was the last time anyone had done that for me? Put themselves at risk? Noticed and appreciated what I'd done for them? It certainly wasn't something I saw in my parents' relationship. The last time my daddy had given anything for Mama, I think it involved not watching a play-off game because she'd broken her tail bone and wanted to watch *Wheel of Fortune.*

I laid back on the dirt, staring up at the stars and chewing thoughtfully. I felt like I was standing with my toes over the edge of something, something special, something that could change the rest of my life. But I didn't know if that change would be for better or for worse. I could have maybe found someone I could love. I could have found someone who could be in my life for years. And at the same time, my family could find out about Alex. I could be pushed out into the cold on my own.

Some weird little voice in the back of my head said maybe one would be worth the other.

5

"What you don't know about your partner's past can hurt you. What you don't tell your partner about your past will hurt you in a far more dramatic (and possibly bloody) fashion."
—*A Gentleman in Any Era: An Ancient Vampire's Guide to Modern Relationships*

The next morning, I woke up to a silent house, which was never a good sign. I padded into the living room. My parents were sitting at the dinette, eating an inordinate amount of sausage and eggs.

"Morning," I muttered, pouring myself a cup of coffee.

"I smell pizza bacon dogs," Daddy said, staring at me.

I froze in the middle of my first coffee sip. How was that even possible with the amount of sausage and coffee in this small space? But instead of making up an excuse, I just said, "Weird."

"Pretty weird, being able to smell them so far away from the drive-in."

"Mmmhmm," I mumbled into my coffee cup.

Daddy stared me down while he chewed. "Where did you say you went last night?"

"Jolene's," I replied, careful to maintain eye contact.

"And if I called Jolene to ask what time she sent you home, what time would she tell me?"

"Well, I got home around 11, so 10:40?" I guessed, sipping my coffee. I was able to stay so casual because I'd already texted Jolene to *tell her* what time she'd sent me home.

I wasn't proud of lying, but life wasn't giving me much choice lately.

"I'll do just that," he said. "Keeps ya honest."

"All right, then." I shrugged, even while I mentally apologized to Jolene.

The front door swung open and Aunt Lurlene walked in without even knocking. Because why would she? It was just our kitchen, where we were sitting, in our pajamas, having a private conversation. I hated it. Almost as much as I hated the way my mother hopped up from her breakfast to plate some sausage and eggs.

The many benefits of living in my own space seemed to scroll through my brain, like a devious voice whispering in my ear. Privacy. Control over who walked in my door first thing in the morning. Meals in blessed silence. But Lurlene was teetering with purpose on her cork wedge shoes, so I didn't have time for that voice or its seductive promises.

"Morning." My daddy just kept chewing as Lurlene kissed his cheek. She didn't say 'thank you' when Mama served her breakfast, which was not helping my mood.

"What brings you by?" Mama asked, pouring Lurlene coffee.

"Oh, just checking in on Tylene," Lurlene said breezily, as if that was a normal thing to say about a grown ass woman, who was standing right there. "I hear you stayed out late last night."

"Yes, as I mentioned before to *my parents*," I said, even while Daddy glared at me. "I was babysitting for Jolene."

"Well, I just think it's weird that you would stay out so late to *babysit*," she said, giving me the stink-eye.

"Okay."

"It would be a shame," she said, chewing on a strip of bacon. "If you were to break the trust of your parents, and your whole family, your pack, the people who have sheltered you and fed you for your entire life, by lying to them."

I tried not to respond, with facial expressions or words. What did she know? Had she seen Alex running through the woods, pizza bacon dog in hand? Had she smelled him on the property? On me?

"That would be a shame," I said, sipping my coffee. Daddy was watching the conversation bounce between us like a very angry tennis fan.

"If you want to go on a date with a boy, he needs to come seek your family's approval," Lurlene said. "He needs to talk to your daddy. If he's not willing to do that, he's not worth having."

"Tylene knows that," Mama said quietly.

"She damn well better," Daddy muttered.

Indignation burned through me—far more indignation than probably deserved by someone who *was* actually lying to her family and dating someone who would not be approved by her family. Even if Lurlene did know something, what right did she have to walk into my home, and question me in front of my parents? For the first time in a long time, the anger I felt being treated this way far outweighed the fear of getting into trouble.

"I promise not to date any *boys* you haven't met yet," I said through an insincere smile.

Six hundred year old vampires didn't count as boys, right?

Lurlene must have picked up on my very specific wording because she seemed unconvinced.

"You just need to be careful who you throw your lot in with,

Tylene." She wiped her mouth and stood, leaving her plate for Mama to clear. "Tyler, we need to talk sometime soon."

With that last comment hanging in the air, she swanned out of the trailer, leaving me to deal with the fallout.

"What did you do?" Daddy demanded.

I scoffed. "I have no idea what she's talking about."

Which was true. I had no idea what she was referring to. She could have gotten a phone call from someone who saw me at the drive-in. She could have seen me sitting out in the field and eating ill-gotten deep-fried food. She could have inferred some random scenario that had no connection with reality as I knew it. The worst part was I didn't know what she planned to do with that information or how to get ahead of it.

Daddy sneered at me.

"Look, last year, Lurlene was convinced cousin Shaylene was pregnant by that cook from the Coffee Spot. Remember? Shaylene was keeping 'odd hours' and Lurlene 'thought maybe' she saw Shaylene's car in the parking lot of the diner once or twice? Lurlene got all the aunties riled up about the new baby and planned a baby shower? But it turned out Shaylene was keeping 'odd hours' because she got her mechanic's certification and was working at a garage in Monkey's Eyebrow."

"And why did she feel like she couldn't tell her family about her new job?" Daddy snorted. "Working for some stranger instead of your cousin Nate's towing business?"

"Because she didn't want to work for her brother, who drives her crazy?" I guessed. "My point is Aunt Lurlene sometimes—"

I paused while Daddy glared at me again. "Misinterprets information."

"You need to watch yourself," he warned me. He stood up from the table and threw himself into his recliner. He picked up the remote and began flipping through channels. I watched

Mama clear the table, knowing that I would get no help from her.

Just last night, I'd been lying under the stars, eating my favorite food, obtained at great peril by my gentleman caller—only to come crashing back to reality this morning. And all I could think of was getting back to Alex.

And possibly getting more pizza bacon dogs.

WITH THE SPECTER of Lurlene's "dangerous information" hanging over my head, I was only too happy to take the kids to music class the next week. Alex's intermediate class was a demonstration their musical skills for the local Junior League. And the Junior League was *delighted* to host them at the fancy old house where they held their meetings, sipping tea from painted china cups in an honest-to-God parlor while the twins and their classmates played simple chamber music pieces. The ladies who lunched—sure, they lunched at the Coffee Spot, but it still counted—were not only impressed by the kids' playing, but the idea that the Hollow had attracted something as sophisticated as a "youth orchestra." We were a small town on the rise.

And Alex being dressed in a crisp white dress shirt and tie certainly didn't hurt.

Because damn.

By the end of the evening, the twins were asked to play a duet by Bach, something in G major. I was still pretty much a classical music novice. I had tried listening to it on my phone over the past few days and while I knew what I liked, I couldn't discuss the merits of one composer versus another. But the music was smooth and bright and reminded me of water falling over stones.

Joe and Janelyn definitely made some errors, but they were savvy enough to act like it was all part of the performance. And that was how Zeb Lavelle found his children, as he entered the meeting room.

Lanky and blond and utterly human, Zeb didn't move with the authority of Alex or Gabriel or even Dick. But I could see the moment that it dawned on him that his children were given the big finale spot in the meeting. And the pride in his smile was enough that I had to blink away a strange warm moisture that seemed to be gathering in my eyes. He *loved* those kids. He didn't care that their hobby was a little out of the ordinary or worry that they were making a spectacle of themselves in front of what passed for the Hollow's upper echelons. He was just happy to see them, pleased that they were excelling at something. That same distant envy I'd felt for Jolene, finding that life outside the pack, pricked at my heart. The twins were very lucky to have this human father—I didn't care what my parents or anyone else said.

If anything, Alex was just as proud of my cousins, leading the audience in enthusiastic applause that eventually spread out to the other students as well. All of them stood, wearing their little performance uniforms of black pants and a green Half-Moon Hollow Music Academy polo shirt. The ladies who lunched increased their clapping, because frankly, the kids were just adorable.

Alex said, "Ladies, if you have questions, please feel free to contact me at the school. Thank you for inviting us this evening. Students?"

The whole class bowed and the ladies gave them one last ovation. Dismissed, the twins launched themselves at their father, who somehow managed to catch them without hurting himself or their instruments.

I watched from the refreshment table as Alex distributed business cards to ladies who were suddenly very interested in his "Strings for adults" classes. (I tried to keep my sarcastic muttering on the inside, but it was a near thing.) Zeb sidled up to me, grinning as the kids hung off of his arms.

"Thanks for driving the monsters, Tylene. It's made our schedules so much easier," he said. "I know it's a lot. Kids, go pack up your very expensive instruments."

"I don't mind," I promised as the twins scampered off. "I've learned more than I ever expected to about fancy-schmancy music."

"Yeah, don't call it that around the kids," he sighed. "They get irritated and they try to explain things with an ear-splitting amount of detail."

"That sounds about right," I said, laughing.

"How are things back on the compound?" he asked, studying me carefully. "Are you doing okay?"

"It's the compound," I told him, shrugging.

"Yeah, that doesn't tell me a lot," he said, patting my shoulder. "I don't know what Jolene has told you, but I know what it's like coming from a family that's…I'm trying to find a nice way to say 'weird as all hell' but nothing comes to mind. But I've been there, and I get it."

I remembered a story when I was a kid, something about Zeb's mother hiring a hypnotist to get Zeb to dump Jolene at the altar. But it seemed like the wrong time to bring it up.

"If you ever need anything, you call me or Jolene, okay? Even if you think it's silly or a bother, we won't see it that way," he promised.

I smiled at him, hoping that he couldn't see how shiny my eyes were getting. "Thanks, Zeb."

"Well, we better get these two home and fed," Zeb said. "Ty, what time are your folks expecting you?"

Suddenly, Alex was at my side. "I can drive her home, Zeb."

Despite being accustomed to vampire movements, Zeb seemed startled with how fast Alex appeared. "Um…is that

okay?" Zeb glanced at me. "Is there something I should know…
what is happening right now?"

"It's fine," I told my cousin-in-law as his eyebrows winged up
to his hairline. "Alex and I are acquainted."

"Is that what the young people are calling it now?" he asked,
his eyes tracking between us.

"I'm very safe with Alex, I promise. He'll probably have to
drop me off a half-mile from the gate, but I'll be safe."

"I don't love that," Zeb muttered.

"I don't either," Alex told him. "But Ty promises me that it's
better that way."

"Just so you know, I'll be calling Jane to ask her to run a
background check on you," Zeb said, shaking his hand. "It's
nothing personal, you would understand if you'd been around
the last couple of years – with all of the various serial killer
types and general mischief makers we've dealt with. And Ty is
family, so it's even more important."

"You trust Alex with your *children*," I noted.

"Dick and Jane already ran a background check on me," Alex
said. "Well, they ran two. One when I moved into town and then
another much deeper check, when Dick found out I was
seeing Ty."

"He what?" I gasped.

Alex put his arm around me. "I respect his protective nature,
especially when it comes to you."

"This is all pretty normal procedure for Dick," Zeb
assured me.

"Yeah, yeah, I've heard the stories," I muttered. "Getaway
cars, incorrect German speeches."

"That one time he helped Cal give Ben Overby an illegal lie
detector test," Zeb added. "He was dating Gigi at the time. And
he was human. In his current state, the test would be pretty
ineffective."

"Dad! It's time to go!" Janelyn called, snapping Zeb out of his thoughts.

He turned to me. "Text Jolene when you get home, okay?"

"I will," I promised. "Night, kids."

The twins hugged me around the waist. Then they gave Alex high fives and ran out the door.

I patted Zeb's back. "Good luck with your assault on the Burger Shed."

"This is going to be so expensive," Zeb grumbled.

The twins were the last to be taken home by their parents. Somehow, we waded through the crowd of Junior Leaguers, some of whom were giving me hard stares. Alex's hand at the small of my back seemed to make a statement. The fancy ladies didn't like what he was saying.

Alex led me outside to his sedate black SUV with Half-Moon Hollow Music Academy written in vinyl on the doors. It seemed like such a *dad* car, but I guessed it made sense. He spent so much energy and time on his students.

"What's the matter?" he asked, loading bags of extra instruments and equipment through the back hatch.

"I don't know, it's just a shame that you won't have kids of your own. You're so good with them," I said. "Unless, you don't want them, which is also a valid choice. This sentence is not turning out as planned. I want you to have whatever you want."

"Well, it's not so much a choice, but a biological impossibility," he said. "And as much as I enjoy working with my students, I think I'm better off as a 'role model' instead of a father. You're also very good with children. Do you want little werewolves running around?"

"I kind of like the 'fun Cousin Ty' thing. I'm there for the holidays and the concerts and the special stuff and then I can just hand them back to Jolene and Zeb before the uncomfortable parent-teacher conferences and the discussions about student loan debt and puberty," I said, shaking my head.

"You know, I've never heard parenthood described like that."

I snorted. "I'll bet."

My phone screen showed a message from Zeb. "*This is Jane-lyn, using Dad's phone. Dad's driving. He's making me type every-thing out with punctuation and good spelling because he's a teacher and text speak makes him sick to his stomach. Anyway, Joe left his math textbook in his locker at the music school. He was doing home-work before we left. Dad asked if you can pick it up. We're already on the other side of town.*"

"Everything all right?" he asked, as I buckled the passenger seat belt.

"Do you mind if we go by the school? Joe left a book in his locker and it contained homework. The consequences could be dire."

"No problem," he said. "I need to drop this off anyway. And it means I have more time in the car with you."

"You're gonna end up doing so many of their errands if they get wind of this," I warned him.

We chatted about innocent nothings as we drove through town. It was nice to be so comfortable with him, compared to how nervous I'd been just a few weeks ago. We could almost be confused with a normal, human couple doing couple errands, instead of two creatures of the night, carrying bags full of expensive noisemakers. I liked this mundane normalcy. No tension. No watching every word and gesture. No fending off aunties.

Though I'd only been there a few times, even I could see that there was something "off" about the music building. Light from the streetlamp glittered against something on the pavement and the pristine pale surface of the building was scarred by red markings.

Beside me, Alex cursed in French under his breath. I didn't speak French, but I knew the sound of heartfelt profanity when I heard it.

"What the?" I whispered as he slowed to a stop. I took in the hateful messages spray painted on the building in a careless hand. "LEAVE TOWN, VAMPIRE!" and "LEAVE OUR LOCAL GIRLS ALONE!" were among the kinder sentiments. The window had been smashed and the glass scattered all over the parking lot was catching the light.

"Oh, no." My heart sank as we opened our doors.

Maybe this was what Lurlene knew? Maybe she *had* seen Alex when he visited the compound, then followed his scent to the school? My cousins had done this sort of thing before, petty vandalism and pointed spray paint messages, but never to someone outside of the werewolf community. What if she'd sent pack members here to harass Alex into breaking up with me? I inhaled deeply, trying to pick up on any familiar scents, but all I smelled was the dry, chemical scent of the paint. That was unusual, but not unheard of. My relatives knew that vampires' senses were just as keen as ours, and they knew how to mask their scents.

Alex yanked the unlocked door open and rushed inside. I followed, my heart in my throat. He rattled the still-locked office door, sighing a bit in relief as I flipped on the lights. The studio was trashed. Mirror glass glittered on the floor, providing a sort of perverse frame for more choice phrases painted on the wall. Chairs and stands were thrown about the floor. It looked like someone had taken a sledgehammer to the acoustic panels.

"I'm so sorry," I whispered.

He shook his head and rubbed his hands on my arms.

"You think I haven't dealt with something like this before? I had most of the spare instruments and equipment with me. This is just a little paint thinner and cleanup. And I've been meaning to upgrade the acoustic panels anyway."

"What about your house?" I asked. "Jane took a report from another vampire in town a week or so ago. Iris something. Her windows were smashed and her porch was spray painted."

He scoffed. "I'm sure it's fine. No one knows where I live. I bought the place under a corporate shell. Besides, I have alarms that communicate to my phone if there's any motion near my property lines."

I nodded. "But not near your school?"

"I didn't want to be driven nuts with the alarms going off every time a truck drove by." He shrugged. "I work at the school. I *sleep* in my house. I see the error of my ways now."

"This could get worse," I told him. "If we keep spending time together. It could get a lot worse."

"What are you talking about?" he asked.

"I'm worried my family could have done this. They know the kids take classes here, and that you're a vampire. They could be lashing out at whatever vampires they think are 'influencing me,'" I gasped. "Oh, no. Jane's shop!"

I pulled out my phone and dialed the number for Specialty Books.

"Why do you think Jane would be targeted?" he asked as the phone rang.

"My family really dislikes Jane. They blame her for Jolene being pulled away from the family and I'm sure they'll blame her eventually if they figure out how far I've 'gone astray.' If they went after you, they'd go after Jane, too."

Dick picked up on the third ring. "Dick! Are you all right? Is the shop okay? Where is Jane?"

"Slow down, Ty, slow down. What's going on?"

I explained about the vandalism and the similarities to what happened at Iris's house. After assuring me that the shop was un-burgled, Dick promised he and Jane were on their way over that moment, "with reinforcements." I didn't know what that meant, but it sounded very official. I hung up the phone as Alex collected the laptop and some files from his office. I guessed he didn't feel leaving them in the building was a good idea, given the smashed windows.

"Well, you saved me the step of calling authorities, so thank you," he said. "We don't know that it's your family."

"We don't know that it's *not* my family," I replied. He paused and stared at me. "Yes, I heard the double negative, too!"

Alex stopped what he was doing, crossed the parking lot and kissed me hard. My knees went a little wobbly and I clutched at his tie. His hands slipped around my waist and pulled me tight against him.

"Take a breath," he told me. I obeyed. "And another."

"That's playing dirty," I murmured against his lips.

"Not as dirty as I could." He waggled his brows. I gasped and he chuckled. "See? Now, you're breathing normally."

"So wrong," I sighed, shaking my head. "I don't know which is weirder, 'persistently genteel' you or 'occasional subtle pervert' you."

"I think we both have our merits," he informed me. "Now, does your family know anything about me, specifically?"

I paused. "No.

"Do they know Iris at all?" he asked as I shook my head.

"Maybe they saw her photo in the newspaper the other day, with Jolene involved in her big group hug on the front page. My mama pointed it out to me, maybe she showed it to them, too," I said, pinching my nose. "Or maybe I'm just panicking. And I'm making it about me, which is wrong, given the situation. I'm sorry."

"Stop saying you're sorry. This is very clearly not your fault." He rubbed my arms again. "It's nothing I can't fix. I'm unhurt. *You're* unhurt, so everything's fine."

I grumbled as he hugged me close to him. A few minutes later, several vehicles arrived, and the parking lot was full of vampires. Jane and Dick jumped out of a black SUV and I threw myself at Jane.

"Oh, thank goodness." I wrapped my arms around Jane and squeezed her tight. Behind her, two figures rushed toward Alex

—men I didn't recognize. One was dark and lithe where the other was broad and blond. However, both of them looked extremely irritated at the situation at hand.

"Not that I mind the public display of affection, but are you all right?" she asked.

"I'm fine, just unnerved by the whole thing," I told her. "I still think it could be my family, but Alex thinks they don't have a reason to hurt him or Iris. I tried to explain the crazy factor, but he's not convinced."

"It's something to consider and we'll keep an eye out," Jane promised me. "But from what we saw at Iris's house, well, not to be rude, but they didn't leave a lot of evidence behind. No prints, no hair, not even strong smells. And unless your relatives spend a lot of time watching *ID Discovery*, I don't think they're capable of that level of forensic countermeasure."

I nodded. "No, that's fair. So where does that leave us?"

"It leaves me and Dick taking reports and handling this just like we would any other vandalism case. And you, take a deep breath and stop assuming the worst. That's my job."

"Just the idea that I could cause Alex this kind of trouble," I said, shaking my head.

"Even if it *was* your family, you wouldn't be causing anybody any trouble. It would be your family," she said. "Don't take that weight on yourself."

"Fine." I rolled my eyes and waved to all the extra vampires in the parking lot. "So, if you're going to handle this like any other vandalism case, why did you need reinforcements?"

Jane waved over two dark-haired vampire ladies who looked a lot alike with their high foreheads and delicate jawlines. The younger of them looked familiar in that "we went to school together but weren't friends" kind of way. I remembered her name was sort of fancy and French, and that she seemed nice. But she definitely ran with a more popular crowd than I did.

"This is Iris Scanlon-Calix and her sister, Gigi."

Gigi. That was her name, Gigi. Like most important information, it arrived in my brain just a few seconds too late.

"Oh, it was your house that was vandalized," I said. "I'm so sorry."

I took a cue from Alex's book and didn't reach for Iris or Gigi's hands. What if they didn't feel as friendly toward werewolves as Jane and Dick did? Gigi seemed to sense my reluctance and grabbed my hand, pumping up and down.

"Nice to meet you," she said.

"The house is already cleaned up," Iris said. "Cal called in some people who took care of it the next day. I know I had a strong reaction."

"There were very specific threats made to the vandal's person and property, should you ever find them," Gigi observed placidly.

"I used the word 'strong!'" Iris reminded her. "I know it's kind of silly, considering the damage was fairly minimal, but I just feel so violated. They messed with my flower beds! Do you know how long it took Mom to cultivate those rose hybrids?"

"Years," Gigi agreed. "But you still have some intact specimens. And Cal can't worship the very ground you walk on if that ground is under a jail."

"Damn your wisdom beyond your years," Iris muttered.

Behind the bickering sisters, I could see the men who had rushed to Alex talking quietly with him. The tall blond stepped toward the building and started randomly touching objects, which seemed like a poor strategy in terms of investigation. Jane excused herself to go take pictures of the damages. Alex lifted his head and nodded to me, waving me over. Gigi and Iris looped their arms through mine and walked me over.

Alex put an arm around my shoulders. "Tylene McClaine, these are two of my oldest friends, Nik Dragomirov and Cal Calix. Iris and Gigi are their mates."

"'Oldest friends' takes on a whole new meaning around this crowd," I said.

"It's true," the dark-haired man, Cal, told me. He jerked his head toward Alex. "But think of all the dirt we can give you on this one."

"So you're the girl that's turned Alex's head," Nik said, shaking my hand. His voice was faintly accented. "My Gigi says you went to school together."

"We've talked about inappropriate possessive pronouns, but he is awfully set in his ways. Claims it's a language barrier," Gigi said, smirking.

He kissed her neck. "I speak the language of love, my dearest."

"You've spoken English for several hundred years," she noted.

Dick and Jane joined us in our little standing group, both looking tired.

"I think we've documented everything," Jane said.

"Maybe I should head home?" I asked Jane. "This seems like vampire business."

"You're involved in this vampire business," she told me. "And it affects you directly. You should stay."

The circle closed around me and I felt more at home in this pack, than I had in my own since before I could howl.

6

"Social media is dangerous, whether you're live or undead. Set your privacy filters carefully."
—*A Gentleman in Any Era: An Ancient Vampire's Guide to Modern Relationships*

*E*ven though I'd been told that Jane's friend group found themselves in peril every six months or so, I wasn't prepared for the "*Law and Order* murder board." They just wheeled it out into the shop like it was normal to have an enormous wheeled whiteboard used specifically for friendship group-based investigations.

"Is this really necessary, for a few acts of vandalism?" Alex said. "They didn't even do that much damage to my building."

"That's how it always starts," Jane said, piling whiteboard markers on the maple bar. "Some small weird thing that spirals into something much larger and weirder and the next thing you know—murders, fires, poisonings, emergency vampire turnings, and I end up with more foster vampirelings. And as much as I love Jamie, Ben, Meagan and Georgie and all the love and color they have brought to our home—I can only handle so many children."

"Georgie counts as two," Gabriel added.

"Half-Moon Hollow seemed to have such a low crime rate when I looked at the Chamber of Commerce website," Alex muttered.

"Don't!" Andrea shouted as Jane's face went thunderous. "Don't get Jane started on the Chamber of Commerce. The sun will be up in a few hours. We don't have the time."

Jane pouted and crossed her arms. "Fine."

"We've learned it's easier if we get these issues out in the open," Gabriel told us as Dick rolled the large white board into the café area of the bookshop. Andrea set a cup of herbal tea in front of me—something involving lavender. Apparently, I seemed too caffeinated at the moment. "If we try to handle the situation on our own, it inevitably gets much worse and someone gets hurt. Some of us had to learn this lesson several times over."

He shot an arch look at Jane, who shrugged. "I never said I was easy to live with."

Alex, for his part, simply watched in awe and the group bustled around the shop, each seeming to know their assigned role. Iris and Andrea made drinks. Dick set up the board. Jane gathered office supplies like pens and paper. Cal and Nik arranged chairs in a semi-circle around the board. Gigi set up a rather intimidating laptop on the bar and logged into an Internet search program that I wasn't sure was entirely legal.

"Once every six months, huh?" I asked Gabriel.

"Well, we had a gap there, about two years long, where we enjoyed a brief period of 'no one trying to kill us.'" Gabriel frowned. "It was weirdly off-putting. Jane does some of her most impressive thinking—and cursing—in these meetings."

"Are you sure we shouldn't call everybody else in?" Andrea

asked. "If someone is targeting vampire-owned businesses here in the Hollow, that involves most of our family. Iris has Beeline. Alex has the music school. Jane has the bookshop. Libby has her accounting business. Meadow owns the tea shop. Collin, Cal, Nik, Luke—they all own mysterious consulting firms we're not supposed to ask about. Erik owns a consulting firm, but if you ask questions about it, he'll answer them and then you're stuck there for hours listening to theories about organizational psychology…"

Several people in the room paused to shudder, so I assumed that was bad.

"We don't know if they're targeting vampire business owners," Nik protested.

"Well, what else do Cal, Nik, Alex and Ophelia have in common?" Andrea asked.

"They're super old." Gigi said. When Cal shot her a look that screamed *betrayal*! she added. "What? You *are*!"

"Yes, but the graffiti was more anti-vampire than anti-business. Andrea, can you expand on the theory you were putting forward before my own flesh and blood insulted me to my face?" Cal asked politely.

"Beeline is one of the biggest vampire-owned businesses here in town," Andrea said. Across the room, Iris grinned proudly. "And Alex owns the music school, which has gotten a lot of attention lately because it's so fancy. It's just what jumped out at me when I heard Alex got hit."

"But it's not like they've done business with each other or have that much in common, other than they're vampires and they're both connected to Cal. And I would think the spray-painted messages would be directed at Cal, if he was the target," Gigi said, tapping on her keypad. "If they were going to target prominent vampires here in town, why not Jane or Dick?"

"Because they have more direct support from the Council? If anything happens to the Council representatives, the Undead

Emergency Response Team shows up within a few minutes," Cal offered.

During all of this out-loud speculation, Jane was scribbling furiously on the whiteboard. She wrote out names, circled them, connected the circles with lines.

"I still think my family should be shoved in the suspect pool. My parents were *not* thrilled to see Jolene in that photo in the paper with you. Between that, and Alex's link to the kids, I think that puts them in the running. Also, my aunt Lurlene made some comments about knowing 'something' about my behavior that she didn't like, and honestly, that could lead anywhere."

Jane chewed her lip before writing, "McCLAINES" on the board. "Okay, I will put them on the 'not likely, but still considered suspects' list."

"Thank you for humoring me," I snorted.

"Forensic countermeasures," Jane argued. "I respect your intelligence and adore your bookishness. But I have spent time around your family...speaking of which."

Through the window, I followed Jane's eyeline to the sight of my cousin walking towards the shop.

"You called her!" I squeaked.

"I told you, we keep things in the open here!" Jane exclaimed.

"Well, don't tell her what I said about the newspaper thing. It would stir up a lot of trouble for me at home," I hissed back.

"Are you okay?" Jolene hollered as she came through the door.

"I'm fine. We weren't even there when it happened," I said, giving Jane a significant look as Jolene strangle-hugged me.

"I'm so sorry about the school, Alex. Zeb's at home with the kids. I didn't have the heart to tell them."

"It's nothing. I'll be open in a few days," he assured her, receiving his own strangle-hug. He awkwardly patted her back.

"Aw, did I miss the murder board... Why did you write 'McClaines" on there?" Jolene demanded.

"Because Ty thinks there's a possibility your family could be involved in the vandalism at Iris's house and the music school," Gabriel told her.

Jolene opened her mouth as if to protest and then paused. "Which family members?"

"I'm not sure," I said. "I just think it's a possibility that should be considered."

"I would protest, but considerin' what they put poor Zeb through, yeah, you should watch them," Jolene said, sitting next to me. "Which is going to put you in a real awkward position… wait, what are you doing here anyway?"

I could see the exact moment that Jolene seemed to recognize how close I was standing to Alex. I could see the emotions shuttering through her eyes like slides—surprise, denial, discomfort. She went through the five stages of "your cousin is dating a vampire" right in front of me.

"I see," Jolene said, pressing her lips shut. "So, who's on the suspect list, besides my relatives?"

"Everybody?" Gigi suggested.

"I didn't pick up anything helpful at the school," Nik said. "I saw hands in gloves, holding a spray paint can. But I couldn't tell if it was one person's hands or multiple hands. I couldn't tell whether they were human or werewolves, or anything else for that matter. All I could feel was…fear."

No one acted as if this was a strange thing to say, so I had to assume that Nik had some sort of psychic talent.

"I guess that would be normal, if it was human vandals," Iris said, frowning. "Hate and fear, fear and hate, they're all sort of wound together in an ugly ball."

"That doesn't really help narrow the list, either," Jane said. "Any other ideas?"

"Newsletter to vampire business owners telling them to be vigilant?" Andrea suggested.

"Alex installs cameras outside of his school," I said pointedly.

"I continue to scan the usual Internet hangouts for local loonies who hate vampires," Gigi said.

Cal raised his hand. Iris put it down. "Don't say 'secret underground lair.'"

Cal grumbled, "One day, I will have a secret underground lair."

"I think I should take Ty home," Jolene said. "It's getting late, for those of us who are awake during the day. And I think she's contributed all she can to the conversation."

"I could drive her," Alex protested. "I promised Zeb I would get her home safe."

"Actually, I have a lot of forms you need to sign," Jane said. "The Council has this thing about paperwork. As in, they like it, very, very much."

"Ah," Alex said, standing. For a moment, I wondered whether he was going to kiss me right there in front of everybody. And he seemed to divine this was a bad idea, based on my neck craning back away from him. He eyed Jolene before bowing over my hand and kissing my knuckles. "Goodnight, Tylene."

My voice wobbled as I said, "Goodnight."

Jolene smirked, tugging me out of my chair. "Come on, lover girl. Finish swooning on the drive home. Night, all."

"Why do I get the feeling I'm being sent to bed like a child?" I asked as we walked out of the shop.

"Because you are, sort of," Jolene told me, unlocking her van with a remote key.

I climbed into the passenger seat. Jolene started the van and turned it towards the compound. I pulled a packet of scented wipes out of my bag and started a thorough cleansing of my skin. Between that and the fresh shirt I'd stashed in the same bag, I hoped my parents wouldn't smell the vampires on me.

Sensing Jolene's pointed silence, I said, "Go ahead and say it."

"I don't know how to feel about this hon." Jolene said. "I

mean, it was hard enough on me and Zeb, with him being human. But a vampire?"

"If this is uncomfortable for you, not wanting to lie to the pack—"

Jolene scoffed. "Oh, hell, honey, I don't care about the pack. I don't want to discourage you, but I'm worried about you. I'm torn because I want you to be happy. But I know how hard it is to be with someone who's not were. And I don't know if you're ready for that, for the whole pack coming down on you. I've been through it and it's not something you just jump into without thinking. You've always been so…obliging when it comes to your parents. Not that I can blame you. Your daddy's always been a nasty piece of work. Anyway, I just wanted to tell you, that if you need help, I'm here for you. You can come stay with us until you get on your feet."

"Really? Won't that bring a lot of trouble down on your head? What about Zeb?"

"It was his idea," she said. Her smile had a dreamy quality to it. "And yeah, it might bring some trouble down on us. But that's the great thing about living off of the compound. If the pack is mad at you, it doesn't feel like the sky is falling because you can get away from it.

"It's tempting," I told her as we pulled onto the compound road. "And I'll think about it. But I really think that if I'm going to get out, I'd like to do it on my own. Otherwise, it will just feel like you're taking care of me, instead of me taking care of myself."

"I can respect that," Jolene said, slowing in front of my trailer. "Even if I think it's dumb."

I snickered. "Thank you. I think that's the very definition of love."

"So can I ask you something?"

"Sure."

"What's it like dating a vampire?"

"Same as dating a human?" I guessed. "Except he's way more polite. Is it weird, how sexy I find politeness?"

"Probably." She nodded.

"Yup." I climbed out of the van. "Goodnight."

"Goodnight, weirdo!"

I SPENT a lot of time considering Jolene's offer. Alex had to spend a few days with insurance adjusters and contractors, repairing his school, replacing the equipment. I continued working at Specialty Books, considering both the murder board and my own work projects. And while I didn't befriend Jane and her family for mercenary purposes, I ended up expanding my own business considerably. When Jane expressed (loud and profane) frustration with the program they used for the shop's email promotions and social media, I offered to take a look at it for her. Within an hour, I'd signed a contract to handle all of her online activity except for sales. And when she told her friends how easy I'd made her life, I had contracts with Beeline, Everlasting Health, Libby Stratton's accounting business, Wade Tucker's garage, and the local free clinic run by Nola McGavock, a human who also happened to be Dick's only living descendant. Jane even talked about handing the Council's regional promotions, if she could get approval from the national office. I was a one-woman public relations empire.

I watched my family in a new light, analyzing every word and gesture from them. Normally, I just got annoyed with them so quickly, I just chalked their behavior up to being meddlesome, but now I wondered—Did Uncle Bill look smug when he was repairing the underpinning on his trailer? Did my cousin Maybelline's eyes narrow when she asked where I'd been spending all my time lately? Was my family capable of vandalizing Alex's school? Yes. But if they had done it, I would have expected them to talk about it. They would gloat and try to assure themselves I'd learned my lesson. And if my parents knew that I was dating a vampire, there was no way they would keep quiet about it, they would rail against me for daring to see someone they didn't approve of, of wasting my time on some guy who didn't even have a pulse.

Still, I watched, and I waited, and tried to work through everything I would have to do if I wanted to move out—whether it was to Dick's apartment building or Jolene's place.

The night of my half-ass blind date with Donnie Ansen came far too soon. While I hadn't "come by" Braylene's trailer as instructed, or even told my aunts when the date was scheduled, somehow Braylene, Lurlene, and several of my cousins crowded into my room to argue over what I should wear.

They were turning into some sort of hen party from hell, giggling and chattering, like I was getting ready for a much-anticipated prom date. My head was splitting from all the damn noise and all I wanted to do was toss myself out of the window just to escape. I also seriously considered showing up to Southern Comfort naked, but that seemed counterintuitive.

"You should wear the green dress," Braylene bellowed, shaking the hanger at me, as if I was some sort of stubborn bull resisting a fight. I guessed she wasn't too far off.

The green print with the tiny sprigs of white flowers was a classic nice girl Baptist church dress. Mama insisted that I wear it to any special occasion from funerals to first dates. She was hovering near the door, again, not quite taking part of the chaos, though she seemed to *want* to. I would have gladly traded places with her—and then bolted for the window.

"No, the yellow!" Lurlene insisted, stepping in front of her and displaying the yellow dress with blue flowers.

I only seemed to own dresses with flowers on them. It was a deep personal flaw.

"Not the yellow! It makes her look all sallow and washed out!" Braylene objected.

"No, the green makes her look flat as a pancake!" Lurlene shot back. "She looks like a twelve-year-old boy in it! The yellow makes the best of what she's got!"

"I don't know why I wouldn't want to spend more evenings like this. It's a damn mystery," I muttered to no one in particular —which was fine, because no one was listening.

"What was that, hon?" my cousin Shaylene hollered over the din.

"I wonder if I could just wear some nice jeans and a pretty top!" I lied.

"Honey, no," Lurlene barked. "We want Donnie to think you're a nice girl!"

"I *am* a nice girl!" I cried. "And I'm sure nice girls have worn jeans at some point in history."

"We want Donnie to think you're *traditional*," Braylene said.

"Isn't that false advertising?" I asked, frowning.

"Honey, that's all dating is."

"True enough," I said with a shrug.

"We could always have Vonnie whip something up for you," Braylene said. "Obviously nothing as fancy as her bridesmaids dresses, but—"

"No!" I yelped. "No dresses from Vonnie."

"Why don't we just put it to a vote?" another cousin, Eugene-lene, suggested. "Who likes the green dress?"

Six of my relatives raised their hands.

"And how many like the yellow?"

Four more raised their hands.

How in the hell did we fit this many people in my room?

"The green dress, it is!" Eugenelene announced brightly.

"Don't I get a vote?" I asked.

"No!" It was the only thing they could all agree on, apparently.

Sighing, I slipped into the green dress and went to my makeup mirror. I'd intended to keep it minimal and somewhat natural, but the brushes were literally removed from my hands. I lost track of how many hands were on my face and it was all I could do not to bite out at them as they reached for my hair. By the time they were done, I was wearing a *lot* more eye makeup than I'd intended and a bouffant hair do that would put Vonnie's 1980s brides to shame.

When they stepped back as a group and let me see the mirror, I marveled, "I look like a redheaded Grand Ole Opry-era Dolly Parton."

"That's what I was going for!" Lurlene crowed triumphantly. I thought maybe I saw sympathy in Shaylene's eyes, but she simply disappeared to the back of the crowd. I hoped my younger cousins were paying attention. They were only seventeen, which meant they were due this sort of treatment in the next couple of years.

I pursed my lips and she smacked me lightly on the arm. "Don't smudge that lipstick!"

"I'll drive you into town," Mama said, holding out a dainty pleather handbag I would never carry in a million years. There wasn't even room for my cell phone in it.

I elbowed my way out of the room, waving off my aunts' advice about good first date behavior and how to catch Donnie's attention. I snagged my backpack on my way out of the trailer. Daddy was nowhere to be found, and I wondered if Uncle Lonnie had done something to get him out of the way.

"Can't I just borrow the truck, Mama?" I asked as I climbed in. "I don't need to be dropped off like some ten-year-old at a playdate."

"No." Mama shook her head. "I want to make sure you get there."

"Because you think I'll get lost?" I asked pointedly.

"Don't you take that tone with me, young lady. You've been

real sneaky lately, disappearing, not telling us where you are, who you're with."

"Well, maybe if you and Daddy believed me when I talked to you, I would tell you more," I replied, pulling the visor mirror down the moment we left the compound. I shook my hair out of its ceiling-high arrangement and pulled it into a much more tolerable ponytail.

"Aunt Lurlene isn't going to be happy about that," she warned me as I started carefully wiping at my eyes.

"Aunt Lurlene will have to get over it," I said, wiping at my lips.

"Don't talk that way about your family," she warned.

"I'm going on the damn date, aren't I?" I shot back. When she looked away, wounded, I softened my voice. "I'm sorry, Mama. I'm just really frustrated with all of this. I'm tired of being treated like what I want doesn't matter."

We turned onto Paxton Avenue and I wished like hell we could skip this whole restaurant thing. I wished I could ask Donnie to meet me at Specialty Books for one of Dick's cappuccinos. But I couldn't imagine he would be okay with going to a vampire-owned establishment.

I did not have high hopes for this evening. I'd been on so many of these setups. Boys who were inevitably disappointed that I was not the agreeable domestic goddess they were promised and cut the dates short. I could only hope Donnie would do the same. I would give this guy thirty-five minutes. That was enough time to have a drink, make polite conversation, get an "emergency text" from a friend who "needed me to come pick her up."

"Ty, it's really important that things go well for you tonight," she said.

I stared out the window, more than a little hurt that she didn't even respond to my feelings. "I'll try my best."

"No, honey, you need to do more than try. If you don't catch this boy's attention, Mimi and Lonnie are bound to give up on you, and you know what that could mean for us."

I didn't want to scoff at my mother's concerns, but in my recent conversations with Uncle Lonnie, he hadn't mentioned my marriage prospects once. He'd been more interested in my happiness, my professional fulfillment. Was it possible my parents were putting pressure on me based on nothing more than their own misperceptions and my aunts' nosiness? If I didn't catch this boy's attention, nothing would really change... other than maybe my aunts would leave me the hell alone.

"Mama, I can't force him to like me," I replied.

"No, but you can put in more effort than you normally do," she told me.

"I'll be sociable and I'll mind my manners. That's all I can promise," I told her.

"I'll go shopping and pick you up in about two hours," she said. "Do more than try, Tylene."

I sighed as I slid out of the truck. I grabbed my backpack, even as Mama opened her mouth to object, and slammed the truck door behind me. Mama gunned the engine and took off down the street.

What did she mean, I needed to do "more than try?" Werewolves didn't take this sort of thing seriously. It's not like his family would be offended if we didn't match up.

I shook it off, rolling my shoulders and walking into the restaurant. Thirty-five minutes. I could do thirty-five minutes.

I had this weird feeling just before I stepped inside. I didn't want to do this. It was a betrayal of Alex. We didn't have any sort of agreement to be exclusive, but it felt wrong to be out with someone else. And this restaurant was owned by one of Jane's friends; what if word got back to him? I didn't want to damage something special just as it was getting started.

I could just say that I showed up and hadn't seen Donnie there...but Mama would sniff out that lie pretty damn fast. She was probably parked outside to monitor whether I bolted. My hand hovered over the doorknob. I couldn't put this off. It was only delaying the inevitable. My aunts and my father would have their way or they would make me miserable at home.

I walked past a meticulously-polished oak bar that seemed to be made from repurposed wood. A pale boy hopped off one of the bar stools carefully circled around the bar. He was in maybe his late teens, and I might have thought it odd that he was sitting at the bar, if not for the dark shadows under his eyes and the sharp glint to his smile. Vampires had to carry special IDs to show their chronological age, otherwise, those who were turned young would never be able to vote or smoke or have access to all sorts of illicit adult things. And this one was dressed in pretty recent styles—a hoodie and jeans—which probably didn't help his case.

I took a step back. Something was sending a note of alarm skittering across my nerves, but I didn't know what—which was incredibly uncomfortable. I took a deep breath, cataloguing the malty smell of the beer, the savory scents from the kitchen, dozens of different perfumes and aftershaves and…this guy didn't smell like anything, which should have been impossible.

Everybody smelled like *something,* even if they didn't wear perfume or deodorant—the musty undercurrent of anxious sweat, the dark, bitter note of their morning coffee. But this guy smelled like…nothing, like a blind spot I couldn't focus on. And rather than relief, it just made me squirm. How was my hind brain supposed to determine if he was a threat or not without data? A little consideration, please, honestly.

"Hey," he said, stepping into my path, grinning. "I've seen you around the library, right?"

I arched a brow, taken aback by the sudden conversational ambush. "Maybe? You didn't knock over a bookshelf there a couple of weeks back, did you?"

He grinned. "Nope. Not me. Can I buy you a drink?"

What was going *on* with me lately? Had I rubbed myself in vampire cat nip or something? He looked sort of familiar and it was possible I *had* seen him at the library. I tried to stick to my own business there, collapsing bookshelves aside. But I had enough vampire-related issues to deal with now, I didn't need to add more to them.

"No, thank you."

"Oh, come on, I'm a nice guy and—"

Suddenly, a tall form appeared at my left. I never thought I'd be *glad* to see Donnie Ansen, but there he was, tall and handsome as ever. "Hi. Tylene, right?"

Like he hadn't known me since we were cubs. And then he turned and walked towards the table, without a word to me. I guessed I was supposed to follow.

I gave the vampire a polite smile. "Sorry. Meeting someone. Have a good night."

He wriggled his eyebrows at me. "See you around."

"I'm having the *weirdest* month," I sighed, walking to the table where Donnie was seated.

"It's nice to see you again," I said, sliding into my chair. Unlike Alex, Donnie didn't pull my seat out from the table. He was too busy staring over my shoulder, watching a baseball game playing on the TV behind the bar. Apparently, I was supposed to be on my best manners, but he wasn't.

He sat there silently contemplating the menu, to the point where I wondered if I should offer to read it for him. His knee bounced nervously under the table and he looked anywhere but at my face. I supposed I could pass the next thirty-five minutes in silence, though I was sure that was *not* "minding my manners."

"So, have you watched anything good lately? I heard Netflix has a bunch of interesting documentaries about people who enjoy tigers and extremely hard drugs."

He frowned at me, turning his attention away from the TV for a whole three seconds together. "What's Netflix?"

I had no idea how to respond to that. I felt almost swoony from the shock of it. How on earth was I supposed to find conversational ground, much less the foundation of a lifetime together with someone who seemed so cut off from the things that I centered my world around? Desperately, I missed Alex and his easy conversation. We had so little in common and somehow managed to find something to talk about every minute we were together. I had so much in common with Donnie and...nothing. I knew I was being more than a little unfair to my fellow were- wolf. Maybe we were having so much trouble finding a topic because I was the weirdo, in terms of our kind. We'd never really clicked when we'd seen each other at pack meetings. He ran around hunting any game foolish enough to loiter nearby and I usually hid in a tree, reading a book. On the rare occasion he spoke to me, it was to ask after Jolene—which was typical.

The Southern Comfort menu was filled all sorts of deli- cious-sounding upscale delights that I would gladly scarf down any other night—seven-cheese macaroni, pulled pork smoked with cherries and apples, buttermilk chicken, next to an impres- sive list of imported bloods for the vampire customers. But a large, delectable meal didn't fit with my thirty-five-minute plan. Donnie ordered a lot and when I stuck with a fried green tomato appetizer, he finally spoke. "You're not one of those salad eatin' girls, are you?"

I smiled, an upward quirk of the lips rather than actually baring my teeth—which I didn't trust myself to do. "Not usually."

"I just mean, your Aunt Lurlene said you were a healthy eater, a healthy girl," he said, frowning.

A healthy girl who would give him lots of healthy babies, was the unspoken implication. It chafed that I was being discussed like a damn brood mare behind my back, but I knew it was no different than how almost any werewolf female was discussed at kitchen tables and wild clearings throughout the country, maybe even the world.

He mumbled, "That seems like a weird thing to bring up on a date, doesn't it?"

My hand froze over the table as I reached for my drink. "Yes."

"I don't think humans talk about that sort of thing on dates, do they?" he mused. "What your relatives might have said about how ya eat."

"Having been on a few dates with humans, I can tell you that they don't," I assured him.

"You've dated humans?" he whispered as if this was some unbelievable feat.

"Well, not dates that my family approved of, but yes." The polite smile became just a little sharper.

"Well, you're a brave one, aren't you?" he marveled. "I don't really go on dates unless my aunts set them up. I'd never hear the end of it."

I stopped, tilting my head as I stared at him. While the girls in my family were badgered about their plans for courtship, their ticking biological clocks, the boys were pretty much left on their own. It was just *assumed* that my male cousins would eventually find someone —even though my cousin Vance was approaching thirty-five and hadn't been on a proper date in years. It struck me that things probably worked differently in other packs, that the guys I was being pressured to date might be going through something similar. Suddenly, I felt really bad for Donnie. And all of the other male werewolves I'd assumed had it easier than I did.

It didn't make me want to marry and/or reproduce with Donnie, but it helped me see him as something other than an obstacle for me to jump over into some other way I'd rather be spending my evening.

My appetizer arrived, and Donnie's plate of eggs deviled with bacon and pimento. We stopped talking while the server set the plates in front of us.

"Did I say somethin' wrong?" Donnie asked.

"No, I just never thought about it from your side," I said, shrugging. "My aunts stick to hassling the girls in my family."

"Oh, no," Donnie said, shaking his head. "Everybody my age gets the guilt trips in my pack. I hear it from the minute I wake up to the minute I go to sleep. My parents, my aunts, grandma, even a couple of my uncles—*When are you gonna find a nice girl and settle down? It's not like you're gonna meet someone new, we know all the werewolves around here. What are you holding out for? Who are you to be so picky?*"

"Yeah, I hear that one a lot, the 'picky' one," I said, raising my hand. "I also hear, 'you're not getting any younger' and 'if you wait much longer, you're going to be the spinster aunt that everybody feels sorry for.'"

"Dang." He recoiled from the table. "That one has to smart."

"You're telling me," I snorted, slicing into the crisply-breaded tomato. Yes, I liked tomatoes in that form. I was a werewolf with layers.

"So, is dating humans a rebellion thing?" he asked around a mouthful of egg.

"Oh, I haven't done that in years," I told him, carefully omitting my recent dates with a vampire. Just because I'd managed to exchange a few sentences with Donnie didn't mean I trusted him. "And it wasn't so much about rebellion as wanting something uncomplicated, you know? Something for myself? Going out with someone I liked, instead of someone I was told I had to go out with."

I paused. "That was a really rude way to put that. I'm sorry."

He laughed. "No, I get it. I really do."

He was staring over my shoulder again. I turned and saw a slim, pretty girl sitting at the bar. She pivoted suddenly on the stool, pretending she hadn't been watching us. I realized Donnie hadn't been watching the game. He was watching the girl. She turned again, and couldn't seem to look away from our table. She couldn't have radiated heartache any more clearly if she'd been carrying a sign that said, "My heart has been run through a paper shredder." And he wasn't looking at her like she was a stranger. I could feel their sadness stretched between them like a string. I didn't want to be the one to make it snap.

"Is she human?" I asked quietly.

He shook his head and whispered. "Mountain lion shifter."

"Really!" I gasped, making him jump. His expression changed from defensive to intrigued by my absolute glee.

Much like humans throughout Kentucky claimed to see mountain lions—which never seemed to be substantiated by photos in this camera phone-infested world of ours—every werewolf I knew *claimed* to have met a mountain lion shifter. But somehow, they never showed up to the shifter meetings. It made sense looking at her, the tawny golden eyes, the feline grace even as she shifted uncomfortably in her seat. I gave her a little wave, which made her frown. She looked caught between wanting to cry and rip my head off. I wouldn't have blamed her, either way.

"That's Mara. My family doesn't accept her cause she's 'not our kind,'" he said sadly. "Who knows what sort of babies we would have, confusing the bloodline, like we're some sort of royal family."

"Why would you bring her here?" I demanded, fully irritated on her behalf. "How could you put her through watching the world's most uncomfortable blind date?"

"It hasn't been that bad," he protested, only stopping when I glared at him. "We don't get to see each other very often. I don't get off of the compound without some member of my family tagging along. If it wasn't for cell phones, I think we'd go nuts."

"What's her name saved under in your phone?"

"Uncle Eustace," he muttered.

I cackled until I had to wipe my eyes. "My special friend is saved under Aunt Myrtle."

I reached across the table to pat his hand, and then, remembering the girl at the bar with the mountain lion fangs, I thought better of it.

"Have you loved her long?" I asked.

"Since we were twelve," he said, swallowing thickly. "But my family acts like I don't know what I'm talking about, that I couldn't love someone they don't want for me. It's the reason I dodge so hard when they try to set me up. I don't want anybody else."

And just like that, my heart broke for poor Donnie and what he must have going through all those times our families got together. He probably spent the whole time running around, being all manly and loud, because if he stood still long enough, they'd ambush him with a surprise ceremony with a "proper candidate" from my side.

We were in the same situation, the three of us—wanting people we were supposed to stay away from. A wave of anger and sadness hit me, so heavy it nearly knocked me out of my chair. I wanted Alex, and I wanted him desperately, right that minute.

With as much kindness in my voice as I could muster, I said, "Donnie, we both showed up tonight, just like we were asked to, with the best of intentions. And if this date were to end abruptly, say I didn't come back from the restroom because I got distracted by a shiny object outside and just wandered off. You couldn't help that, right? You tried your best. You bought me a nice dinner—"

"An appetizer."

"You made conversation. You told me all about yourself," I said, nodding toward the lovely lion lady. "And your interests."

"But I saw your mama drop you off," he objected, even as I groaned. "If you call her to take you home, they'd know we didn't make it all the way through dinner. Your family will hear about it. My family will hear about it. I couldn't let you take the blame for that. And I couldn't lie to my family about what I'd done tonight."

"You mean you couldn't tell them that you took a pretty girl to dinner?" I asked, nodding to the bar. "Because I see a *very* pretty someone who would be more than happy to take my place. The trick in trying to get what you want while staying under the radar is being careful with details."

He blinked at me rapidly, as if it had never occurred to him to be sneaky. The poor, sweet honest doofus.

"And as for blame, well, you let me worry about that. My family's used to being disappointed," I added.

"Are you sure?" he asked.

"Absolutely." I cleared my throat. "Would you excuse me for just a second? I need to powder my nose, my face, just everything."

"Thank you, Tylene."

"Have a good night, Donnie."

Pasting on a smile, I grabbed my backpack and walked toward the restrooms. That vampire boy seemed to have left, a bit of good luck I needed to get the hell out of dodge without him blocking my path. I turned abruptly, ducking around a waitress. I stopped by Mara at the bar and hugged her fiercely. She seemed prepared to take a swing at me, until I put my arms around her. She relaxed ever so slightly and patted me on the back.

"Just do whatever you can to be happy," I whispered to her.

Without another word, I dashed out of the door, sucking air into my lungs like I'd just broken through the surface of murky, silty water. To my relief, I didn't see my parents' truck parked outside the restaurant. But for all my bravado with Donnie, I was frozen, completely at a loss for what to do. I couldn't go home this early. I didn't want to just wander around town until it was time for my mom to pick me up. (Which was, honestly, so freaking sad.) Not to mention, she was going to be furious with me for not "doing more than trying." And that was nothing to what my family was going to do when they found out. And still, I couldn't go back in. I just couldn't stand it for one more minute, sitting there and acting like it was normal for two adults to be miserable because it would make everybody around them happy. I was caught between despair, knowing what was waiting for me at home, and the resentment of that being a problem in the first place...and then, maybe I was a little bit proud, because I hoped that what I had done would shake Mara and Donnie up a bit and they might pursue their own happiness. Or, I might have just led them to do something that would make their situation even worse and blown up their lives entirely.

Shit.

I scrubbed my hand through my hair. I should be a grown woman, leaving a relatively unspectacular date with minimal emotional turmoil, looking to soothe my jangled nerves with ice cream and fucking *Netflix* at her own apartment. And yet, here I was, unable to move because for me, a bad date could throw off my whole freaking home life. I glanced down the street and saw a familiar vehicle.

"Oh, come on." I seethed, ducking behind the nearest truck. My aunts Braylene and Lurlene were sitting there in Braylene's, thumbing through magazines and sipping coffee like it was a damn stakeout. Mama may not have trusted me to show up for the date, but they didn't trust me enough to stay. They sat there outside the restaurant to make sure that I stayed for the entire date. I mean, obviously, they were right, but that was entirely beside the point.

Fortunately, the latest celebrity divorces were so fascinating that they hadn't bothered to look up since I'd walked out. I turned, no longer frozen, and ran like I was being chased by Donnie's mountain lion girlfriend.

7

"If your friends have been single for several centuries, consider what their relationship advice is really worth."
—*A Gentleman in Any Era: An Ancient Vampire's Guide to Modern Relationships*

I didn't know where I was running, only that I was moving away from the restaurant, from the window where my aunts could see me fleeing. I didn't know if they could see me. I only knew I needed to be far, far away.

Alex—I wanted Alex. I I just wanted to be somewhere I felt safe, preferably with Alex, but I didn't want to bother him with what seemed to be an emotional breakdown. Before I knew it, I was in the library parking lot, headed for a gap in the retaining wall on the far side of the building. There was a fountain hidden inside, a sort of walled-in garden that hadn't been maintained in years. I remember Mrs. Stubblefield saying something about liability and kids with the fountain, and probably the rotting wood of the benches.

It was beyond overgrown, every flower bed gone to seed a long time ago and completely choked with weeds. The fountain, a bronze of the *Alice in Wonderland* characters, was covered in a thick patina that was more neglect than art. I could tell it used to be a pretty space. A little glassed-over picture posted on the entrance sign showed a little oasis of quiet, probably meant for mothers who needed a break while their kids were attending Story Time.

For now, I was content to just sit in the dark and try to figure out what the hell I was going to say to my family. I wanted to scream at them, tell them it was none of their damn business who I dated, and they needed to just back off. I wanted to tell them I was dating someone who made me happy. And some small, frightened part of me wanted to tell them I was sorry, that I was just angry and scared and Donnie and I clearly weren't meant for one another anyway. And I was very ashamed of that small frightened part.

It was terrifying to me, how easy it was to just say I was sorry, how appealing it was to just fall in line and try to go along. It was so unfair, to have to fight this hard just to try to live with some damn dignity.

As if on cue, my phone buzzed in my backpack. It was a text from Mama. *"Where are you? Lurlene said she looked inside the restaurant and Donnie was out with some other girl! Explain yourself, right now, young lady!"*

I sighed and stuck my phone back in my bag. It was immature, but I just didn't want to deal with it. I reached into my backpack for a packet of tissues, rubbing at my eyes. Suddenly the makeup my relatives had applied felt like it was suffocating my skin. I pulled the little papers away from my face and saw thick black smudged across them. My eyes stung, hot and bright, and I could feel the drip-drip-drip of tears against my hands as they slid down my cheeks.

It was all just so stupid and pointless. Alex wouldn't want to be with me long term. Sure, I aged slower than the average human, but I still aged. I would go through middle age, menopause, become stooped and wrinkled and he would just go on forever and ever preserved in perfection. It wasn't like he could turn me. At least, I didn't think he could turn me—as far as I knew, it hadn't been tried before. He would lose interest. I would eventually find someone my family approved because *not* doing it meant losing my place in the pack. It was what my parents had feared my entire life. They'd always made it sound like a fate worse than hell. How was I supposed to face hell alone?

I indulged in a bit more crying. I was not proud of it, but I spent so much time actively dodging my family that I guess I hadn't really processed how hopeless I really felt about the whole thing. Something had to change, or I was going to snap.

"Ty?"

My head whipped up at the sound of my name. Alex was standing there in the moonlight like the answer to a wish I hadn't even made. I wiped furiously at my cheeks, hoping I wasn't all streaky and tragic looking.

"The library isn't even open," he said, walking towards me. "What are you doing back here?"

"It's a long story," I sniffed. For the first time that night, my smile was genuine. I stood and made myself hold absolutely still so I wouldn't throw myself at him.

"Are you all right?" he asked, pulling me close. I buried my face in his shirt, breathing in the scent of cedar. I couldn't answer. The tears would start all over again and that was the last thing I needed, to make the situation even worse with a red nose, swollen eyes, and runnier makeup.

His hands slid under my chin and tilted my face toward the moon. "Are you hurt? Did something happen?"

He frowned, but he didn't flinch, so I guessed I wasn't completely hideous. His cool hands felt so good against my flushed skin that I nuzzled my cheeks against his hands. "No, it's more of a feelings issue. Don't worry about it."

"Why wouldn't I worry about your feelings?" he asked, looking so genuinely confused by the concept that I laughed, because otherwise—red nose, swollen eyes, etc. He guided me onto the bench, sitting next to me with his arm around my waist.

"Is there anything I can do?" he asked.

I glanced down, so I wouldn't have to look him in the eye. "Doubtful. What are you doing here? I thought we'd agreed to avoid the library for a while."

"Oh, I wasn't trying to get in the library. I was in town, fetching a package from the post office—replacement supplies for the school. I picked up your scent and followed it here."

I chuckled. "Usually that's my line."

"What were you doing tonight?" he asked, glancing down at my dress. "You look beautiful, if a bit uncomfortable."

I plucked at my skirt. "I don't usually wear dresses. I'm more of jeans and t-shirts girl."

"Well, it looks very nice. But I like the jeans, too. I can't help but notice you didn't answer the question—what are you doing here?" he asked again.

"Hiding a little bit?" I offered, the corner of my mouth pulling back.

"Hiding from who?" He pulled back, holding my elbows while he looked me over for potential damages.

"No, nothing like that. I had to, I know this is going to sound lame and awful—My family set me up on a date with a were-wolf," I confessed.

"I see." He stepped away from me slightly and I felt something in my heart crack a little bit. "Do I see?"

"There's a lot of pressure on me to marry and have future werewolves, and this guy is considered a good candidate," I told him.

"And—I'm sorry, I don't know how to ask this, but was it a good date?" he asked.

"Lord, no," I laughed. He sagged against my side. I liked to think it was relief. "I mean, he wasn't awful or anything. I've known him since we were children. And he's nice and all, but I knew there was no chance of anything. He wasn't any happier than I was. He is definitely in love with someone else, who was also there…which sort of made it worse, and better at the same time."

"Wait, what?"

"I'm sorry. I should have told you. I should have told them no. I should have—I should have done a lot of things," I told him. "I went because my family wanted me to. It's something I'm trying to change. I can't be myself with them. Everything that makes me…me, they think is bad. Not just like, 'morally wrong,' but actively bad for me, like cancer bad. They spend a good amount of time trying to talk me out of being myself for my own good."

He frowned. "I can't say I'm thrilled about it. I don't like the idea of you agreeing to something you don't want to do because of your family. And to be honest, I *really* don't like the idea of you being courted by someone else. Isn't there some way you can talk to your family about this? Would they listen?"

I burst out laughing, which seemed to alarm him. Alex may have come from a family a lot like mine, but clearly, the centuries of separation from them made him forget what it was like.

"I'm sorry. No. The pack wouldn't listen. The pack thinks of itself as a unit, what's good for one is good for all. It's considered selfish to put yourself ahead of that. And it's not just our pack, that my family is thinking of, it's a global thing. The number of werewolves who can shift is dwindling and more of us are marrying humans, which is reducing that number even more. My family clings to the way things have always been because they're trying to protect what they know. They do it because they're scared."

He seemed to think about that for a long time. "Cal and Nik explained to me—that it takes a spoken agreement, a commitment for an 'exclusive' relationship these days. They also mentioned becoming 'Facebook official' and when I didn't understand what that meant, they told me you would explain it," he said, tilting his forehead against mine. "I want to be with you and no one else. And I would very much like it if you wanted to be with me."

"For how long?" I asked.

"However long we can manage it," he said. "However long you want me. Do you agree?"

"I would like that a lot," I said. "The way I feel about you, it's not just something that comes along so often that I can ignore it. I like you so much. I more than like you. It sounds so silly to use a word so small for what I feel for you. I'm just not ready to say I love you."

He leaned close, pulling me into his lap and kissing me firmly. "I'll wait."

"If my family tries this whole set-up thing again, I'll do whatever I can to get out of it."

"But you can't tell them about me, I suppose?"

I stayed silent for a long moment. "I don't want to hurt your feelings by laughing again. No. Jolene was accepted after she married a human because her parents insisted on that acceptance. My parents? They're so terrified that they'll lose their place. They wouldn't bother with any sort of defense for me. I would be disowned, tossed out. For a werewolf, that's a terrible fate."

He nodded. "I'm only sorry you didn't think you could tell me. I understand what it's like to be pressured by your family. My family wanted me to be a priest."

I giggled. "Clearly, you went in a different direction."

"Yes. I was the third son. And while my father had purchased a modest second estate for my brother, by the time I came along, the only options were the church or the army."

I relaxed against him as his voice rolled over my nerves like warm honey. "How Austenian of them."

"Well, it was several hundred years before her time, but that was how my family operated."

"Sorry, I interrupted you. Frock or firearms, only options. Continue."

He grinned at my airy hand wave. "You have a charming way of cutting to the heart of a matter."

I beamed at him, which made him kiss my temple before continuing. "Well, my father was soldier, you see. He was a second son, never supposed to inherit. His elder brother died of a fever and suddenly he was the heir. Military life was good enough for him and who was I to aspire to something else? Someone had to represent the family, to lead our family's small legion. But I had no passion for it. Fencing, riding, shooting for exercise, well, that was one thing—though I was always worried about hurting my hands, ruining my ability to play. I told him I wanted to make music my life and he laughed. It wasn't even something he would consider. He told me that if I didn't fall in line, I would be disinherited entirely, tossed out of the family home. He was genuinely confused when I packed my things on the one horse I owned and rode off for Paris.

"I wrote to them on occasion, to tell them what I'd learned, the masters I was learning from, but I stopped after a few years. To read letters from my family at the time, you'd think I was engaged in acts of cannibalism and heresy. They begged me, over and over, to just forget the life I made for myself, the life that defined me, and come back to a place that made me feel unwanted and useless. And then I was turned, and it was more a protective measure for my family—never seeing them again."

"Do you ever regret that?"

"Sometimes," he said. "But living a life that made me happy? No, I can't say I regret that."

"I get your point," I told him quietly.

"I'm sorry tonight has been so unpleasant for you," he said, brushing his fingertips along my cheek. His brow furrowed when I smiled. "Your teeth look sharper."

"It's close to the full moon."

"I thought that was a myth," he said. "I thought werewolves could change whenever you want."

"It is. We can," I insisted. "But the pull is harder over the full moon, the change is more complete. And it makes us a little crazier, decision-wise. Most of us lock up our credit cards and booze to prevent regrettable Internet shopping and fistfights."

His thumb brushed across my bottom lip, barely grazing the tip of my right top canine. His skin tasted like mint.

"They're so much like mine," he said, tilting his head. "But warmer. You're so much warmer."

He bent to kiss me. I groaned at the cool relief of it, the taste of iron and mint and Alex. His tongue slipped over my lip, licking ever so delicately at mine. My hand slid into his hair, relishing its silkiness. And even as all the thoughts ebbed out of my head, I heard familiar voices echoing on the street.

I gasped, breaking away from him.

"What?"

I crossed the garden and looked over the wall. Several of my relatives—Uncle Creed, my daddy, Cousin Deacon, and my aunts—all running around the library parking lot, sniffing deeply. They couldn't take the chance of being seen in town as wolves. Half-Moon Hollow residents might accept one wolf running through town and write it off as an oversized coyote— but a whole pack? People would freak—though I wasn't sure a bunch of McClaines running around town like they were bloodhounds on two legs was *less* scary in comparison.

"Tylene!" my father yelled.

"Who in the hell is that?" Alex asked.

"My family. We need to go."

"I'm not going to run like a thief in the night," he protested.

"That's about a third of my pack, and where they are, others follow. I don't care how tough you are, you need to run."

Sighing, he pulled on my hand. "Come with me."

I weighed the options—how angry my family would be for running versus how angry they were going to be if they found me here in the garden.

"Turn around," I told him. I stripped out of my clothes and shoved them into my backpack. He was trying not to look, which I appreciated. My other body melted away and I rolled into my more comfortable form.

"I still love seeing that," he breathed, rubbing his hand over my ears.

I jerked my head toward the fence, away from where my relatives' voices could be heard. I leapt onto a bench and launched off of it, using the leverage to jump over the fence. I realized I didn't know where we were going. My only clear thought was to get away.

I could hear my uncles calling me.

"Ty! Come on out, don't make us track you!" Uncle Creed yelled.

Creed was ancient, but he could still smell blood in the wind at a hundred paces. I was running from them. I'd never run *from* my family before. I didn't know what would be waiting for me when I got home, but I didn't care. It felt so good just to do something for myself for once. Alex passed me, and I whuffed at him, enjoying the game of it.

He could keep up with me. Better than that, he could beat me! I didn't have to hold back my natural speed to protect his feelings. He offered me a challenge. I *loved* a challenge.

I pushed my legs even harder and caught up. He led me out of town, down long dark tree-lined country roads. The smells of exhaust and garbage made way to the green scent of grass and the wild woods. Prey scurried away as two predators bolted through their territory.

"Turn here!" Alex shouted, hooking dramatically down a gravel road.

Through the trees, I saw a small, sturdy log house done in a sort of Adirondack style, definitely fancier than most of the older cabins around here. The moon reflected in a small lake behind the house, with a long dock extending over it. The whole scene was very cozy, and I could see myself being very comfortable, surrounded by so many trees.

"What happened to being part of life and a community?" I asked after I shifted to two feet.

"Baby steps," he said, dropping his dress shirt around my shoulders. I tried not to stare at his half-dressed state, because he'd been so polite when I'd stripped down in front of him. But damn. When had he had time for all the sit-ups required for those abs when he was supposedly practicing music for hours? It was like he was carved by some sort of hyper-perfectionist sculptor. I generally wasn't self-conscious about my body, but it just seemed unfair.

Unaware of my silent perving, he continued, "Cal talked me into buying some property in town, and there's some apartment space there, but I've lived on my own for so long, it just felt like too much all at once. I had this built just before I moved here. Nik was good enough to oversee the construction. He likes that sort of project."

"That makes sense, I guess. It certainly smells better out here —no cars. No people. No dumpsters."

"You wouldn't want to live in town?"

"I think I would live just about anywhere, if it meant having some peace and privacy."

"You could, you know."

I scoffed, waving at the haphazardly buttoned dress shirt. "Yeah, right. This is about as reckless and impulsive as I get."

"I have something for you," he said, stepping onto the porch and unlocking a very solid looking door.

I wanted to object. He'd already given me that book. I'd learned over the years that unexpected gifts came with obligations and guilt, but I also didn't want to offend him.

The house was exactly what I'd expected of him. The open-plan room was clean and orderly, except for the space set aside in the far corner, near a window, for practice. It was littered with sheet music and various instruments. He'd used a mix of clean contemporary pieces with the intricately carved wooden music stands and chairs that looked like they might have fit in his time. The floors were the same warm maple as the school, but the walls were a soft, buttery yellow. You could almost imagine you were standing outside on a sunny day and that made me a little sad for him. There might be a lot of inconveniences and annoyances that came with being a werewolf, but at least I wasn't trapped indoors before sunrise.

He crossed to a carved wooden box he'd put on the river stone mantle and took out a small metal cylinder on a keychain. That certainly hadn't been what I'd expected in terms of romantic gifts, but at least I didn't feel weird about accepting it... right?

"Since you're out here on your own now, you need some protection." He pressed the cannister into my hand. "Colloidal silver spray. We're highly allergic to it, so it's basically mace for vampires. I figure you know how to fight your own kind, but I wanted to give you an edge against mine."

I stared at the little cannister. He was giving me a weapon that I was able to use against *him*. He was that worried about my safety. I wasn't familiar with people putting me before themselves. That's the only explanation for the way I jumped on him. I literally threw myself at him, using the momentum to wrap my legs around his waist. He stumbled back a bit, "oofing" in surprise, but he caught me as I plundered his mouth. He groaned into the fiercely sloppy kiss, sliding his hands under my bare bottom as I nudged my tongue against the tips of his fangs.

I couldn't get close enough. I wanted to wallow in him, rub my scent all over his body so everybody with a nose would know that he was mine. I felt myself growing warm and wet against him and for the first time in my life I wanted to follow that feeling.

Sex was one of the few things werewolves took very seriously. Even with my generally rebellious attitude toward most traditions, I'd never gotten past a few fumbling make out sessions with boys that my family most definitely did *not* know about. Werewolves mated for life. Once our partners were chosen and the bite marks were exchanged, that was it. We could only have cubs with that person. We simply couldn't afford casual sex, conceptionally speaking. If you picked the wrong person, you were stuck with them *forever*.

But with Alex, I wouldn't have to worry about that. Vampires didn't have the, um, material. I had complete freedom of choice and I wanted to choose him so, so badly.

Meanwhile, he still had one hand under my ass while blindly attempting to lower us onto the couch. I stuck my foot out against the couch cushion to stop our descent. "Bedroom."

I watched as waves of lust, concern, and "yay!" crossed his face. "Are you sure about that?"

"I wouldn't have said it if I wasn't," I promised.

"It's not that I don't want you," he swore. "I want you so very much. But I don't want you to do something you're not ready for."

"So we're going to have to stop in the middle of all this, so we can have a very adult conversation about consent?" I suggested. He nodded, so I added. "Being a grown up is difficult."

"Yes, but worth it," he promised.

I kissed him again, hoping that I could pour all of my enthusiasm and certainty into it. He laughed against my mouth, pivoting so he could turn into a bedroom just as open and comfortable as the rest of the house. And the bed was huge, like, almost to the point of being questionable, but I wasn't about to bring it up. Instead of dropping me on it, he bent at the waist and crawled up the length of the mattress while I still clung to him.

"I want to have sex," I told him plainly. "All of the sex. But I don't think we should bite each other. I don't know how my blood would taste to you and that's probably not something we should try right now. Also, biting means something different to werewolves, which I would rather not get into right this second."

"I agree to all of that," he said, nodding sharply.

"Excellent." I paused to pull his shirt over his head. "Proceed."

Laughing, Alex skimmed back down my body, nosing aside his shirt to nuzzle at my chest, which was only half-buttoned and covered almost nothing. He teased each nipple in turn until I was whimpering under him. It felt like he spent hours mouthing at my belly button, my hip bones, my knees, and calves. I was boneless against the bed. I felt like every inch of me had been well and truly kissed.

I shrugged out of the shirt he'd given me. I was already half-dressed, which took some of my natural awkwardness out of the situation. But then I reached for the button on his jeans, and fumbled badly, because I'd never tried it from this angle. He grinned against my lips and reached down to help.

Expecting some panic at Alex's closeness, I was surprised at how right it felt to be there. Every inch of his skin was pressed against mine, cold to my warm, and all I wanted was more. I had chosen this man and this time, and the freedom of it was a heady thing. He rolled his hips and could feel the rigid weight of him rubbing exactly where I needed him.

I hissed and dragged my blunt teeth across his earlobe without biting down. He shivered, which just increased that lovely friction between my thighs. I moaned, following the motion of his hips. He swept his hand down the length of my ribs, down my belly, his deft fingers sliding inside me to find me ready and wanting. He thumbed at the rigid little bundle there, twisting and thrusting his fingers as the tension built in my belly. He seemed to know all of the right motions to coax a response out of me and before I knew it, the tension had become a rolling wave of energy. I fought to stay in the moment with him, instead of letting those ripples of pleasure pull me under. But then everything surged all at once and I was falling, spasming, arching off the bed as I cried out against Alex's skin.

He pressed featherlight kisses over my shoulders as I came down, floating blissful and breathless. Kneeling suddenly, he pulled me up into his lap, straddling him. "This might be a little more comfortable for you," he murmured.

I nodded, still kissing him, as he moved to slide into me. It was a little clumsy, all knees and elbows as I tried to find the best way to settle over him. He was smiling up at me, his dark eyes almost glowing in the dim light. He pressed his forehead to mine, and I gasped as he slid home. My nails bit into his back as I sank down, moving experimentally against him.

All those nerves inside me, still firing from my release, sang as he moved inside me. I rolled my hips, trying to keep up. Alex's hands brushed up and down my spine, comforting me as we found our rhythm. I watched the expressions change on Alex's face, pleasure to contentment and back again.

Alex's hips were stuttering, like he had to concentrate to keep moving. An echo of the orgasm I'd just enjoyed was already building. He pressed his mouth against the curve of my breast, his blunt teeth barely touching my skin. My breath caught, half-worried that he would sink his fangs into me, and half-hoping he would. Instead, he reached between us, bent his hand at an unnatural angle to reach that same place.

The echo became a full-blown song and I was riding him, howling. His thrusts went wild and he was right there with me. He spilled into me, his seed almost cold, and slumped to the sheets, dragging me with him.

My heartbeat filled the room, not quite drowning out my heavy breathing. It might have been embarrassing, but I figured I had to have the "live responses" for the both of us. He got up, not bothering to dress, and left the room. I heard the fridge open and the microwave beep. I threaded my fingers through my sweaty hair and tried to catch my breath. I wished desperately for an elastic to tame this mop on my head.

Alex returned with a tall glass of water and a mug full of what smelled like blood. He offered me the glass and I happily drained it. He slid under the covers with me and sipped at his mug.

"So, now that I'm not completely blinded by lust—"

"I take that as a compliment," I said, grinning brightly.

"You should, you relentless minx," he snickered, kissing me. I thought the taste of blood on his lips would be off-putting, but it was just a part of him. He leaned away and kissed me on the forehead. "So, what does biting mean to werewolves?"

"It's how we mark our mates. You exchange bite marks and then you're connected for life. You can't have children with anyone else. For life. And while the kids thing isn't really an issue for us, I didn't think we were ready for it."

"Interesting," he said, nodding. "So we both just made very responsible and mature choices in the midst of passion."

"Good for us," I said, reaching out to shake his free hand.

"Yes, three cheers," he said very seriously, before bursting out into a laugh.

I giggled until I had tears streaming down my cheeks. I

pressed my face against his skin, breathing deeply, feeling more at peace than I had in a long time. "I didn't know it could be like this."

"Like what?"

"Fun," I said. "I mean, I knew you were supposed to get some enjoyment out of it, obviously. But I didn't think you could laugh and talk in the middle of everything and not feel awkward about it."

"Well, it hasn't happened for me very often," he conceded. "I'm glad it happened for us, though. I don't know what I would do if we didn't laugh together. It's one of things I like most about you."

"Same," I said, yawning.

I guess it should have surprised me when I drifted off to sleep. It only felt like a few second later when I sat up, gasping for breath. Panicking, I searched the bedside table for the clock and saw that it was after four. My parents were probably still awake, waiting for me. And I could only imagine what sort of rage was going to be waiting for me when I got home.

For the first time, I considered not going back. I had somewhere else I could go now. In fact, I had several other places. Even if I didn't want to stay right here in bed with Alex, I could go to Jolene's, or Dick's, or even Jane's. But it felt wrong to just not go back without a word. Somehow, I felt like I owed the pack an explanation before I left.

Alex was dozing next to me, which seemed sort of weird for a vampire at night, but I liked to think I had worn him out. I slid out of bed and padded out to the couch, where I'd left my backpack. I dressed in my backup clothes and searched the kitchen counter for a pen and paper so I could leave him a note.

"Do you want to know what you smell like to me?"

I turned to find him standing behind me at the counter, a contented grin on his face.

"Not right now!" I laughed. "I'm covered in dried sex sweat and I don't have time for a shower!"

"All right then," he sighed. "Do you want me to drive you home?"

"Definitely not."

"But it's late and dark outside," he objected.

"And I'm a werewolf," I reminded him as I kissed him soundly.

"Is this because of your family?" he asked. "I don't think they would sense me close to the compound if they're all asleep. I don't like you putting yourself in danger just to avoid trouble with them."

"No, it's because this is faster," I lied.

"I don't like it!" he called. "But I like you!"

"You, too!" I called, dashing out of the house. I sprinted back to the compound on two feet, my head full of romance and moonlight and sorts of general foolishness. I had done something for myself, for no other reason than because it felt good. I felt absolutely decadent. I'd sort of skipped this silly teenage romance phase, where I dreamed of dark, handsome strangers and happy ever afters. It felt good to indulge now.

I snuck back into the house before dawn. My parents were propped against each other on the couch, sleeping, with the TV blaring informercials in the background. I tiptoed past them, praying that their sensitive ears wouldn't pick up my footsteps. I turned on the shower and triple-washed with the most perfumed soap I owned. I listened at the bathroom door, but all I could hear was the enthusiastic voice hocking some sort of 'nutritious' food blender.

I glided down the hallway to my room and pulled the covers over my head, hoping that in the morning, my parents would have moved onto to something besides cutting my date with Donnie short. Maybe, for once, they would just pretend it didn't happen and we could ignore it?

8

"Whereas in your time, you might have focused on impressing your paramour's family, modern relationships are keyed in on friendships. If you don't have the support of your partner's friends, they will quietly and efficiently undermine your relationship. Probably by text. Probably while you're in the room."
—*A Gentleman in Any Era: An Ancient Vampire's Guide to Modern Relationships*

I woke up to the sensation of my blankets being ripped off.

Again.

But this time I was smart enough not to shift and confront the blanket snatcher. My parents stood over me, with my aunts behind them, all looking absolutely furious.

"What were you thinking?" Aunt Lurlene demanded.

I blinked up at my father. "What was I thinking?"

"You just walked out on your date with Donnie. Not a word," Daddy thundered. "Your mama didn't know where the hell you were. And then you don't come home until God knows when. What happened?"

"Nothing. Donnie and I had a good time together, but we didn't click."

He stared at me. "What do you mean, you didn't 'click?'"

"We had a perfectly nice date, but neither one us sees a romance happening between us."

"Well, what does romance have to do with anything?" he cried.

I glanced at my mother, who didn't respond at all to this statement. I felt very sorry for her.

"We had a good conversation and parted as friends. If anything, I think I made a good connection with their pack we can build on, which was the point, wasn't it?" I asked.

"All right then, if you had such a 'nice time,' why did you leave so early?" Braylene asked. "We kept watch outside the restaurant, and we saw you leave about thirty minutes after you got there. That's not enough time for any sort of date!"

"Yeah, we need to talk about that, because y'all having date night stakeouts is a real problem for me," I told her, sliding out of bed.

"Don't you talk to your aunts that way," Mama said quietly. "They're just looking out for you. If I had any idea you would leave in the middle of dinner, I would have stayed there myself."

"Where did you go?" Daddy asked. "Your uncles, aunts, and I spent all night running around town, looking for you."

"I went for a run," I said, jerking my shoulder, all innocence. "You know how it is when the moon gets like this. My blood was up. I just needed some time in the woods. First, I went by the library garden and—"

"Don't you feed me that library bullshit again," Daddy insisted. "We went to the library and you weren't there. Did you sneak off to meet someone else? Is he a human? Is that why you're being so cagey this morning?"

I opened my mouth to reply, but my mother was faster.

"Of course not," she said, giving me a significant look. "You probably just missed her. A she-wolf needs to run on her own every once in a while. It's normal."

The look worried me. What did my mama know?

"Well, you're just lucky Donnie didn't say anything to his family about you being so unsociable. He told Alvin that you seem like a sweet girl and he had a good time. His daddy is real excited to have you go out with him again," Daddy told me. "Alvin thinks you're a real good match for Donnie. So just clear your schedule when we plan your next date."

I rolled my eyes. Poor Donnie. Maybe we could figure out a way for him to get time with Mara on these dates while I sat at the bar or something. Maybe we could double with Alex and Mara...except that would involve telling Donnie and Mara about my dating Alex and that seemed like a bad idea.

"If we go out again, y'all are staying home," I told him. "It's the only way I'll agree to it."

"I don't care what you agree to," Daddy snorted. "But we'll talk about it, if we feel like we can trust you."

Temporarily pacified, my aunts and my father trooped out of my room. Mama lingered near the door. "I picked your dirty clothes of the floor earlier. Put them in the laundry."

My dirty clothes, meaning the dress I'd worn the night before, around Alex. While I'd been careful to wash my body, I'd figured I would launder my clothes in the morning, so I didn't wake anybody up. Unfortunately, I'd underestimated how tired I'd be from all the sex and the sneaking around. Mama had woken up before I did and grabbed my clothes before I could wash them. It wasn't all that unusual, except my clothes didn't usually reek of man.

But at least she wasn't yelling?

I watched Mama carefully as she stood in the doorway. I doubted very much she was keeping silent out of any instinct to protect me. She just didn't want Daddy any more riled than he already was.

"I'll have 'em washed back on your bed by this afternoon," she said, walking out of the room.

WHY WAS it so hard for me to make a decision that was good for me?

I sat at my usual table at Specialty Books, reviewing my business schedule for the next few months, my bank accounts and my bills. I could afford the new apartment for at least a year, and long afterwards, if my projections held out.

I wanted it so badly. It would obviously be healthy for me to get some space from my family, to take care of myself and become the adult I was meant to be. And yet, the idea of telling my parents that I wanted to leave, telling my Alphas, going through all the steps of packing up and leaving while my family pressured me to stay—it all just felt so impossible. A mountain I couldn't begin to climb.

Surely, grown humans didn't go through all this uncertainty and turmoil when they moved out of their parents' homes. I turned the leather-bound copy of *The Princess Bride* over in my hands. Maybe I just needed to ask myself WWIMD—What Would Inigo Montoya Do?

He'd probably kick down the door to the apartment, sign the lease, and tell his neighbors that they should prepare to die if they mess with his recycling bins. Okay, probably not, but he would at least be able to tell his parents he was moving out without dithering on about it like a character in a Fitzgerald novel.

Dick carried a box of coffee grounds into the café area and noticed the frown on my face. "What's up, Buttercup?"

"Buttercup? Is that my new nickname, or are you just going for low-hanging fruit that rhymes?"

"Well, you've picked up that book every time you've come in here," he noted.

"That has more to do with me being a cheapskate," I muttered, holding up the book.

"You all right?" he asked. "You seem a little off tonight."

"I just have a financial decision to make. And some personal decisions. And it feels like they're getting all jumbled up in a big yarn ball of confusion and I'm not sure I like it."

"Well, I don't think you're supposed to *like* confusing emotional yarn balls," he said, sitting across the table from me. "But if you're feeling all of this over a decision, it's pretty obvious that it's an important decision. And over my epic and storied lifetime—"

I snickered.

He wagged his finger at me. "No laughing. No one likes a smart ass. Over my epic and storied lifetime, I've found that when an important decision comes up, I usually know what I want to do. The dawdling and indecision usually comes from knowing that what I want to do is going to be pretty difficult. You know what's right for you, hon. You just have to find the courage to do it."

"That was incredibly thoughtful and helpful advice, Dick."

"Why is everybody so surprised when I am helpful and thoughtful?" he asked.

I glanced pointedly at his t-shirt, which read, *"Ninety-nine percent bad decisions, one percent redeeming snark."*

"What's your point?" he asked just as Jane emerged from her office.

"Ty, how's the promotional-stuff-that-I-do-not-have-to-worry-about-and-therefore-I-will-be-happy-no-matter-what-the-results-are coming along?" she asked.

"Really well, you had a seventy percent open rate on your

last email about the book club meeting. That's almost unheard of," I said. "I can prepare a report for you, if you'd like."

"Nah, I trust you. As long as I don't have to do it, I'm happy," Jane assured me. "So, I hear you had an interesting evening with Alex the other night."

"Alex told you about the sex?" I gasped. "Or wait, did you see it in my head? What is going on?"

Jane's jaw dropped. "I was talking about that date you abandoned at Southern Comfort. Tess said the awkwardness was so thick, you could see it spread all over the table like mayonnaise. And then after you left, the guy invited some other girl to the table."

"Oh." I shuddered. "Also, that mayonnaise thing is gross."

"But you had sex with Alex, that's…interesting!" She gave me the world's most uncomfortable thumbs up.

"I can't believe I'm having this conversation with you two," I moaned, covering my face with my hands.

"Um, I'm back here, too," Gabriel called from the office. "Congratulations, I think."

"I'm not happy with it," Dick said, shaking his head. "I mean, really, Buttercup, a French guy? I thought we raised you better than that!"

"You didn't raise me, Dick."

"Well, we have a deep personal emotional investment in you, so it feels like we did," he scoffed.

"I've known you for like, a month," I reminded him.

"Alex is a perfectly nice man," Jane reminded him. "And he treats Tylene with respect and affection, and that's all we can ask. Besides, he's a good friend of Cal and Nik. They wouldn't be friends with someone who wasn't boyfriend material."

Dick grumbled as he walked towards Jane's office. "Excuse me, I'm going to go learn the shovel speech in French."

"Well, that was unexpected," I said.

"I know it seems a little infantilizing, but for Dick, this is normal," Jane said. "Zeb mentioned he told you this already, but for Dick - once you're family, you're family forever. And he will violate a lot of state and federal laws to protect his family."

"I don't know if that makes me feel *better*."

She shrugged. "That is also normal."

Without warning a huge man burst through the door at full vampire speed, yelling in what sounded like Russian. It was alarming enough to make me shift into werewolf form, standing in front of Jane and snarling viciously before I recognized the vampire was Nik Dragomirov.

"Aw, look at you, jumping in to defend me," Jane cooed, scratching my back. Nik was sorted into the "not a threat" part of my brain, so my hackles dropped. Gigi practically baseball-slid into the shop, yelping at the sight of an enormous wolf occupying retail space. I huffed what I hoped sounded like an apology at Nik, who had at least stopped yelling.

Nik threw an arm in front of Gigi, pulling her behind him. I was no longer growling or snapping, but I didn't blame him for not wanting her near me.

I transformed back into a human, ducking behind Jane. "Sorry! You startled me!"

Of course, it wasn't just that he'd startled me. It was that he'd barged into the shop, an apparent threat, and the wolf-y part of my brain had considered the shop to be my home territory.

He was a threat to that home and the people there that I cared about, and I'd shifted without a thought to protect them.

I gripped a nearby stool as the full force of that thought hit me. The compound wasn't home to me anymore. The shop was home. Jane and Dick and Alex and all of them—they were my home. Somewhere inside my chest, the ropes that kept me bound to the packlands seemed to snap, the weight of them easing away. I felt like I could breathe freely for the first time since…ever.

The shock of this unnatural change in instinctual loyalties

was almost enough to distract me from the fact that I was standing naked in the middle of the shop. My clothes were shredded in a pile on the floor.

"What's going on?" Dick yelled, coming out of the office. He blanched and covered his face. "No! My eyes!"

"Um, Dick, can you toss out an extra t-shirt and sweats?" Jane yelled.

"I'm just going to stay in the office, where it's safe!" Gabriel called.

Dick backed into the office, his eyes still covered and knocked several books off of the shelves in the process. For his part, Nik was staring up at the ceiling, respectfully studying the light fixtures. A purple shirt and sweatpants came flying out of the office.

"I'm just going to stay back here for a bit!" Dick called. "I think I'm coming down with hysterical blindness."

"Family forever," Jane sang to me as I slipped into the clothes. "Nik, as much as I enjoy drop-in visits, care to explain your dramatic entrance? Is everything all right?"

"I'm afraid not," Nik said. "I need to speak to you in your capacity as Council Representative, Jane. Dick, too, when he's comfortable."

"Is Ty dressed?" Dick called.

"Yes!" I yelled back.

"Sorry, Buttercup," Dick said, walking into the café area. "I was not prepared for werewolf nudity."

"No one ever is," I told him. "But I think Nik needs your attention."

By this point, Nik had calmed down considerably. I supposed unexpected nakedness tended to shock people out of their emotional states.

"Yes," Nik cleared his throat while Gigi settled on the barstool nearest to me.

"You all right?" I asked.

"Just preparing myself for the protective shenanigans to come," she said. "You should know, he called Alex and Cal over here, too. So, you're in for it."

"In for what?"

"The 'secret underground lair' treatment," she said darkly.

Gabriel and Dick poked their heads out of the office, presumably to make sure everybody was clothed.

"I'll start the coffee," Gabriel said.

Dick replied, "I'll get the murder board."

"It is always this dramatic? Is the new 'weekly terror' element in my life because I'm dating someone that's so much older than me or is it because he's a vampire?" I asked Gigi quietly, while the "adults" tried to return the room into something like order.

"A little bit of both," she conceded. "It's not always like this. And relationships with vampires are always sort of high tension, even the super functional ones like Cal and Iris. Nik basically had to rethink everything he thinks about women, relationships, culture. And I have to be patient. It's all about making that effort and knowing that it's worth it in the end."

I nodded, my expression thoughtful.

"If you need anything or have any questions, give me a call," she said. "It's not that Jane and Dick couldn't give you good advice, but I'm a little closer to your age."

"Definitely, I'll text you my number," I said, taking out my phone.

"Oh, I already have it. I found your info through the Council's databases ages ago. Jolene had to fill out paperwork when she joined Jane's committee. You're listed on her forms as 'one of the few normal relatives you could contact in an emergency,'" Gigi said, tapping on her own phone, "and I just sent you the contact information for everybody in the family. And you're on the emergency phone tree."

I don't know which part was more touching—that Jolene

listed me as someone she trusted in an emergency or that I'd been added to the "family" phone list. I was included here. I was appreciated. Maybe I could forge this new life with these new people and not lose everybody in the pack. Maybe I could have everything I wanted.

This was a dangerous line of thinking, and I was grateful when Andrea got Nik calmed down enough to explain why he'd damn near torn off Jane's shop door. There was a large mug of Calm Your Ass Down blend tea involved. "Gigi went to check the mail earlier tonight and retrieved a package from our mailbox. She found this, mixed in with the bills and junk mail," Nik seethed, tossing a large clear plastic bag containing a small carboard box and some sort of mangled metal cannister. Both were splattered with a shiny grey substance that rolled around inside the bag.

"It took me longer than it should have to realize there was something wrong with the package," Gigi admitted. "It was addressed to Nik, but there were no postage marks. I was walking back to the apartment when I heard the noise."

"Colloidal silver," Nik spat. "The cannister inside was loaded with it and rigged to spray when the package was opened."

"A nasty trick," Jane murmured. "And painful. It happened to me a few years ago. If Dick hadn't been there to help me, I would have died."

She paused to smile fondly at Dick, who winked back at her. Andrea leaned her head against her husband's, clearly proud of his heroics. Even Gabriel, as reserved as he was, put his hand on Dick's shoulder.

"If the cannister hadn't been jostled loose and sprayed early, if Gigi hadn't heard the cannister spraying and tossed it down the hall, *she* could have died," Nik said. "As you can imagine, I find this beyond unacceptable. Jane, Dick, I believe this is an escalation of the harassment Cal, Iris, and Alex have experienced. Please, tell me what you are going to do about it."

Jane had donned latex gloves to handle the contorted bit of metal evidence. "Why is the cannister so beat up?"

Nik peered down into his teacup. "When I recognized the threat to Gigi, I may have kicked it away from her."

"But first, he stomped it into oblivion," Gigi noted.

"That's a pretty big escalation, from vandalism and spray paint to a colloidal silver bomb. Are you sure it's the same person?" Jane asked.

"Look at the handwriting on the package," Nik said. "Even when you use spray paint versus a pen, your handwriting remains the same. Look at the curious way the R curves. And the A, a perfect right angle creating the inverted V shape. That's unusual."

Dick wheeled the murder board out into the open and Nik pointed to the R and A shapes in the word "VAMPIRE" painted on Iris's house and Alex's school. "See? They're the same."

"I have video this time," Nik said. "He placed the package in our mailbox around seven, just before we rose for the day. I've sent it to your Council email address."

"How do you have video of him?" Jane asked.

"I keep a video camera trained on our mailbox," Nik replied, as if this was a completely normal thing for someone to do. "It sends motion capture clips to my phone."

Jane didn't comment on why you would want to surveil your mailbox, which was probably wise. "Did you get his face?"

"No, he is wearing a baseball cap that covers his face from the camera angle." Nik played the video, showing a thin, tall masculine shape, his face shielded with a UK cap. He approached the mailbox, just as casual as you please, and placed the box inside their mailbox. He seemed to know the camera was there and was careful to keep his face tilted away.

"Do you see that?" I asked, tilting my head as the man pulled his hand away from the box. "Can you pause it, Nik?"

"Of course." He poked a finger at the screen.

I squinted at the screen. "What is that?"

"It's just a regular phone, Ty," Nik said. "It's not like the video enhancement software they use on TV shows."

"No, but I have werewolf vision," I noted. "Also, you're a damn vampire. So, your vision is probably better than mine."

"Good point," Nik noted, pausing the video on the wrist that was reaching toward the mailbox. A dark symbol seemed branded on his skin.

"It's a tattoo," I said, squinting at the screen. "And not your typical misspelled Asian typography you see on today's youths. It looks...what's a fancy word for 'old and scary?'"

"It seems familiar," Nik mused.

Just then, Cal burst into the shop, followed by Iris and then Alex. Iris sniffled, throwing her arms around Gigi. Cal wrapped them both in his arms, creating a sort of triple hug.

"Told you," Gigi mouthed at me, just before Alex pulled me close.

"I am not and was not in any danger," I promised him. "But the hug is nice."

"Cal called me on his way over. I was sure you'd be here," he said. "I just needed to see you."

"Jane. I am displeased," Iris said, her voice deadly calm as she pulled away from her sister. "Please, tell me there is a plan."

"We will do everything we can to address the situation," Jane promised. "Nik managed to get the guy on video, but not his face. But it's more than we had before."

Nik handed Cal his phone. Cal replayed the video several times, his frown deepening with every repetition. Alex watched, too, over his shoulder. Again, I was struck by how comfortable the three men seemed together. They seemed to communicate without words, just gestures and facial expressions.

"I recognize this mark," Cal said. "It's a brand. It marks a man as the descendent of a noble house of Rome. The idea was that if he fell in battle, even his enemies were supposed to know who he was and send his bones home to his family."

Nik's jaw dropped. "The little Roman twerp?"

Alex nodded as if to confirm it. "The little Roman twerp."

"His name is Augustus. No one knows the last name. That's how old he is," Cal said. "We met him in Paris, around the same time we befriended Alex. We could see how unbalanced he was, even then, and tried to stay away from him. He didn't appreciate the rejection."

Jane gasped. "Oh, even I've heard of him. I wasn't sure if Ophelia was trying to scare me or make my job easier, but she gave me a list of some of the most destructive psychotic vampires in history. Augustus No-Last-Name was two or three on the list. She said he was a butcher, the illegitimate spawn of some creepy Roman emperor. He mowed through entire towns to slake his thirst. The Council was formed in its infancy to deal with vampires like him."

Gigi leaned toward me, whispered. "Ophelia was the head of the vampire Council around here before Dick and Jane. She was turned when she was about fourteen, so picture an adorable teenage sociopath with fangs."

"Sociopath?"

"Oh, yeah, in an indirect yet-entirely-still-her-fault-way, I was turned because she thought I was getting too close to her boyfriend," Gigi said, pursing her lips. "She's the literal worst."

"Augustus was a prick," Nik added. When Alex showed him a startled look, he said, "You can say it. If you don't, one of the ladies here will. On the night we met him, we had to stop him from going into an orphanage for a 'quick snack.'"

"Well, if the Council was founded to take care of vampires like him, why didn't they?" I asked.

Alex shrugged. "We thought they did. After the orphanage stunt, the three of us worked with what was eventually became the Council to help them track him down. It was how our friendship was formed, mutual disgust with Augustus."

Jane nudged Dick's ribs with her elbow. "Some meaningful friendships have been founded on far less."

"I saved you from a parking lot ass-kicking," Dick reminded her.

"And you were amazing at it," she assured him.

"The Council set fire to a tavern where he'd spent weeks holed up, drinking from the kitchen maids. We thought he died in the blaze," Cal said.

"Do you think that's why he's targeting you?" Dick asked. "Revenge?"

"It very well could be," Cal said. "Even that imbecile could have figured out that we were involved in informing the Council of his activities. And when the Council burned the Inn, we were standing right outside, carrying torches. It would make sense, that he escalated to silver with Nik. He was the one Augustus hated most. The night of the orphanage, he threatened to rip Nik's head off and use it for lawn bowling."

"He failed, of course," Nik scoffed. "He was a spindly boy who vastly overestimated his power. Even vampire strength can only do so much."

Jane frowned at him. "Well, now we have to kill him for real. I can't have a lunatic like that loose in my region...and I just realized that for the first time I've made a decision that Ophelia would have made. And now I'm questioning my decision."

"Wait, the messages at Iris's house and Alex's school were 'get out of town' and 'stay away from local girls,'" I objected. "Wouldn't they be different if he was trying to get revenge? Something like, 'Remember the orphanage?' or 'Surprise, I'm not dead!"

"You don't still think your family was responsible for the vandalism, do you?" Jane asked.

"I don't know if it's a *better* theory, but do you really think he waited hundreds of years for the three of you to move to the same tiny town so he can get back at you for an attempt on his life?" I asked. "No one is that crazy."

Iris put her hand on my shoulder. "Orphanage snack."

I sighed. "I don't like that there is a place in my life for phrases like that."

"I want Ty to be safeguarded," Alex insisted. "Jane, please request that a UERT unit be stationed outside the shop when Ty is working here."

"I was going to do that anyway," Jane agreed.

"And I would like other units stationed outside the perimeter of her pack's compound," he added.

"Whoa, whoa, that cannot happen," I told him. "My family will *definitely* notice a bunch of vampires in SWAT gear hanging out on the edge of their territory. And that will result in all sorts of questions that I can't possibly answer without being sent to the werewolf version of military school."

"So you're not willing to protect yourself? Is that what you're telling me?" Alex asked, his brow furrowed. "You're all right with being hurt?"

Slowly, the vampires around us seemed to sense this was a conversation they should not witness. Nik and Gigi, and Cal and Iris, slowly backed into the historical section of the stacks. Andrea and Gabriel pretended to be occupied with something near the emergency exit in the back. But Dick and Jane remained, presumably because they needed to know whether I agreed to my own personal security army.

"Do you know what would happen if they found out what I've been doing the last few weeks?" I countered. "Did you not hear me when I was talking about being kicked out of the pack? What that would mean for me?"

He shook his head. "But if you explained to them—"

"No," I told him firmly. "I'll agree to being guarded while I'm working here and while I'm running back and forth to town, but that's as far as I'm willing to go," I told him. "And if you can't accept my word on this, maybe we don't have the relationship I thought we were building."

It was as if an emotional shutter closed over his entire face. Suddenly, he was remote, colder, and I could feel a space open up between us that wasn't hadn't been there before.

IT WAS spring cleaning day on the compound. The McClaines might have a dozen or so defunct cars in our yards, but the grass was always trimmed around them. The barns were cleared of junk and the trailers were shiny clean, even if they were worn. I stood in my room, trying to decide whether I needed half of the stuff I'd accumulated over my lifetime.

Over the past few days, I'd found I didn't mind the "guard" from the Council. A van full of them waited outside the shop, 'surveilling' me. And another, Ray McElray, a beefy vampire with a dark curly mullet, sat at one of the tables in "civilian clothes" pretending to read a book on the Honey Island Swamp Monster. Ray reminded me of one of my family members. He and Dick spent a lot of time talking about the various improvised anti-vampire weapons he was making at home. He was trying to get the Council to invest in an idea he had for an air gun that launched tiny silver spikes at vampire intruders. Dick liked the idea on principal, but said it was unlikely.

Alex was distant. He hadn't called in days and rarely stopped by the shop to see me. I tried to tell myself that he was just busy, getting the school back up and running. But I'd really hurt him with my refusal to be protected. I understood why he was upset, but was bewildered by his refusal to see my point of view. I was walking a fine line between peace at home and staying safe. He couldn't just walk into my life and tell me how I was going to handle things. And I certainly didn't want him making decisions for me.

I was torn between wanting to beg him to forgive me and being angry at his lack of understanding. And while the idea of him being upset with me or even wanting to leave me sent me into a state of panic, part of me thought that maybe it was inevitable. Maybe I was fooling myself, thinking that a relationship with Alex was even an option for me.

These were deep, depressing thoughts to have while I was trying to clean out my closet, which was already a depressing task. I stood, staring at the empty bar. There was a lot of extra room. You couldn't tell what I owned and what I'd cleared out. Not even Mama would know for sure what was clean, what was dirty, what was missing.

Suddenly, my jeans and t-shirts were in my hands and being stuffed into an old gym bag. I told myself it was just for emergencies, like those "go bags" the federal disaster types were always telling you to keep packed. But it could be more. It could be something I didn't dare put into words for anyone else. Hands shaking, I crossed to my desk and took anything I didn't think I could live without. A few of my favorite books, a framed photo of my late grandparents, a moonstone necklace my parents had given me for my sixteenth birthday. My ears almost twitched as I heard someone walking down the hall. I shoved the bag under my bed and returned to the closet, shaking out a dress and folding it.

"What are you doing?" Mama asked.

"Just setting some things aside for Marlene's girls," I told her, nudging the suitcase under my bed with my foot.

"Well, that's nice of you," she paused, frowning at the pile of discarded clothes, neatly folded on my bed. "Those are your date night dresses, Tylene."

"Yes, and I'm sure Marlene's girls can make good use of them. They're getting a little tight for me."

"How are you going to go out on your date with Donnie if you don't have any dresses?" she asked.

"I don't plan on going on any dates with Donnie, Mama. He's in love with someone else."

"Well, that doesn't mean that you just give up! Does his family approve of this girl?"

"No, but he *loves* her, like really loves her and I refuse to torture a man who told me to my face how much he loves someone else," I told her, taking a deep breath and steeling my nerves. "And I think you've figured out that I've started seeing someone. And I don't want to confuse that whole situation by dating someone else."

For the briefest moment, relief and joy flashed across my mother's face. "But that's great news! Why wouldn't you tell us anything about it?" she cried. And as quickly as it appeared, that joy drained out of her face. "Oh, no, he's not a werewolf, is he? That's why you didn't want to tell us. He's not human, is he?"

"No, he's not human," I admitted. "He's a vampire."

She shot to her feet and slammed my bedroom door closed.

"Tylene McClaine! Only you could take Jolene's mistake and make it worse," she hissed. "You can't breathe a word of this to your daddy or your Uncle Lonnie or anyone. Do you understand? This never happened. Did you go anywhere that people could see you?"

"Yes, because I wasn't doing anything wrong!" I told her. "He's a good man, a kind man. And he makes me feel special, loved. Isn't that what's important?"

Mama looked absolutely bewildered. "NO!"

"Can you please help me with this?" I asked.

"You don't understand. When your daddy brought me back here, it was a huge upset. He was supposed to marry a girl from the Ansen pack. It was all arranged. And then he left, which was bad enough, but then he found me. I was unattached, but we got pregnant with you and we married without permission from either pack. I couldn't go back home, do you understand?"

My mouth dropped open but no words would escape. I knew that my mother didn't have contact with her pack in Florida, but I thought it was because of the distance and how possessive my dad's pack was. We just didn't have the time to visit them or keep up socializing. I'd never really thought about it.

"He brought me back here and nothing was the way I thought it would be. Lonnie had been chosen as the next Alpha, passing over your daddy. And that was bad enough, but I just didn't fit in here. It was nothing like my pack and the harder I tried, the more the aunts pulled away and ignored me. So I just followed. I did exactly what they wanted, and they finally accepted me."

"Have they really?" I asked.

"Well, as close as they'll ever come to accepting me," she said.

"I don't want that sort of life , Mama. I need your help. I can't keep this up. I'm going to make changes. And if those changes make them as mad as I think they will, I'm going to need your support."

Mama's shoulders curled around her. "I can't honey. If that's what you want, you're going to have to do it on your own."

"Even if it means you might never see me again?" I asked.

She turned to me, her dark eyes full of tears. "I can't lose your daddy, the pack. I've put too much time in to lose it all now."

I nodded, trying not to let it hurt that she didn't consider me part of what she could lose.

"Can you at least promise not to tell anybody anything until I'm ready?"

She laughed, a brittle, rattling sound. "You think I want to be the one to tell him?"

She got up, and without another word, walked out of my

room. For a long time, I sat on the bed and stared at the wall. I don't know why I'd hoped my mother might make this situation easier, but now it was clear I was on my own. And if I didn't do something, I would end up just like her, unhappy, gray and constantly afraid.

No more being afraid.

I pulled out my phone and scrolled through the contacts. The phone rang several times before I realized that it was daytime and Dick wouldn't be awake for hours. Friendships with vampires was very rewarding but this whole "dead during daylight hours" was sort of inconvenient. I waited for the voicemail to pick up.

"Hey Dick, it's Ty. I know you're sleeping right now, but when you get up can you call me back? I was wondering if that apartment is still available."

9

"Being left 'on read' can be very frustrating. But showing up at someone's door to ask why they haven't responded to your text? It's an overstep."
—*A Gentleman in Any Era: An Ancient Vampire's Guide to Modern Relationships*

Contrary to what my parents had told me, once I told Dick that I was interested in the apartment, it was all very simple. They didn't even run a credit check on me and gave me a "family discount." My savings, considerably padded by the extra income from my new clients, were more than enough to cover first and last month's rent, plus deposit. I had utilities set up in my name within twenty-four hours of calling Dick.

For the first time in my life, I felt like a real *adult*. I was buoyed by this strange sense of hope. I had been so sure for so long that nothing would ever change. I thought I knew exactly how my life was going to play out and now, suddenly there were so many possibilities. I could do anything, go anywhere. I just had to have the courage to complete this first step.

Dick and Andrea were the only people who knew. I didn't want to tell anyone else until I told my parents. And I kept putting that off. I set a deadline for telling them after I had the application filled out. And then I thought maybe I wouldn't say anything until the utilities were open, because that was the real point of no return. And then, I didn't want to ruin their weekend, especially when I hadn't even signed up for recycling pick-up.

At this point, I hadn't even had the nerve to tell Alex yet. I told myself that I just wanted to surprise him when I had everything settled; but really, despite all this hope for change, there was still this lingering doubt in the back of my mind that I might not follow through with it. I didn't want to get his hopes up only to disappoint him.

I'd finally gotten in contact with Alex to set up a date night, but for the first time since we met, he seemed…off. I'd had to lie to my parents, tell them that I was babysitting Jolene's kids for the night, and he knew it. He was quiet, still just as distant as he had been for weeks, and I just wanted to go home. I didn't think that was a good sign.

We were trying to have a nice, normal night in, like a regular couple. We'd curled up on his couch, watching a concert streamed live from Vienna—a collection of Mozart pieces that sounded like heaven's soundtrack. But my phone was dinging steadily all night, with messages from my aunts about my next date with Donnie Ansen.

They'd collectively decided that we would go out to a movie that weekend. They'd even picked the title and the time for us. I was surprised they didn't dictate what snacks we could order.

And then there were texts with Donnie, coordinating excuses as to why we couldn't go on another date. Donnie offered to say he had some sort of skin fungus that required him to stay indoors, which was awfully sweet of him.

"Why is your phone chirping like a hyperactive canary?" he asked. "Is everything all right?"

I rolled my eyes and shoved the phone down in my backpack. "My family is trying to set me up with Donnie again, that werewolf boy from the other night. Both of our families have decided we're perfect for each other."

"I suppose telling them 'no' is out of the question?" he asked. When I gave him a scathing eye roll, he added, "I only mean, have you tried to definitively tell them that you're not willing to cooperate with their schemes to set you up with a mate of their choosing?"

"You don't know what it's like to live with them and you don't have any idea of what I could lose. Do you know what it's like for a pack animal to be threatened with exile? Or what that would mean for my life?"

"Jolene did it," he pointed out.

"Because Jolene had *Zeb*! She had someone who wanted to build a life with her. I don't know what you want. *You* don't know what you want. You say it's me. Maybe it is. Maybe it's domesticity and security. Maybe it's running back to your shiftless musical nomad life. Maybe it's a hot tub full of supermodels on some yacht in the Seychelles."

"*What?*"

"I don't know what you do with your spare time when I'm not around!" I cried, rising from the couch.

"No one goes to the Seychelles at this time of year. The weather—"

I pinched the bridge of my nose. "Oh, my god."

"I thought that you liked that I didn't put pressure on you! I was trying to respect your wishes! You don't think I hear the fear in your voice? The uncertainty? Every single word out of your mouth rings with how little you think of my love and my place in your life. But I kept trying because I thought we're growing! I thought if you had other things in your life, the idea of losing your pack wouldn't be so frightening," he said.

I shook my head at him. "You really think a lot of yourself. Like you're just going to come along and change my whole life with a few dates and some sex? It doesn't work like that. I need to work through it on my own."

"Why do you care so much about what they think of you?" he demanded.

"That's easy for you to ask," I told him. "You didn't care about what your family thought of you. You left them and you didn't look back. And it was such a long time ago, I'll be you've forgotten how hard that was."

"I want you to be mine, out in the open. I don't want to have to sneak around. I don't want to hide. I don't want you even pretending to belong to another man."

"I don't belong to anybody, buddy," I said, grabbing my backpack. "Least of all, you."

"Buddy?" he jumped up from the couch as I walked to the door. He took my arm carefully. "Please don't leave like this, Ty. I don't want you walking out there on your own. Not with Augustus out there somewhere."

"Don't start that again!" I cried. "I think we're done here. I haven't felt right about us for a while now. You've been weird ever since we found about Augustus."

"You mean the night when you said you would much rather get injured than have your family find out about me?" he asked. "Is it really that important? Being their good agreeable girl? Are you willing to die for them?"

I shook my head. "I'll have the UERT guys follow me home. I know you had them park out by the end of your driveway to monitor your house while I'm here. You're constantly underestimating me. Don't call me. I don't want to talk to you in the near future. I hope that clears up your uncertainty."

"Tylene, please!" he called after me while I stomped down the driveway.

I made it home to the compound in record time, even with stopping at the end of the road and spraying on perfume. The UERT guys had to drive at top speeds to keep up with me, flicking their headlights at me when I turned off the main road towards our land.

It was quiet, and my parents were in their usual seats. Mama was working her puzzle book and Daddy was in his recliner. Always the same.

Mama eyed me suspiciously as I walked into the living room. "Jolene and her husband make an early night of it?"

"Mmhmm," I said.

"Did you eat?" she asked. "I made meatloaf."

"I'm not hungry," I said, backing toward my room.

"Are you all right, Ty?" my father asked, his voice softer, worried. It was more concern than he had shown for me in a long time. "I've never known you to turn down your mama's meatloaf. And your eyes look a little red."

"Oh, sure, I'm fine," I said, sniffing. "Just allergies."

"All right. Your Uncle Hank needs you tomorrow at the butcher shop. And Donnie Ansen's daddy just called to say he can't go out this week, something about an intestinal fungus. Poor boy."

So Donnie had followed through with his offer. And he'd given himself a pretend fungus to get out of it. I didn't know whether to laugh or cry.

I went to my bedroom and flopped down on my mattress. I'd lost something significant, something real. How had it gone so wrong, so quickly? No warning, just a huge explosion of wrong and suddenly it felt like everything was over. It was like a death.

I wasn't wrong. I knew that. He was asking too much of me

and he was holding himself apart from me. And I—I couldn't even think. I was just too heartbroken. This was the drawback of missing that stupid teenage romance phase. I was completely unprepared for just how *awful* this felt.

To make it worse, I'd probably just lost the friends I'd made at Specialty Books. Jane and Dick might like me, but Alex was their kind, not mine. And Gabriel would follow Jane. Cal and Nik were Alex's friends, and I wasn't close enough to Gigi or Iris for them to cross their partners for me. They would choose him over me. It was instinct. With one stupid argument, I'd swept all of those friendships I'd built off of the map like a tidal wave.

In a way, I thought this might be better. I didn't want to see that. I didn't want to watch them make polite, squirming conversation as they tried to gently shoo me away from the bookstore as quickly as possible. All of the places I'd carved out as mine, I would lose. Except for the library, as long as Mrs. Stubblefield didn't have security video of me stripping down in the garden. I couldn't imagine she'd let me back after that.

And it wasn't just the personal that I'd lost. I'd just blown a hole in my business as well. All of the contracts I'd just signed? I doubted my new clients would honor them once I was the undead's *persona non grata*. Dick would withdraw the apartment offer. It wasn't official until he handed over the keys. I would be lucky if Jolene and Zeb didn't drop me.

I couldn't keep my parents happy and live the life I wanted. I couldn't be a good werewolf and a good girlfriend. I'd spent too much time trying to play both sides of the card and it finally caught up with me.

I was right back where I started, without having moved at all.

I scrubbed my hand across my cheeks, my palm wet with tears I hadn't even realized were there.

I sniffed and tried to tell myself to be brave about it. I would just have to find new places. The fact that I'd managed it was proof that I could. And maybe I could find a place of my own that I wouldn't have to lie about, friends that I could have, while also holding on to parts of my own life. Maybe this would be better. I doubted it was possible, but maybe.

But I would really miss Dick's coffee drinks.

10

"Sometimes, to hold an important relationship together, you will be asked to do things that uncomfortable. Whether you're willing to do those things is a measure of whether you're committed to the relationship. Either way, if those uncomfortable things are illegal, you should probably rethink the relationship."
—*A Gentleman in Any Era: An Ancient Vampire's Guide to Modern Relationships*

*M*y next Friday night was spent staring at an eight-foot-tall carved wooden possum, holding a pepperoni pizza.

I didn't have to lie this time. I was really babysitting Jolene's kids. She and Zeb wanted a nice quiet evening out, so I agreed to take the twins out for pizza. There was a place in Murphy called The Hungry Possum run by a possum shifter named Barnaby who didn't ask questions when a party of three ordered five large meat lover's pies.

We sat in the rustic wooden booth, munching on triple-cheese bread, talking about their weeks in school. Spending time with the kids was surprisingly relaxed. They didn't have high expectations. They didn't ask difficult, emotional questions. They just wanted to eat and complain about fourth grade math, and how unfair it was that they had to do math at all.

And toilet humor. There was a lot of toilet humor.

Jolene, however, looked at me like she was afraid I would fall apart any minute. She knew *something* was going on, but when she asked if everything was okay with Alex, I just shook my head and changed the subject to the twins' dietary restrictions. She kept trying, telling me that Jane was worried about me and wanted me to call when I was ready, but I was sure it was just something to do with whether she should withdraw the UERT unit following me around town. It was hardly necessary anymore. I mostly stayed on the compound, trying to work. And dodging my aunts' attempts at ambush makeovers.

I managed to get out of the conversation when Joe spilled grape juice down the *back* of his shirt and had to be mopped up.

"So, school is good. Math is bad. Recess is your only refuge in this cruel, cruel world," I said, dropping a wad of grape-soaked napkins on the table. "What else is new?"

"We started music lessons again," Joe said. "The school opened up."

"Oh?" I said, carefully. "That's great, sweetheart. I'm glad for you.

"Mr. Alex seems sad, though," Janelyn said, staring at me. "He's had us playing nothing but Samuel Barber all week. He only plays American composers when he's depressed."

"Well, that sucks," I replied. Even though a tiny vicious part of me was glad to hear Alex was as dejected as I was. Even if I was alone, at least I wasn't alone in my misery. "You guys want another order of cheese bread?"

"I'm gonna stick with the meat lover's," Joe said, grabbing his seventh slice of pizza.

"Probably wise," I said, picking up another piece of cheese bread.

"You seem sad, too," Janelyn noted.

I attempted a smile for her. "Do I?"

She nodded. "Yeah, and that's not a real smile. It's a scary thing adults do with their faces when they're trying to convince children we're too dumb to know a sad person we they see one."

"Dang it, Janelyn," I winced. "Could you be a little less observant, please?"

"Probably not," Joe told me. "Just think of how annoying it is to live with her."

"You have my sympathies," I replied.

"So why are you sad?" Janelyn asked.

"Grown-up problems."

She lifted a brow. "And now I'm too dumb to understand grown-up problems?"

"No, I'm too private a person to share them," I retorted.

She shrugged. "I guess I'll accept that."

"Thank you."

"Tylene?"

I glanced up to see Donnie standing next to our table, his arm around Mara's waist.

"Hi, Donnie," I said, smiling up at them. "How are you?"

Mara pulled me out of the booth and wrapped me in a bone-cracking hug. "We're great. Thank you so much!"

"You're welcome?" I said, confused.

"I decided you were right," Donnie told me. "That I wanted to be happy, and that meant being with Mara. So, I went home and told my family that I was in love with her."

"We eloped!" Mara cried, showing me a tiny, earnest diamond sparkling on her finger, part of a wedding set.

"Wow, when you rebel, you guys go full out." I laughed. "Congratulations. And how did your family respond?"

"Tossed me right off the compound," he said, grinning. "I'm the family shame."

"But no one has said anything to me," I said. "My aunts still think we're going to the movies next weekend. They said you had a fungus!"

"Yeah, my daddy hasn't had the heart to tell anyone. They might send one of my cousins to the movie theatre and try to convince you that's how I looked all along," he said.

"Well, I'll try to be nicer to him than I was to you," I said.

"Oh, hell no," Donnie objected. "You were nicer than I deserved. We wouldn't have been able to do it without you."

I wrinkled my nose. "Do me a favor and don't tell your family that, okay?"

"We promise," he said as Mara wrapped me in another rib-crusher of a hug.

"Have a good night," I told them, as they left for their own booth.

As I sat down, I looked at the twins. "You didn't see anything."

"I don't know what you're talking about," Janelyn said.

"I'm not sure we saw *you* tonight," Joe told me.

A FEW DAYS LATER, I was back at the library, and everything felt so shabby after the charms of Jane's shop. Mrs. Stubblefield was not pleased to see me and somehow, despite all being empty, none of the study carrels were open for me.

I checked my email, again, expecting to find some cancellations from Jane's friends. But all I had was a note from Libby, saying she really liked the new Facebook business page I'd set up for her and a thank you from Meadow, who said her customers had mentioned how much more user-friendly her website was now.

What if I'd misjudged all of them? What if I could go back to the shop and work and see Dick and his magical coffee creations? I would feel like an idiot if I was suffering the pains of the library tables for no reason.

"Now, what's making a pretty girl like you frown like that?"

I looked up, finding a vampire standing over me. It was the same guy who had tried to talk to me at Southern Eclectic, the one without a scent. He was a perfectly nice-looking guy, I supposed—light brown hair in a spiky, tousled style, deep brown eyes, almost cherubic lips that could have been seen as sensitive if they weren't turned in a smirk. He still didn't smell of anything...except rubber that was so new it reeked of chemicals. It was all I could do not to gag as I glanced under the table. Yep, brand new sneakers in a neon-colored European brand I didn't recognize. Was he trying to impress me with new shoes or something? Did I seem like the kind of girl who would be impressed by that sort of thing? I hoped not.

My phone buzzed. I shoved it into my backpack, unwilling to even let him see who might be calling.

"Nice to see you again," he said, giving me what I'm sure he thought was his most winning smile.

"Hello. I don't want to be rude." I paused to gesture towards my laptop. "But I'm working and don't have time for company."

"You're working? At the library?" He flopped into the chair across from me.

"I didn't invite you to sit down," I noted.

He shrugged lazily. "It's a public library."

"The fact that you have to say that should tell you what a bad idea this is."

He smirked at me, as if it was adorable that I thought I had the right to say who could be near me. I didn't like the way this guy was looking at me. I wanted to put my laptop away, to make it as easy as possible to get up and get away, but I also didn't want him to think he'd rattled me. Apex predators recognized a standoff when they saw one.

"So, I guess your date the other night didn't go so well, huh?"

"I don't think that's any of your business."

"So, what's your deal? Where are you from? Why do you spend so much time in the library? Was that guy the other night your boyfriend?"

"Why would I answer any of that?" I scoffed. "I don't know you. I don't even know your *name*."

"It's Greg."

"Of course it is," I sighed. My phone buzzed again, almost insistent. I wondered if it was Mama, trying to get me to come home.

"What's yours?"

"Not interested."

"That's an unusual name."

"Not really. I come from a long line of Not Interested's."

"So, how about I take you out, sometime?" he asked, giving me that grin again.

"Not. Interested."

"Why not?" he demanded, his tone getting whinier with each word. His jaw set in an irritated line as he stared at me. "You know, they say once you start dating vampires, everything else is just pointless. Usually, sayings rhyme, but not much rhymes with vampire."

"Ew." I frowned at him. The good news was that I hadn't objectified Alex sexually because I was fascinated by his vampirism. This guy was a vampire and I was pretty repulsed by him. He seemed to think he was *owed* something, specifically owed something *by me*—for reasons I didn't understand. And to my surprise, I couldn't care less.

He was getting really upset with me, and the anxiety I usually felt in situations like this seemed non-existent. The annoyance that *I* felt burnt through it like the sun through fog. Was it because I had started to see the shop as home? Like I'd broken some sort of programming?

"Oh, come on. What's the worst that could happen?"

"This?" I noted. "Spending time with someone who starts so many sentences with, 'Oh, come on' and doesn't see anything wrong with that? Someone who won't take a hint?"

"But I see you with vampires all the time," he objected.

"Vampires that I know, that I like. That has nothing to do with you."

"Just one drink," he said. "What do you have to lose?"

"Nothing. I'm just not interested."

I shoved my stuff into my backpack and walked out of the library. I could hear him following me and I was immediately annoyed. I didn't want to go home and show him where I lived. But I didn't want to walk around town, vulnerable, either. I was just as strong and just as fast as this guy, but he seemed to have a lot of skeezy on his side. You couldn't underestimate skeezy.

I kept my head up and my ears alert. I wanted to hear him coming if he decided to rush me from behind. I couldn't shift here out in the open. I didn't know if there were witnesses or security cameras around. I reached into the side pocket for the cannister of silver spray Alex had given me. I closed my fingers around it and held it near my thigh so Greg wouldn't see me with it.

An old red El Camino pulled into the library parking lot. Dick hopped out and made a beeline for me. I turned to see whether Greg was still following me. I hated the idea that he might learn my name by virtue of Dick. But he wasn't there. Given the way the library door was swinging, I wondered whether he'd seen Dick and decided he didn't want to tangle with the older vampire. Or maybe he knew that Dick was a Council representative? Either way, I was glad he was gone.

As Dick approached, I slowed down, not quite sure how he

would respond now that I wasn't part of the "circle" anymore. Apparently, he saw the uncertainty on my face. "Oh, sweetheart, c'mere," he said, opening his arms.

I hugged him fiercely.

"If I had to breathe, this would be a real issue," he wheezed.

My voice was muffled by his t-shirt, which read, *"Don't Worry. I'll Make This Awkward For You."* "Sorry. I just didn't know if any of you would want to talk to me after everything with Alex."

"Oh, Buttercup, no. That's not how this works. You're ours now, whether you're dating Alex or not. If it makes you feel better, I threatened to kick his ass all the way back to France," he said.

"It does, a little bit."

He pushed me back a bit so he could see my face. "Is that why you haven't come around?"

"Well, I didn't know if I would be welcome. And then you didn't call, so I just thought—"

"We were trying to give you space!" he cried. "Jolene said you were taking the breakup really hard. Oh, man, is that why you haven't been taking Jane's calls just now?"

"Jane's been calling me? What's going on?"

Dick grimaced. "The music school's burning down."

I TRIED to dash across town before Dick stopped me and drove us over in the El Camino. The school was fully engulfed by the time we got there. There would be no saving it. And he'd just re-opened it. I jumped out before Dick came to a full stop.

Alex was standing in the parking lot, arms crossed as he watched the volunteer fire department aiming hoses at his building. Bright red spray paint scrawled across the pavement, "LEAVE HALF-MOON HOLLOW OR ELSE." Jane was there, talking to someone in a fancy firefighter's uniform, while Dick took a seat in the back of the El Camino, filling out paperwork.

When he saw me, I forgot about our stupid argument or how angry I'd been just a few hours ago. He pulled me into his arms and hugged me tight. "I'm so sorry for the things I said," I whispered.

"No, I'm sorry. I know how hard it is to break free of a difficult family. I pushed too hard."

"I should have been braver," I insisted.

"We were both wrong," he agreed. "Though maybe I was a little less wrong in the grand scheme of things." I pulled back to glare at him. He shook his head. "Right. Not the time."

"Your school," I sighed. "And you'd just re-opened it."

"It's insured," he said. "And the instruments inside, too. Though I'm glad to have video to show the insurer to prove I didn't do this myself. They're probably starting to get suspicious," he said, pulling out his phone. "When you pointed out how silly it was not to have a camera on my business, I installed one there, on the utility pole."

He showed me footage where a single person was painting across the pavement at lightning speed. He was some sort of supernatural creature, moving that fast. But there were so many of us in the Hollow, it was impossible to guess what kind. He was smart enough to hide his face. I couldn't see his hands, to check for the wrist mark.

"I just want to point out that my mother now knows about you," I said. "Just to put the 'it's my family' theory back in the running."

"I'm sure your family didn't do this. Unless you believe they would hire an arsonist to burn down my school."

I pursed my lips. "Let me think about it."

Tonight was the night.

I was supposed to meet Dick and Andrea at the apartment to sign the lease in an hour. I couldn't put it off any longer. I couldn't make more excuses. I was leaving home and my family would just have to accept it. Of course, there was always the option of moving out and *not* telling them…

No, that would be cowardly. And I'd probably end up on the werewolf version of a milk carton. I didn't know what that was, really, but it was bound to be unpleasant. I took a deep breath and opened the door.

"What do you think you're doing?" Daddy asked.

"I'm leaving."

"What time will you be home?" he asked.

Mama stared down at my hands, dread drawing her features back into a grimace. "Why do you have bags with you?"

"I've found an apartment in town. I'm going to live there now."

"You wouldn't." A hoarse whisper rose from Daddy' recliner. "You wouldn't do that to us. Not even you."

All of the color had drained out of his ruddy face. His pupils were practically pin pricks. He looked *terrified.* To my surprise, my father wasn't just upset or angry. "You wouldn't. You wouldn't shame me like this. You wouldn't do *this* to me."

"I'm not doing anything to you, Daddy. I'm doing this *for* me."

"That's not how we do things in this family!" he barked, shooting to his feet.

"I love you both. Lord knows you haven't given me much reason to over the last couple of years—"

"What are you talking about! All we've ever done is work ourselves to the bone from you!" Mama cried.

"I love you," I said again. "But I can't keep living like this. I need to live like an adult. I need some control over my life. I'll call you after I get settled."

"This is all because of that vampire, isn't it," Mama exclaimed.

"What vampire?" Daddy yelled.

"This has nothing to do with the vampire," I said, rolling my eyes.

"What vampire?" Daddy yelled again.

"I've been dating a vampire."

I stood back and waited for Daddy to explode, but to my surprise, it was Mama that went off. "What do you mean you're dating a vampire?"

I gaped at her. She was glancing nervously at Daddy. And I realized, she was pretending not to know about it. To save her own skin, she was willing to blatantly lie. And that was the moment I knew, my relationship with my mother probably wasn't salvageable. I had to leave. And Mama would have to live with her lies and the consequences. I couldn't try to protect her anymore.

"That's right, I'm dating a vampire. A really old one," I said. "And while we're at it, are you the one who destroyed Alex's music school?"

"What in the hell are you talking about?" Mama demanded. She turned to Daddy. "I told you. I told you this would happen. First, Jolene marries a human and then she moved off of pack-lands to live in that *house* next to the vampire lady. I told you where that would lead, but no, you spoil that girl! And this is where it leads. The whole pack is ruined."

"Nothing is ruined," I told her.

"Well, don't come crying to me when he bites you and leaves you for dead!" she cried.

"No problem," I said, starting towards the door.

Daddy caught me by the arm and tried to drag me back from the door. "All you had to do was go along, date Donnie. Even you shouldn't be able to mess that up."

"Also, why do you keep saying 'even you?'" I asked, shrugging him off. "By the way, *Donnie* is not at all interested in me. He just got married to a very nice mountain lion shifter and they're ecstatic."

"The whole world's gone crazy," Mama whispered. "But that's still not as bad as dating a vampire."

"What's so wrong with dating a vampire?"

Mama pulled a disgusted face. "They're unnatural and wrong!"

"*We're* unnatural and wrong! I don't know if you know this, but most people can't turn into giant wolves!"

"We don't hurt people!" Daddy yelled.

"Last March Madness, you waited outside an Applebee's and bit a U of L fan on the ass because he cheered too loud," I countered.

"This isn't about me, it's about you and your ungrateful, lying ways," he said, he tried to shove me back towards my room, but I planted my feet. "I won't let you do this. I will lock you in this house until you come to your senses."

"Is that really how you want to live? Would you really rather have me trapped in your house, instead of just living on my own?" I finished. "Is that really what you want?"

"You know what happened to me when I left," Daddy insisted. "You know how we were barely accepted back and now you want to put us in danger again? We could get kicked off the packlands right along with you."

"Uncle Lonnie would never do that to you. As long as you want to stay, you know he'll let you."

"Don't act like I should be *grateful* for that. I have a right to be here!" Daddy thundered.

"Then why did you leave?" I asked.

"Because I wanted to see what was out there!" he cried. "It was something I just had to do. I was always going to come back. They knew that. I should have been able to do what I wanted, as the Alpha. They should have held my place."

I stared at him, my mouth hanging open. I may not have been the biggest supporter of pack structure and life, but even I knew that's not the way it worked.

"And when I came back, they told me I could pick any spot I wanted for our place. Like I would want any place but the farmhouse. I didn't want to wake up every morning and see what I should have had."

"I thought they *gave* you this spot on the outside of the compound," I said carefully. "That's what you always told me!"

"No!" he yelled. "I wanted to be as far away from my brother as I could get! I didn't need his charity!"

My whole life, I'd thought that my parents had been ostracized by the family, that my being born had somehow led to their marriage, their punishment, their unhappiness. They'd told me that they'd been *forced* to take this spot as a reminder that they were barely accepted back into the fold. But my father had chosen his distance from his brother. How much of his so-called "mistreatment" had been in his own head? In mine? Since I was a child, I'd thought I couldn't trust my family not to reject me. How many of my perceptions were wrong and how had they led to the state of my relationships with them?

I still didn't want to live on the compound. I still wanted my own life, on my own terms. But maybe I wasn't risking quite as much as I thought.

Daddy continued. "You'll be worse off than Jolene. We only let her back on the compound every once in a while because she has the kids. You're not even gonna have that if you date a vampire."

"I'll bet that's news to Uncle Lonnie," I scoffed, reaching for the doorknob.

"If you do this, that's it," Mama told me. "No coming back."

I nodded. "I know."

I walked out of the trailer, with my backpack on my shoulders. All of my aunts and uncles were waiting outside, probably drawn in by the noise. I braced myself for the yelling, the pitch-forks, but they just stared. Uncle Lonnie was waiting, too, but unlike my parents, he looked sad rather than anything else.

I cleared my throat and adjusted my grip on my bags, ready to run. "Uncle Lonnie, I'm sure you heard. I'm going to leave. I've found an apartment in town. I'm going to live there. I know this is probably going to make you unhappy as my Alpha. I'm ready to accept the consequences."

While there were mumblings and whispers all around us, to my shock, my family stayed quiet. And Uncle Lonnie? He didn't yell. He didn't even look mad. He just opened his arms to hug me and kissed my cheek. "If you don't want to be part of the pack anymore, that's up to you, Tylene. I won't say it doesn't hurt, but pack life has never been about keeping people some-where they don't want to be, no matter what my sisters say. It's about making a place for everybody, making them feel loved and needed. If you don't feel that here… that has to be awful. And I'm sorry we didn't do a better job."

"I don't want to leave, necessarily. I just don't want to be pinned down and have no options."

"Well, I can't recommend living like Jolene, half-in and half-out. I'm sure it's painful for her. But I'm grateful to her for making the effort. I just love seeing the twins," he said. "But I want you to know that you're welcome back on the compound any time you want. I don't care what your parents say."

Warmth and relief flooded my chest and it was a hell of task, keeping my tears at bay. "I really appreciate it, Uncle Lonnie."

"Call me when you get settled in," he said. "Let us know where you land."

As I walked down the stairs, Lonnie called, "Let her through!" And my aunts, uncles, and cousins parted for me, their expressions grave. I walked down the pebbled road faster than I thought possible.

CARRYING my suitcase up the stairs of my new apartment building, I didn't quite believe I lived there. I knocked on the door and Dick opened it seconds later. He gave me a confused smile.

"You're knocking on your own door?"

"Doesn't feel like my door yet," I told him.

"Well, it is," he said, dropping a keyring into my hand. The plain old housekey was attached to a little plastic plaque that said, "*Inconceivable!*" in bright red medieval font.

I snickered as he tugged my hand and led me through the door. "Funny."

My new apartment was not a palace, but it was mine. I looked around the empty room. The walls were painted a soft, impersonal white. All of the rooms were so empty they echoed whenever I moved. But it was mine. I could come and go whenever I pleased and not have to ask permission. I could put whatever I wanted on the walls. I would decide when and what to eat. I had all of the authority and if I paid for it, it belonged to me.

"Did you rent a truck?" Dick asked, peering behind me into the parking lot.

"No, I didn't need one."

"Well, where's your stuff?"

I raised the shoulder carrying my backpack and waved my suitcase. "Right here."

"But what about furniture? And the rest of your clothes?"

"The great thing about not really owning much is makes moving super-simple. You don't need to bug your friends for help!"

"Well, you can't stay here with no furniture!" Andrea exclaimed.

"Sure, I can. I'll get some pieces in here tomorrow. I'll get to go shopping. It will be great."

"Well, we wanted to do something for a housewarming gift for you, so we stocked your fridge. It's only enough for a few days, but it will get you started. Zeb told us what a werewolf can go through in terms of groceries in a week."

Andrea opened the fridge with a flourish and showed me shelves filled with produce and meat.

"Thank you so much," I said, throwing my arms around her neck.

"Meadow left you some plants as a welcome."

"Oh, that's so sweet," I said grimacing. " But I will kill them."

"We can take them to Iris," Andrea told me.

I pressed my lips together as I nodded. "Please don't tell Meadow."

"Are you sure you don't want to come stay at our place for a night? It would be a lot more comfortable for you," Dick said.

"It's important for me to stay here tonight, on my own. I made a pretty big step today and I don't want to take another step back by relying on someone else."

"I get it." Dick kissed my forehead. "I don't like it, but I get it."

"Goodnight," I told them, hugging Andrea tight. "Thank you for everything."

"Sleep well," Dick told me, and they closed the door behind them.

Surveying my new digs, I pulled my phone out of my backpack. Alex picked up on the first ring. "Is everything all right?"

"Everything is fine," I assured him. "I have news."

"Lately, 'news' has all sorts of horrifying potential," he said.

"I have a new apartment," I told him. "I didn't want to say anything until it was all settled, but I literally just moved in a few minutes ago."

"What!" I heard noises like he'd dropped his phone. "When did this happen? Do you need help? Can I come by and see it?"

"Just a few minutes ago, no, and no," I said. "I'd like to have some time to fix it up first."

"What about your family?" he asked.

"Um, not happy, but I'm not fully disowned. Uncle Lonnie said I can come back any time. But I won't. I'm already in love with it."

"I'm very happy for you," he said. "Very proud. I know this wasn't easy."

"You're right and thank you." I paused. "I don't want to tell you I love you for the time first over the phone. That seems weird."

He cleared his throat. "You're right. I should definitely wait to tell you I love you too when we see each other next."

I smiled. "I'm glad we have that settled. Goodnight, Alex."

"Goodnight, Tylene."

I hung up the phone, turning in a circle, squealing. Even though it was only nine, I was exhausted. I'd been through a lot of emotions in the past few hours. I shifted into my wolf form, which was far more comfortable with sleeping on the floor. I balanced my muzzle on my backpack. Fortunately, my warm nature kept me from needing a blanket.

Every movement echoed in the empty space. I had no furniture. I didn't even have a glass to drink water from. But it was mine. All mine. I could do what I wanted, when I wanted. I felt lighter than I had in years.

11

"The thing about past relationships and the baggage you carry from them, is that they can spring up when you least expect it and bite you on the ass. If you figure out how to minimize the damage, you have mastered life. Or at least, you have figured out how to dodge."

—*A Gentleman in Any Era: An Ancient Vampire's Guide to Modern Relationships*

*N*ever in my life had I gone on a shopping spree. To me, money was something that you saved because you never knew when you might get more. You didn't just go around spending it at random.

Moving into an empty apartment, I found I needed, well, everything. Curtains, sheets, towels, dishes, lamps, silverware, pots, and pans. I was literally starting with nothing. I ran through Sheets and Things like a madwoman on a game show, tossing everything that caught my eye into my cart. And a lot of things caught my eye. Apparently, I liked green, which was something I didn't know about myself, in terms of interior design. It's hard to know what your preferences are when you're not allowed to choose.

Unfortunately, all of that stuff came in an unreasonable amount of packaging, meaning I was making a lot of trips back and forth to the dumpster in the parking lot. I was afraid I would fill the thing up before I finished unpacking, and I hadn't even started on the furniture yet.

I stepped out of the apartment, taking a deep breath of what I liked to think of "the free air." The instinct to return to my pack's territory was like an itch in the back of my brain. I couldn't reach it, couldn't stop it. Only the distractions of work and moving-in chores kept my feet from running right back to my family. But it was becoming more manageable every day, because my freedom was worth more than the potential relief of that itch being removed.

"Hey, Tylene, how's it going?" I heard a rich baritone call from across the lot.

My neighbor, Sammy Palona, was one of the nicest people I'd ever met. He was tall, built like a professional wrestler, *and* he smelled like coffee and cocoa all of the time. (He worked as a barista in the coffee bar at Council headquarters.) If I wasn't already committed to a perfectly nice vampire, I could be in real trouble there.

"Hey, Sammy," I called back. I nodded at his car. "Heading into work?"

"Somebody's gotta keep the vampires caffeinated," he said. "Just so you know. Jane and Dick and Gigi, and several other high-profile consultants at the Council have all told me to keep an eye out for you. So, if seems like I'm checking in on you too much, I'm not being a creep. I'm just trying to protect my job."

"Understood," I told him. "And I'll try to get them to back off."

"Eh, if that many people are looking out for you, it says good things about my new neighbor," Sammy said with a shrug.

"Or I could be completely insane and they're worried about *you*," I countered.

Sammy grimaced. "You know, I had not considered that."

"I'm kidding," I assured him. "I'm only mildly insane."

"Well, that makes you just like all my other neighbors." He seemed to think that over for a moment. "You don't think you'll have private investigators coming by, do you? That last guy smelled like tobacco and ass."

"I don't think so…but if you see a couple of redneck types sniffing around, asking questions about me, you don't know anything."

"Exes?" he asked, his dark brows knitted together.

"Relatives," I replied. "They're not thrilled I've moved out. Dick and Andrea know all about it."

"Okay, good. If you have any problems, I'm just a few doors down."

"Thanks, have a good night," I told him. "I definitely will not poke holes in your walls for my cameras while you're at work." He stopped and turned, his expression alarmed. "I have got to stop making jokes."

"Nah, that was a good one," he conceded as he climbed into his car.

I waved as he pulled out of the parking lot and pinched the bridge of my nose. "Note to self, ask Jane for a book on how to talk to normal people."

My phone buzzed in my back pocket. I steeled my nerves as I checked the screen, praying it wouldn't be my mother again. She'd been calling and leaving messages pretty much nonstop since I'd moved out. It had gotten to the point where I just deleted the messages and texts unread. I didn't need any of her pleading or accustations in my head right now. I would go to the cell phone store and get a new number that week. I didn't think my parents were tech savvy enough to use a phone tracking app or anything, but some of my cousins were a little more advanced.

To my relief, the message was from Jolene's phone. *"Hey, Cousin Ty, this is Janelyn, I sent you an audio file. Video call me after!"*

I pressed the attachment and immediately regretted it. Never in my life had I heard such unpleasant, shrieking sound. It felt like being stabbed in the ears with an ice pick covered in poison ivy. Covering one ear, I fumbled for the "stop button," and felt relief flood my head when the unholy noise stopped. Grumbling, I dialed Jolene's number and Janelyn's puckish little face popped up on the screen. "Hi, Cousin Ty!"

"What in the hell was that?!" I cried, making her and Joe, who was hovering over her shoulder, crack up.

"It's the highest note you can play on a violin," she chirped. "I've been trying to figure it out for weeks."

"Why would you send that to me?" I demanded.

"Because she could?" Joe guessed.

Janelyn nodded. "Yep. Besides, if anybody annoys you, just play that. It will mess them up. It's gotta hold me over until Mama lets me get pepper spray."

"It messed *me* up!" I cried. "And you should never get to have pepper spray, for the greater good."

She jerked her shoulders. "Uncle Dick will get it for me."

"Mama says we're gonna come see your new place soon," Joe said. "We're gonna have a party for you!"

"As soon as I get some furniture," I promised them. "I better get back to unpacking, okay, kiddos? Love you. No more audio files."

"Love you!" they called back as I hung up.

"I am better off an auntie." Sighing, I went upstairs to retrieve what I hoped would be my last batch of boxes for the Dumpster. Doing little chores like that was something I wasn't used to. My parents did most of the maintenance things like that around the house. But I liked being responsible for it. It was my space and I was in charge of keeping it clean.

Though, I was going to have to get a broom if I was ever going to get all those Styrofoam bits of my floor. My floor. Just the thought was enough to send a little wave of contentment through me.

As I slid the cardboard into the recycling bin, I heard a strange noise behind me, like a foot being dragged across the gravel. I turned around, scanning the darkness for a sign for…I wasn't sure what. But all of my predatory instincts were triggered. Someone was watching me, from the shadows and all of my nerves screamed for me to get away. Which was a little embarrassing. I would analyze my fight versus flight responses later.

I had freaking super powers. I shouldn't be afraid of walking through a dark parking lot on my own. I closed the lid on the recycling bin, using my inhuman speed to get to the stairs. I didn't care if anyone saw me and asked questions. I just wanted to get inside my door and lock it.

I was almost there. I sucked in huge lungfuls of air to propel my legs. So close to home, but just as I reached the bottom step, I felt a rush of motion behind me. I turned to confront whatever it was and felt a heavy object smack against my temple. Stars exploded behind my eyes as I dropped to the ground, my cheek scraping against the gravel. From this angle, I could see obnoxiously neon European sneakers on the feet standing over me. I tried to raise my arms, to get up and fight, but my limbs didn't seem to be obeying my brain. In fact, I felt like I was still falling, hurtling to the ground where I was already splayed across the gravel.

My eyelids fluttered shut, but just before the darkness took me, I recognized the strange Roman mark against the wrist of the hand reaching for me.

Shit.

EVEN BEFORE I was completely awake, I remembered thinking that it was embarrassing to have been ambushed by a pubescent douchebag vampire.

I mean, sure, he was hundreds of years older than me, but I should have least seen those loud, horrible shoes coming.

It seemed that Greg, the hoodied dude from the library who couldn't seem to take a hint, was also Augustus, the orphanage snack enthusiast who hated my boyfriend. Small world.

I felt pretty stupid, not picking up on the hints. My only excuse was that I'd pictured Augustus as a snotty teenager in a toga with one of those weird curly Roman haircuts from the sculptures—which just went to show you what happened when you pre-judged people. But like Cal and Alex, "Greg" had adjusted to the times. And obviously, he'd been following Alex for a while. Now that I thought about it, I remembered seeing him the first time I met Alex, the night of the book avalanche. And he must have followed us, watching us get closer and decided to follow me to Southern Comfort, the library, my apartment. I guessed the silver lining was that he didn't have any real romantic interest in me.

Yay?

I pretended to be unconscious for a few more moments, just to assess the situation. He was close.

I was tied up, I knew that much. And my ass hurt from being in one position on cold concrete for too long. I couldn't hear traffic noises or voices. Grumbling softly, as if I was shifting in my sleep, I scraped my foot across the concrete, trying to determine the size of the room I was being kept in. I guessed it was pretty big, given the sound of the echo I made. And then I realized that my shoes were taped together, which made no sense at all. Was my kidnapper aware that my shoes were not a permanent part of my foot?

I was suddenly very ashamed I'd been waylaid by someone who was such a bad abductor.

What could I do to get out of this? I could wait to see if help arrived, but no one really knew I was in danger. Alex wasn't expecting to see me tonight, so unless he called and became alarmed when I didn't pick up, no help there. Dick and Jane knew I planned on spending the evening unpacking and weren't expecting me at the shop. Sammy might notice my door standing open when he got home, but he wouldn't be back from work for hours. If I was still living on packlands, my parents definitely would have noticed I was gone after a few hours, but that was a moot point. There was no backup coming for me, no rescue. I was going to have to find a way out on my own.

The cannister of silver spray was in my purse, but who knew where that was. I couldn't feel my phone in my back pocket. I thought about shifting to four feet, but while I was unnaturally strong in either form, I didn't know if the shift alone would be enough to rip the tape. And then I would be bound in my wolf form on the cement, which didn't seem like an improvement. Also, getting duct tape out of wolf fur would *really hurt.*

"You can stop pretending, you know. You're awake. I heard your heart speed up a few minutes ago."

Annoyed, I let my eyes open, glaring at him.

"Congratulations to you," I muttered as I squirmed to a sitting position. "So the whole 'dopey guy who doesn't know how to talk to girls' thing was a ruse? You were just trying to get to Alex?"

I glanced around the basement storeroom where he was holding me. I wasn't sure where we were, but he'd taken the time to board over the windows. Did he spend a lot of time down here? My phone was on the floor next to him. And he appeared to be listening to my classical music with his earbuds.

Apparently, he'd stolen a bunch of instruments from the music school before he burnt it down, because they were piled in the corner, next to a pile of cell phones still in their manufacturers' boxes and flat screen TVs. And UK sweatshirts. And food dehydrators? Was he planning to sell them? Was that how this creep made his creepy money?

He'd taken instruments from Alex's students to make money off of them, before he burned their damn school down. He was the *worst.*

"So *you* did all that stuff to Alex's school," I sighed. "Oh, man, I owe my family an apology."

So what did my Aunt Braylene mean by all that stuff about lying to my family and seeing boys that they didn't approve of? I also owed her an apology. I probably wouldn't give it to her, even if I lived long enough to see her.

"Wait, go back." Greg looked honestly insulted. "What do you mean, doesn't know how to talk to girls?'"

"Oh, please," I scoffed. "I went on a date with a guy who openly admitted he was in love with someone else and *he* had more game than you."

When it became obvious that I wouldn't elaborate on his poor people skills, he shrugged. "Well, it wasn't just Alex, I was targeting Nik and Cal, too. We've known each other for a long time. Hasn't he ever mentioned me?"

"I'm afraid not," I said, smirking. "Cal and Nik did, though. They said you were a twerp. Is that your vampire power? Annoying people on an advanced level?"

"Well, that's insulting, isn't it?" He scooted closer to me. "And no, that's not my special vampire power."

I scoffed, a hysterical laugh bubbling up my throat because, well, this was my first kidnapping. "Don't tell me, it's not having a scent. That's how you managed to get sneak around the vampires' houses and businesses without being detected—not to mention sneaking up on me," I muttered. When his eyes narrowed at me, I gasped. "Oh good grief, is that it?"

He sniffed. "I prefer to think of it as having the power of invisibility."

"Just like unscented deodorant or detergent," I said, snickering. "And I thought the sunrise thing was lame."

He drew his arm back and backhanded me across the cheek. I grinned at him, which he seemed to find very off-putting—probably because of the blood seeping between my teeth.

"I'm much older than them, did you know that? Maybe even older than all three combined. And just because I was turned at a younger age than they were, they call me names? I am their elder! I deserve their respect!"

"And that's just it, isn't it? I think you don't want to be invisible," I said, laughing. "I think it drives you nuts that you don't matter to them, but you know you'd get an ass-kicking of a lifetime if you made yourself known. You're not brave enough to be seen, but you hate to be ignored. It must be driving you *crazy*."

"You don't understand anything about me."

"Well, I do fail to understand why you've been such a dick about it," I conceded.

He rolled his eyes at me, which probably meant I was doing something right with my life choices.

"So all of this—the spray paint, the silver bomb, the fire—this is all because they kept you from getting a meal a couple hundred years ago?" I asked. "Wait, no, I forgot about the Council thing, and the Council trying to set you on fire. Dang it, what in the hell did you hit me over the head with?"

"A tire iron."

"You are *such* an asshole," I hissed.

"Well, I can't say that didn't hurt my feelings. I mean, all I did was try to befriend them, and they went to the council like a bunch of tattletales," he huffed. "And the Council's fire? Well, I didn't mind that so much. Convenient, really. I pretended to die so I could reinvent myself without the Council's interference. I took the name Gregory, pretended to be a French peasant." He held up his wrist. "No one really knew what this mark meant, so it was easy enough."

The whole time he was talking, I was rubbing one foot against the other. I hoped he was so caught up in his whining that he wouldn't notice that I was slipping my shoes off. My feet would be freed and then I could do all sorts of fun damage. With one of those uncased violins. Probably to his face.

"To be honest, I didn't really think about the three of them that much until I moved here a few years ago. I wasn't about to check in with those upstart morons at the Council office. I moved under their notice, bought a home, established a business. I made a *life* here. But then, I saw that photo in the newspaper, with Cal and Nik celebrating Cal's wife's stupid little company, and wherever they were, I knew that Alex would follow. Those three can't seem to stay apart for too long. It's sickening, really. Sooner or later, they'd realized I lived here, and they wouldn't be able to stop themselves from ratting me out to that nightmare Jameson woman. And I wasn't about to lose what I'd built. I *deserve* to be here. I deserve what I have. Not them."

"But you've lived here for years without them realizing it. In fact, *you* didn't know that they lived here—which is sort of miraculous, considering how small this town is. It shows you how little you have to do with the vampire community around here. Why did you think they would notice all of the sudden?" I asked. "Did you really think they've been thinking about you all this time, just waiting for you to show up so they could sabotage your life?"

I could tell that the possibility that they had not been thinking of Greg/Augustus this whole time *had not,* in fact, occurred to him. Wow. This guy took self-involved to a whole new level, and that level was scary.

"But why don't you just *move?*" I demanded. "You wouldn't even have to go that far! Murphy, maybe, or Scadwell. I mean, what sort of business could *you* possibly operate? Never mind, I don't want to know."

He smirked. "Well, it's not quite legal."

"Shocker," I rolled my eyes toward the food dehydrators. I leaned against the wall, subtly flexing my wrists to test the strength of the tape. Yep, it was duct tape. This was not going to be easy.

"So, murdering multiple people is somehow less work than moving?" I asked.

He sneered. "Have you ever tried moving without any friends?"

"Yes, I did it just recently!" I cried.

"I sent this to Alex." He held up my phone, showing me a picture of me trussed up and passed out on the cement. I groaned. If those were the last pictures ever taken of me, I was going to be so pissed. "And the coordinates for this stupid wreck of a building. He should be along shortly."

"You really are the worst," I told him. "And how do you know he's going to come for me?"

He smirked again. "Even if he doesn't show up in time to save you, losing you will break him. He won't want to stay in a place where he lost you. And when he's gone, I'll go after Nik's Gigi and her sister. They're very stubborn women, they won't tolerate being limited. There will be an opening and I will take it. I'll get Cal, Nik, Jane Jameson, Dick Cheney, her whole stupid so-called family. I've heard how her weird little family responds when one of their own in threatened. I can sweep the lot of them off of the board, set myself up a nice little fiefdom here in the backwoods."

A wolf growl rippled out from my chest. The idea that he

would attack my friends, take advantage of how much they loved each other for his own gain, his own *convenience*, was infuriating. How dare he? How dare he use people's feelings against them? He was going to go after my family—my real family. The people that loved me for no other reason than myself. He was going to take them away. I had to make him think that there was nothing to gain in keeping me. I had to make him think that Alex didn't care, that it was easier just to let me go. Or at least stall him long enough to work this stupid tape loose.

I thought of all I stood to lose—Alex, the love of my life, the only person I'd ever met who seemed to truly understand me and want me in spite of it. Dick, my surrogate father-slash-brother figure who would be so upset when he realized I'd been hurt. He would blame himself for not protecting me. Andrea, who would have to spend so much time comforting him. Jane, who had helped to give me a place, a family, a life of my own. If he killed me, I would miss out on that beautiful, chaotic life I'd started to build, and the thought of that was enough to make the tears burn my eyes.

I sniffled and to his growing horror, the tears tumbled down my cheeks in twin rivers. "Well, the joke's on you because I'm not one of their own. I never was. They only kept me around because I was Alex's and he lost interest a few days back. He said he was finished with me, bored." I paused to give a bitter laugh that wasn't entirely false. "And now that he's done with me, I'm not even part of my pack anymore. You went to all the trouble of kidnapping someone you can't even ransom."

I giggled and I'm sure it sounded like madness. I wriggled my wrists, loosening the tape, flexing the muscles.

"But I saw them. I saw how they were with you. The smiling. The laughter. The disgusting amount of hugging."

"They're like that with everybody who dates within their circle, but once you're out, you're out."

Greg shook his head. I guess I wasn't selling my heartache well enough. I hadn't found those words. "That whole group just folded you right in like there was a space waiting for you. How do you do that?"

So, selling my broken heart wasn't going to get through to him. But his absolute bewilderment that violence and betrayal did not result in friendship? That I could work with. For a moment, I almost felt sad for him. I knew what it was like to be lonely, to want acceptance.

"I tried to be nice when I met them?" I suggested. "I listened when people talked? And I didn't try to kill them or set their stuff on fire?"

"What's your point?" he asked, shaking his head.

I stared at him for a long moment, trying to contain the urge to call him a litany of colorful names. I took a deep breath and kept my voice calm. "Honestly? I don't know. It's never happened for me before. Most of the time, I've been pretty lonely. I don't fit in with my own kind, but I fit in with them. How do *you* manage to go like a thousand years without making a single friend? That's the real question."

Given the cold rage that swept over his features, I had definitely not found the right words. "Is this what you and your *friends* sit around doing? Talking about your stupid feelings? If that's it, I don't need any friends. I just want to keep running my life the way I want, without you and your idiot friends messing things up for me."

He stood so quickly I didn't have time to react and kicked me in the ribs, practically launching me across the room.

"I'm tired of waiting. I guess I'm going to have to send your boyfriend another photo, just to drive home exactly how serious this situation is." He held up my phone and opened the camera function. "Smile pretty."

I did smile, and I could feel the blood seeping between my teeth from biting my lip. It would heal quickly, but it definitely stung like a bitch. And the sight of my bloody grin made him pause, revulsion clear on his face. I laughed, twisted into a sitting position. I kicked off my shoes, freeing my feet.

He dropped the phone, the photo forgotten. "What's so funny?"

"I'm going to guess you've only kidnapped humans over the course of your whole bullshit campaign of terror, huh?"

He scoffed, "So what?"

Inhaling deep, I used all of my strength to force my wrists apart, tearing through the loosened duct tape. His eyes bugged out like something out of a cartoon.

"Surprise." I sprang to my feet, jamming the palm of my hand under his chin as I threw myself at him. I felt his jaw snap under the force of it. He howled, swinging out wildly at my head level, but I was already shrinking to four paws. I lunged, sinking my teeth into his ankle and sweeping him off of his feet. As he writhed on the floor, I used his leg as a sort of handle and swung him against the wall. He hit the cement block with a dull *thud,* hard enough that I felt safe to dash for the stairs.

But he was fast, scrambling to his feet and grabbing at my back left leg, dragging me into the basement. He flung me back, and I rolled, sinking my claws into the cement to slow my momentum. It made an awful screeching noise and left shallow furrows on the gray surface.

I sprang again, landing against his chest with all four paws, shoving him against the pile of food dehydrators. I lunged for his right arm, tearing at the wrist until I tasted blood. The foul bitterness of it had me dropping his limb and attempting to spit it out in my wolfy way. He kicked me in the muzzle, knocking me back. And then he threw a food dehydrator box at me.

Who throws small appliances?

He seemed to be running out of tricks. He didn't know what he was doing once hitting me in the face didn't knock me unconscious. He was used to overpowering someone quickly.

And he seemed like the type of dick who would only target people who couldn't fight back. Well, I'd grown up in a family where casual fistfights were a way of life. I had all of the tricks.

Game on.

I changed into my human form and scooped my phone off of the floor, scrambling through the menu options until I found the file the twins sent me. I pressed play, cringing as the horrific shriek of the highest-slash-most obnoxious violin note filled the room.

Greg shrieked, covering his ears with his hands and screaming at me to shut it off. I tried to run past him, but he slapped my phone out of my hand, shattering it against the wall. I grabbed a violin from the pile of instruments. With mental apologies to Alex and his students, I swung it up in a tight arc. The wood collided broadside against his cheek, exploding into splinters. I was left holding the neck of the violin, broken off to a jagged wooden point.

I swung the makeshift stake at him, and he ducked out of the way. He honestly seemed intimidated by me for the first time, but I wasn't sure whether it was because he knew I was a werewolf, or because I was a naked woman attacking him with a sharp implement. He scrambled back and I made for the stairs again.

Technically, I had a stake in my hand, but I didn't know if I could kill him, even with everything he'd done. I knew that members of my pack had shed blood in self-defense, in defense of the pack, but I didn't know if I could. With a choice between sinking the stake into his chest and getting away, I just wanted to get away. If I could get out of the basement, I could run to the book shop, get help, tell Jane and Dick about Greg and his stupid plans.

Greg wrapped his arm around my waist, yanking me off of the stairs. I squirmed out of his arms, repulsed by the sensation of his cold hands on my skin. He backhanded me, sending me flying into the pile of boxes again. He tried to grab the stake, but I clung to it as if my life depended on it.

"You don't have to be alive when he gets here, you know," he seethed. "It works either way for me."

"Neither do you," I panted.

"You don't have it in you," he said, laughing. "It's why I picked you first. You're not a killer. Every time I watched you, you let someone push you around. You're not even fighting me with your full strength. I could probably let you go, and you'd come right back and tie yourself up again. You're weak."

My arms dropped and my shoulders slumped. There was a certain amount of shame in the fact at, at one point, he'd probably been right. I was weak. I spent far too much time letting people control me, worrying about whether I was loved, whether I would be accepted.

But I'd changed. I'd done things in the past months that I'd never believed I'd be able to do—establishing a real adult life of my own, loving the person I chose, making real friends. I was a hell of a lot stronger than the girl who had nearly been crushed by a falling bookshelf.

He'd stepped closer, watching my shoulders fall, thinking that he'd gotten to me. I gripped the makeshift stake and lunged forward, shoving it into his gut. "Not anymore."

He screamed, dropping to his knees. He glared up at me. "It's supposed to be the heart, you stupid bitch."

"I don't want to kill you," I told him, kicking at the violin neck so it sank even deeper. He yelped and flopped to his side. "I just want to slow you down. I don't want your dust on my hands."

He rolled on the floor in agony as I grabbed one of the UK sweatshirts and threw it over my head. I ran up the stairs and out the unlocked door. By the time I'd reached the outside of the empty building where he'd held me, I had the time to be a little insulted by his not locking it. Did he really think I didn't have a chance of getting out? Also, was this the business he just couldn't stand to leave behind? An abandoned Circuit City where he stored a weird assortment of stolen merchandise?

Why was I even thinking about that sort of thing? Maybe he'd hit me a little harder on the head than I thought.

I glanced around the empty parking lots surrounding the former Circuit City. I was about a half-mile from the Half-Moon Hollow Mall, a dying collection of retail stores that was steadily losing traffic to the downtown area. But there were still enough cars circulating the dark streets that I wasn't thrilled about the prospect of walking through it, only wearing a sweatshirt.

Changing in the middle of town would definitely be noticed, I thought. Or someone would call Animal Control on the giant wolf running down the highway. As I mulled over my options, I heard my name called from behind me.

"Tylene?"

Alex was standing in the parking lot, his phone in his hand, surrounded by vampires. Dick was carrying a First Aid Kit the size of a microwave. I did not know where or how he'd gotten it. Gabriel appeared to be holding Jane in some sort of gentle wrist lock to keep her from running into the Circuit City. Andrea was carrying a baseball bat. Cal, Nik, Gigi, Iris, Meadow, Erik, they were all there. Hell, there were some vampires I didn't even recognize. And then a black van marked Undead Emergency Response Team pulled up and some SWAT types came pouring out in full gear.

"Hi," I said, waving weakly. "Does anyone have some spare pants?"

Alex folded me into his arms and I damn near collapsed against him. He kissed me and I could practically taste his relief. I was safe. I'd survived a nasty fight with a nastier man. And I was proud of myself, but I really just wanted to go home to my little apartment and have a bath.

"We're here to rescue you," Alex whispered against my neck.

"Too late," I said shrugging. "He's inside. I couldn't kill him, so I just wounded him pretty good."

"That's my girl," Dick said, patting my shoulder. He shouted to the UERT guys. "Go get him. Feel free to rough him up as you handcuff him. No holds barred. Maiming allowed."

"Dick," Jane sighed.

"Light maiming only!" Dick called as the men trooped into the storefront. Ray McElray tossed me a pair of sweatpants as he passed.

"Glad to see you're all right, Ty," he called over his shoulder.

Aw, that sweet mulleted goofball.

"No maiming!" Jane yelled. "Alex, do you think you could let her go long enough to let us take a statement?"

"Probably not," Alex replied.

"Come on, Frenchie, there are other people who would like a hug and an assurance that she's okay, too," Dick chided him.

Alex growled.

"If you don't let go, I will just drag him into this hug and it will get real emotional and real awkward, real fast," I told Alex.

Sighing as if I was forcing a great burden on him, he relinquished his hold on me. I pulled on the sweatpants and felt more secure for it "I'm going to go help with the maiming."

"No maiming!" Jane cried before pulling me into a hug. "I'm really, really glad you're okay, Ty."

"Thanks for coming to get me," I told her. "I would like to fill out all of the paperwork and file all of the complaints, because this guy had some very bad plans."

"Well, we're just lucky Alex was with Cal and Nik when that psycho sent him the photo," Dick said as he and Jane stepped away from me. "By now, we know how to activate the emergency group text."

Suddenly, Gabriel rushed out of nowhere and threw his arms around me, almost bowling me over.

"This is unexpected," I said, awkwardly patting his back.

"Gabriel, honey, she does need to breathe," Jane reminded him.

"It's just that she's such a calming influence on the group," Gabriel said. "And she was going to take over all the email promotions for the shop. You always curse so much when you have to do those."

"I appreciate it, Gabriel."

Dick was hanging back, his hands clutching the strap of the First Aid Kit. I opened my arms and he stepped into them. He pressed his face into my neck, and I wasn't sure, but I thought I felt his shoulders shake. "We thought we'd lost you," he said. "I didn't like it."

"I didn't either," I told him.

"I don't know what I would have done if he'd…oh, Tylene," he sighed. "I'm probably going to file official adoption papers after this. I'm a good late-in-life surrogate grandparent figure. Just ask Nola."

"Okay, Dick," I said, patting his back.

"I still don't think Alex is good enough for you," he said.

"Well, that's your job as my late-in-life surrogate grandparent figure," I said, making him smile.

"I'm going to go see to the maiming," Dick said, kissing my forehead.

"No maiming!" I yelled after him, realizing that the other vampires, particularly Cal and Nik, were still waiting to check on me, arms open, ready for hugs.

Alex followed the UERT team has they hauled a bound and gagged Greg out of the store, his belly still bleeding where I'd stabbed him.

"What's going to happen to him?" I asked Jane.

"Well, I'm going to consult the international Council muckity-mucks to determine what they want to with him," Jane said. "But I don't think he's going to be anybody's problem anymore."

"And it's probably better that you don't know the details," Dick told me.

I nodded. "I gladly accept that."

"We'll give you two a minute," Jane said.

Alex wrapped his arms around me, pressing his face into my neck. "Do you know what you smell like to me?"

"Cement dust and nervous sweats?" I guessed, making him laugh.

"You smell like home," he said, kissing me.

This was what Greg had tried to take from me. I had family. I had a life. I had a pack.

12

"So much of the modern world is temporary and transitory. When you finally find a place where you want to spend a long time, do whatever it takes to stay there for as long as you can."
—*A Gentleman in Any Era: An Ancient Vampire's Guide to Modern Relationships*

I may have survived a vampire kidnapping, but the difficult-to-pronounce and even more difficult-to-assemble Swedish desk had almost broken me.

I stood, stretching my aching back, still twinging from sitting on the floor for hours. Completed, it looked nice in the corner of my living room and would give me a comfortable workspace that I didn't have to worry about locking up every time I got up. I wouldn't have to worry about someone rummaging through it to find private paperwork or if I did— well, I guess the person had already broken into my house and I would have more to worry about than privacy. That was the sort of thing I hadn't had to worry about when I lived on the packlands, protecting myself, but I wasn't afraid. It felt right to take care of myself, to see to my own security. I wasn't at all sorry for leaving the packlands. I was only sorry that I hadn't left years earlier.

So far, my desk, a nightstand and a brand-new bed were the only furniture I had assembled in the apartment—which was a shame because I had a lot of people coming over and there was nowhere for them to sit. Dick and Jane had insisted on doing a housewarming for me. They wanted to celebrate me taking steps towards my independence, knowing what a big deal that was for a young single werewolf.

A knock at my door startled me out of my deep thoughts. I put aside the tiny screwdriver that could only be used to build this stupid desk. I opened the door to find Alex, holding a vase full of tulips of all different colors. And because I'd stumbled on a guide to Victorian floral messages in Jane's shop, I knew that yellow tulips meant cheerful thoughts. Pink tulips meant affection. Orange meant enthusiastic passion. Cream colored tulips meant "I will love you forever." I was glad that he hadn't given me lime blossoms because that was basically the f-word of floral meanings—which I had always found to be weird. What the hell were Victorians doing with limes?

Of course, this was all probably moot because most people didn't know the meaning of flowers beyond, "these are pretty and smell nice."

"Are you trying to figure out the meaning of the variegated tulips?" he asked. "I read somewhere they mean 'you have beautiful eyes' but that's never made sense to me. I just had the florist throw them in because they looked nice. The rest of them I mean, whole-heartedly."

"Thank you," I said, smiling as I kissed his cheek. "Come on in."

I opened the door wider so he could step inside. "I don't have much more put together than the last time you were here, I'm afraid. What is that?"

"It's a bag. With various items that I might need…should I stay the night," he said carefully. He lifted a soft-sided cooler out of his bag and placed several units of donor blood in my fridge. "It's not that I didn't enjoy camping out here with no supplies last time, but I like to be more prepared."

"Are you trying to slowly but surely move into my apartment one overnight bag at a time?" I asked. "Because I think we can agree that I need to live on my own for a while, develop adulting skills."

He held up both hands in surrender. "No, I'm not even pressuring you to give me a drawer, hence the overnight bag."

I squinted at him. "You came up with that answer too quickly."

He wrapped his arms around me, murmuring against my lips. "I will wait until you're ready. I'll wait forever. I've got the time."

"I can't decide if that's a nice sentiment or a vampire dad joke."

He pulled a gift purple bag out of his luggage and held it out to me. "A little bit of both."

"But you already gave me flowers," I objected.

"It's something for your desk," he said as I opened the bag and found Funko Pop versions of the Stark direwolves from *Game of Thrones*. "Dick mentioned that you liked the TV show. And I thought you would like the wolf connection."

"Thank you!" I exclaimed, carrying my treasures to my desk and arranging them carefully.

"That is a lovely home office," he said. "I can tell I'm going to have to fight very hard for your attention if I'm going to tear you away from it."

"I have faith in you."

My phone rang and my mother's phone number appeared on my screen.

"Do you want to answer it?"

"I haven't talked to them since I was kidnapped. It feels like I should tell them that I'm okay."

"I think this is a case where you should do what you *want* to do, as opposed to what you think you *should* do," he said.

I sighed. "I'll give her five minutes. Time me."

"I'll hold you to it."

I slid my thumb across the screen. "Hi, Mama."

Her voice was muffled, like she was holding her hand over the receiver and whispering into. "Tylene, don't you think it's time for you to come on home?"

"I'm fine, and how are you?" I responded dryly.

"I don't have time for you to be smart with me, right now, Tylene. Your daddy's only going to be over at your Uncle Creed's for so long."

"Okay then, no, I don't think it's time for me to come home. I have a very nice apartment and I'm happy here," I told her.

"But Jolene said you ran into trouble with those vampires," she objected. "You'd be much safer here with us."

"The trouble wasn't Alex's fault," I said. "And I got out of it just fine on my own."

"Well, you see what happened when you're on your own," she sniffed. "That's why it's not right, you being away from your family."

"Nah, I'm sure I won't be kidnapped again," I scoffed. "That's sort of a once in a lifetime thing."

"I'm gonna hang up if you keep bein' so hateful," she cried.

"Well, hang up if you want to, but if you do, you need to know I might not pick up when you call next time. Our relationship is going to change, Mama," I told her.

Alex mouthed the word "wow." He leaned in and kissed me again.

"Are you still seeing that vampire?" she asked after a long pause.

"Yes."

"I'm still not happy about that," she huffed.

"I know."

Mama sighed and asked, "Could you at least apologize to your daddy?"

That was the point to the call, then. She didn't really care if I was safe or happy. She was worried about herself, about Daddy's foul moods making things uncomfortable for her every living minute. As usual, she was putting herself first. Which meant, I would have to fend for myself. As usual.

"I'm not going to apologize because I didn't do anything wrong."

"It doesn't matter who's wrong! You know he doesn't care about right or wrong. He just wants you to say you're sorry!"

"Which is the whole problem. And it's *his* problem, not mine," I told her. "I've got to go. I've got a bunch of people coming over for a housewarming party. Call me again if you want to talk about something besides Daddy."

I hung up the phone. I didn't feel like crying. I definitely didn't feel like laughing. I just felt…okay. My parents were upset with me, and I didn't feel like the world was closing in on me. My parents were upset with me, and I would have to live with it. Alex took me in his arms. "Is it condescending to tell you that I'm proud of you?"

"Never." I nuzzled into his neck. "I don't know if I'm ever going to be able to talk to them again. And I don't think there's anything I can do to change it, not without losing everything I've gained. And I've gained so much, it almost makes it worth it. I love you."

"As I love you," he murmured against my cheek.

Just then, a fist rapped at the door. I turned, scenting a dozen or so people on the other side.

"Why, whoever could that be?" Alex asked cheekily.

"Door-to-door salesman?" I guessed.

"We heard that!" Jane shouted through the door. "Open up, or we take back all your presents!"

I laughed as I ran to the door and threw it open to a shout of "Congratulations!" The crowd was so thick, I couldn't see the parking lot. Everybody I loved was there: Jolene, Zeb, the twins, Jane, Gabriel, Dick, Andrea, Gigi, Nik, Iris, Cal—even Meadow and her boyfriend, Erik.

"Happy housewarming!" Dick crowed, handing me a wire carrier with four bottles of champagne. I'd watched enough British TV to recognize a quality label when I saw it. My brows raised as I turned my face up to him.

"You don't want to know where he got it," Andrea assured me.

"I will ask no questions," I promised as they filed through the door. Andrea reclaimed the champagne and set to work opening the bottles.

Zeb lifted a wrapped box. "Hangers and closet organizing stuff."

"Towels," Gigi said, holding up a large gift bag.

"Tupperware," Iris said. "I know how much Jolene cooks and you can never have too many containers for leftovers."

"What are these leftovers you speak of?" Jolene scoffed.

"I brought you some furniture," Jane said, jerking a thumb over her shoulder to a truck I knew had to belong to the Council. "We'll bring it up in a bit."

She paused to take in the lack of chairs in the room. "Or maybe we can go do that now."

I gasped. "I can't let you do that, Jane, it's too much!"

"I can. It's just a bunch of extras we have from redecorating River Oaks," she told me. "It was just sitting in storage. I'd much rather you put it to good use...unless I'm over-stepping, in which case I will never speak of it again, because I realized I'm being very pushy and unintentionally repeating some unhealthy patterns. Sorry."

Seeing someone with all of Jane's influence and power feeling bad for trying too hard to help me just made me love her more. The corner of my mouth lifted. "The couch isn't plaid, is it?"

She grinned. "No, it is a sturdy and comfortable plain blue. We got it when Jamie was going through a 'didn't know his own supernatural strength' phase. There are chairs to match and a couple of end tables. And a dinette set. And I'm, like, ninety percent sure there are no elderly ghosts attached to any of it."

"I'm sorry, what?"

"Gigi, Iris, you want to give me a hand?" Jane asked brightly, ignoring the question.

"Thank you?"

As his wife and sister-in-law filed out, followed by Alex, Cal approached to press a brotherly kiss to my forehead.

"What was that for?" I asked.

"Making my friend happy. Keeping him here in the Hollow, where we can keep an eye on him. You don't know how much that means to me and Nik, Tylene."

"Happy to help."

Uncle Lonnie stepped into the doorway holding a cooler. I could smell the meat inside: steaks and chicken and mmm, Hank's applewood smoked bacon. I barely withheld my drool. Hank's bacon was one of the few things I missed about living on the compound. Aunt Mimi was at his side, holding several bags of groceries, far more than even Dick and Andrea had brought for me. They were re-stocking my kitchen. It was the ultimate sign of werewolf acceptance—making sure I was fed. Some little crack on my heart that I didn't even know was there sealed back together.

"Uncle Lonnie."

"I'm not here as your Alpha," he said, shaking his head.

"Former Alpha," Jolene murmured.

Uncle Lonnie shot a look at her and she just grinned.

"I'm here as your uncle, who loves the heck out of you. I want to make sure you're fed and that your home is safe."

"Thank you, Uncle Lonnie. Please come in."

He cleared his throat, looking around the apartment. "It's a nice place."

"I might not understand it, but I think you're very brave," Aunt Mimi said, kissing my cheek. "And I have ideas for curtains."

"I'm sure you do," I acknowledged.

They opened the fridge and saw the donor blood Alex had left inside. They paused and I froze. But instead of staying anything, they just stocked my fridge with half a cow. Jane and Gigi trooped in with some very attractive furniture. It was probably nicer than anything I'd ever had. And now my friends had a place to sit, so *even better.*

Erik and Meadow placed some potted herbs by my window. When Meadow looked around, obviously searching for the plants she'd already left for me, I crossed to them. Where was Iris when I needed her? "Hey, not-quite-neighbor! Is it weird, being in an apartment that used to be yours?"

Meadow nodded. "A little, especially with new stuff in here. But it's going to be great for you. This was the first place I called home and meant it. Jane told me a little about your parents. And I can definitely relate. Living in a new place, I think you'll find it's not the place that's home, it's the people."

Alex approached, carrying all four dinette chairs on his shoulders, as only a vampire could. He paused and kissed me. I growled lightly and nipped at his earlobe.

I looked around the living room, at all the people who were there for me. It was almost too much happiness for me to bear. I had people in my life who loved me for me, who sought out ways to make me happy, who made me feel safe. That was what I had gained, and so much more. I had a life and a place and people I cared about—and somehow, I'd managed to get those things on my terms.

I turned to Meadow. "I'm sure you're right."

EXCERPT FROM HOW TO DATE YOUR DRAGON

A MYSTIC BAYOU NOVEL

CHAPTER 1

JILLIAN

*J*illian Ramsay, PhD, was driving a panel van without air-conditioning through an area known as the Devil's Armpit.

She wished that was an exaggeration, or a misprint on the map. But there it was, in bold print on the highway sign, "You are entering the Devil's Armpit."

She supposed she should be thankful that her destination wasn't the Devil's Armpit, an unusually sulfurous section of southern Louisiana that smelled of rotten eggs and damnation, but a small town just beyond it—Mystic Bayou. She hoped the more attractive name also indicated a more appealing odor. Dr. Montes hadn't left anything in his field notes about bringing air fresheners with him. But then again, she'd come to learn Dr. Montes's methods were less polished than anyone hoped.

Jillian fanned her face and dabbed at the perspiration dotting her upper lip. The air-conditioning had crapped out within fifteen minutes of her leaving the New Orleans airport, but after a flight from Chile involving two layovers and a lengthy argument with customs over her audio-video equipment, she just didn't have any fight left in her.

She rolled down the window, just a crack, hoping the muggy late May air would be cooler than the interior of the van. Almost immediately, her nostrils were flooded with the smell of what could only be described as Satan's BO.

"Mistake! Huge error in judgment!" she gasped.

Jillian rolled up the window, her hands so sweaty that her fingers actually slipped off of the handle a few times before she sealed herself inside the van. Eager for some form of odor-free distraction, she used her hands-free dialer to call Sonja Fong at the League office. She grumbled as the call went to voicemail, *again*. But when the machine went *beep*, Jillian tried to make her tone more suited for a friend she was actually fond of, as opposed to a telemarketer.

"Hey, Sonja, it's me again. I'd really appreciate a call back, so maybe you could explain to me what's really going on back there. The League keeps assuring me that everything's just fine, as they turn my life completely upside down. But I keep getting the feeling I'm a heroine in one of those awful seventies horror movies, where the unwitting outsider ends up a human sacrifice. Cell phone reception is getting pretty spotty, so if you can, call back soon. Love you, bye."

Jillian pursed her lips. This was not a very auspicious beginning to her first real field assignment. She'd flown all the way to Santiago, only to get a call that her mentor and boss had been seriously injured on his assignment in northern England, and the International League for Interspecies Cooperation was sending her in his place to southern Louisiana. Her in-depth study of the *mohana* and their mating habits would just have to wait.

All that background reading on malevolent sex-obsessed dolphin shapeshifters for nothing.

Nearly an hour later, Jillian had sweated completely through her clothes and was beginning to worry that she was lost. The gnarled trees dripping with Spanish moss were all starting to look the same. She was pretty sure she'd passed a carnation-pink shack on stilts twice, and she'd realized those "logs" resting against the banks of the swamp, dangerously close to the road, had legs and very large jaws. She was beyond jet-lagged, couldn't remember her last application of deodorant and was starting to think maybe the League could go jump into the murky, gator-filled water looming on either side of the highway.

Just as Jillian started to search for a place to either do a three-point turn or sleep for the night, another sign came into view. It read, *Welcome to Mystic Bayou, Home of the Fighting Marsh Dogs*, over a caricature of a large rat with its fists raised *a la* the Fighting Irish.

Jillian nodded. "OK, then."

Maybe it was better for her to stay lost.

Jillian opened the van window again, hoping that maybe the air in Mystic Bayou was more palatable. She took a tentative breath. She could almost taste the sweetness on the air, redolent with honeysuckle and dried grass and earth. She took several gulps of it, lifting her mass of honey blond hair off her sweaty neck. She balked at the reflection in the rearview mirror, wondering who let that pale, sweaty woman with the under-eye luggage into the driver's seat.

She was due to meet her community liaison in just a few minutes and she was a mess. Maybe she could duck into the back of the van to freshen up before she met Mayor Berend? That was something legitimate scientists did, right? Change their clothes in vans?

The town quickly came into view in that "suddenly there are buildings and if you blink you will miss them all" way unique to tiny rural towns. Main Street was pretty much the only street from what Jillian could see, with the occasional short side street branching out into clusters of two to three small homes. Dr. Montes had written that few families lived in town, preferring to keep almost clannish compounds in the outlying areas of the county and only venturing into town limits for errands.

Main Street led to a town square centered on a gazebo, and, behind that, a large white-washed building topped with a golden shape she couldn't quite make out. The street boasted a freshly painted collection of businesses with flower baskets hanging from every surface, giving the town a cheerful, neatly kept air. Aside from the inordinate number of them that seemed to involve taxidermy, there was a bank, a boat dealership, a grocery, an "apothecary," a beauty salon, a book shop, a newspaper called the Mystic Messenger, and finally, Bathtilda's Pie Shop, which boasted the world's best chocolate rhubarb pie. Jillian had never heard of chocolate rhubarb pie, but frankly it sounded a bit gross. Each business had a little addition under the shop name stating, "Owned and Operated by Bonner Boone" or "Owned and Operated by Branwyn Boone," or in the sweet shop's case, "Bathtilda Boone." Was every business in town owned by a Boone?

Dr. Montes's instructions were to go to City Hall, which appeared to be the tall, white building at the end of the street. With a gold spire rising from a bell tower-like structure on the roof, it was the tallest building in town. As she drove closer, she spotted a gold-and-green SUV marked "Sheriff" parked out front, next to a rather large Harley Davidson with custom-painted claw marks raking down the body.

She parked the cursed van in an empty spot, near the fountain that stood across from Mystic Bayou City Hall's door. She glanced down the street at the sweet shop and wondered if she could duck in unnoticed and change clothes in the restroom. It would probably cause a bit of a stir. She couldn't imagine a town like this got a lot of tourists hauling luggage into public restrooms with them. But it would be better than—

Jillian shrieked. "What the hell!"

A huge man in an extremely tight black t-shirt and even tighter jeans was staring at her through her driver side window. He stood several inches taller than the van, and his hands were the size of picnic hams. He had thick, wildly curling black hair tied back in a ponytail and a matching beard that spread across his barrel chest. His smoke gray eyes seemed to penetrate through the window glass, making her shiver despite the muggy heat.

He raised a hand, and it was all she could do not to flinch. "Hi, there."

A friendly grin spread across his face, warming his features as he waggled a massive hand.

Should she roll down the window? Was it safe? At this point, it would be rude not to, but she'd always read that a woman traveling alone should ignore their instincts to be polite and err on the side of not letting an enormous man pull her through a van window and onto the human trafficking market.

OK, yes, this was becoming terribly awkward. She rolled down the window. "Can I help you?"

"Dr. Ramsay?" his voice boomed, practically shaking her van windows. "I saw you from the sweet shop window, thought I should come over and introduce myself proper."

Jillian sagged against her seat in relief. "Oh, thank you, but I'm just here to meet the mayor. Mayor Zed Berend?"

"Yeah, you right!" The man grinned again, showing perfectly white, razor-sharp canines. "You must be the League doctor. *Bienvenue!*"

Without an invitation, he yanked the van door open and pulled Jillian to her feet. He gripped her much smaller fingers in his very warm, very rough hand. Jillian stared up at him, mouth slightly agape. This was the mayor of Mystic Bayou? He looked more likely to be driving a long-haul truck route or forging lightning bolts on Mount Olympus. Who had dared challenge him for the position? Did he chew all of the ballots in half to remove his opponent from the election?

"Everybody's been waitin' for you to show up," he told her. "Well, they were waitin' for Dr. Montes, but they'll be just as happy with you. I can't say the whole town is gonna be thrilled that you're here, but like my *maman* always said, learnin' never hurt nobody. The guy at the League office said I have to sign a buncha papers before you can get started? Didn't I already sign enough? Y'all tryin' to steal my house and my firstborn?"

Jillian laughed at the rapid-fire questions. "No, but with Dr. Montes being replaced so quickly, the League just wanted to make sure the paperwork reflected the appropriate names, in case issues came up later."

Like the "issues" that came up with the cave troll study in the Reykjavik sewers. No one liked to talk about the incident that led to a League scientist being mailed back to headquarters in a shoebox, not even for training purposes. Jillian shuddered.

"What happened to Dr. Montes anyway?" Zed asked. "He was plenty keen to hit the ground runnin' and then he just stopped callin.'"

Jillian chewed her lip and tried to compose an appropriate answer. Currently Dr. Montes was in a League-funded ICU, ten stories below the surface of London, recovering from a unicorn impalement to the gut. Jillian couldn't imagine what he could have done to provoke that response from a unicorn. Hector Montes was a senior member of the paranormal anthropological staff. He wrote an actual book on approaching and interacting with sapient creatures. How had Dr. Montes underestimated the will (or the ticklishness) of a creature as old as a unicorn? Had he become too arrogant to consider his subject's feelings? Or had his clammy hands, combined with breath that smelled of old coffee and gingivitis, pushed the unicorn into a panic?

Zed was staring at her, waiting for an answer.

"Oh, um, he ran into some medical problems and couldn't travel," Jillian said, smiling through the awkward lie. "It happens sometimes. But I assure you, Dr. Montes trained me in field work. I'm fully qualified to handle this."

He jerked his shoulders. "Oh, I'm sure y'are, *cher*. No worries. You've probably taken dozens of these research trips, right?"

Jillian cleared her throat. "Well, not exactly."

Zed paused and tilted his enormous head toward her. "How many have you taken?"

Jillian pursed her lips and admitted, "One."

Zed asked, "One before Mystic Bayou?"

Jillian shook her head. "No, just this one."

Zed's cheerful demeanor faded. "You've never done this before?

"I was heading out on my first assignment in South America before the League called me back in and redirected me here," she told him. "I know what I'm doing. I've studied the process over and over. I've collected and interpreted other researchers' data… This is just the first time I've done it on my own."

Zed practically deflated, leaning against her van with a dumbfounded expression. "I don't mean to be rude, but I just don't know about this, Doc. It was hard enough to talk my neighbors into participatin' when they knew that they were gonna be dealing with an expert. I just don't know how people are gonna react to someone your age, without any real experience."

"Well, we don't exactly have to include that information when I introduce myself. I'm not planning on handing out copies of my CV to random citizens," she protested.

Zed's cheerful demeanor returned full force. "Good point, smart lady. If I've learned anything since takin' office, it's that less is more when it comes to information and your public image. It's why I deleted my Facebook. Nothin' good can come from your constituents knowin' you unfriended them."

The radiating heat of his hand on her elbow as he led her into the building had her sweating even more. She cast a mournful look over her shoulder, to the van, where fresh clothes and her trusty dry shampoo were waiting in her bag.

Zed shrugged. "We'll just have to see how things play out. I'magine you're pretty tired after all that flyin'. The sheriff says there's nothing like it, but I never took to it. Prefer to keep my paws on the ground, if ya know what I mean."

Zed flung the heavy wooden door open so fast Jillian didn't get a chance to study its carved details. He led her into an open office, divided into sections with lines on the floor. One corner was marked "Revenue" with gold lines. Another was marked "Public Works" with green lines. "Schools and Social Services" was marked in red and "Everything Else" was marked with blue.

"The whole parish government operates from this one room?" she marveled.

Zed seemed very pleased with himself as he pointed to the various departments. "Well, I get my own office over there and the sheriff gets his own office on the opposite side. But it works just fine. We don't have much room here and it keeps things simple if we can just holler at each other from across a room instead of callin' and leavin' messages and cursin' the voicemail and gettin' so stirred up you can't remember why you called in the first place. End-of-work was a little while ago, but usually this place is a beehive. Theresa Anastas keeps us all lined up and running without smacking into each other. She runs the Everything Else department. Gigi Grandent—she's a seventy-seven-year-old human and more terrifying than I could ever be—runs Public Works with an iron fist. Mr. Chiron retired as superintendent, but he's good at keepin' the schools running. And Betchel Boone may be a bit of *couillon* but no one can keep the books balanced like he can."

"Boone? As in the family that seems to own all of the businesses in town?" She gestured toward the street.

Zed grinned. "Caught that, did ya? Nice enough folks, the Boones, I suppose. They're used to gettin' their way and get plenty fired up if they don't. We let 'em throw their money around because it makes them happy and keeps the town in clover. And then we mostly get things done when they're not around."

A sharp voice interrupted him, "Not all of us are like that, Zed."

Zed's cheeks went a little pink under his beard, when another man, lean and tall with almost preternaturally sharp cheek bones appeared in the doorway marked, "Sheriff's Department. Check all firearms with the mayor before knocking." The man's light hair was shorn close, which only emphasized his large, amber-colored eyes and sharp features. He was wearing a tan police uniform and a gun belt that seemed to have a lot of "extras," but Jillian wasn't super-familiar with law enforcement gear... And she was staring at his narrow waist, which he had noticed. Awkward.

Zed shook off his embarrassment by flashing that winsome grin again.

"'Course not. Sheriff, you are the exception to all the rules," he said in a condescending, teasing tone. "Dr. Ramsay, this is Sheriff Boone. Sheriff, this is Dr. Jillian Ramsay."

"Sheriff, I'm pleased to meet you." Jillian did not reach out to shake his hand, another etiquette issue. Some species of the supernatural world, like the Irish spriggans, could lose their glamour when touched by humans, so casual physical touch with strangers was taboo. Also, some species, like the rainforest-dwelling *nagual* were extremely prone to colds and therefore a little germaphobic.

The Sheriff said nothing. He simply stared at her with those strange eyes of his, as if he was categorizing her every freckle and flaw.

Zed sighed. "I told you all about her, Boone. Twice. This is the doctor that's gonna be studyin' how well we run things in our little town, so she can help other little towns do the same," Zed said, in a tone that was probably meant to evoke some sort of friendly response.

Instead, the sheriff growled, "Seems to me that those towns should figure that out for themselves."

Jillian scoffed, "Well, that's an interesting approach to interspecies cooperation."

The sheriff crossed his rangy arms over his broad chest. "Never said I planned on any approach."

Zed cleared his throat. "Doc, you got those papers for me to sign? I'll leave you two to your howd'ya do's."

Jillian reached into her enormous canvas shoulder bag, handed him a carefully labeled manila envelope full of reprinted paperwork. Zed opened the sheaf of official documents and beamed at her. "I get to use my official mayor stamp. I love doin' that."

Boone muttered, "To a point that might embarrass any other man."

Ignoring the sheriff, Zed strode into his office. Jillian turned her head toward the sheriff. The hair elastic keeping her thick blond mop off of her neck gave up the fight. It snapped and her hair fell around her face like a slightly damp gold curtain. The sheriff's eyes flashed and not with annoyance at the mayor.

There were actual rays of light shining behind his irises. Which she now realized were longer, and narrower than average, like a cat's. He had to be a shifter of some sort. The mayor also had "double corporeal forms" written all over him, for that matter. But there were far too many varieties to guess just from eye shape or build. From what Jillian understood of shifter etiquette —or any other sort of etiquette, really—it was rude to ask someone, "so what are you?"

So, she would just have to wait.

"Sheriff Boone. Do you have a first name? Is there a reason the mayor doesn't seem to use it?"

The sheriff cleared his throat. "'Course I do. I'm Bael Boone. And the mayor doesn't use it, because he likes to needle my ass at every opportunity."

"I sure do!" Zed called from the next room.

"I'm sorry. Did you say *Bill* Boone?" she asked.

"Bael."

Jillian repeated what she heard, "Bill."

"Bael."

Jillian shook her head. "I don't understand. It's *not* Bill?"

The sheriff was starting to look annoyed, or, at least, more annoyed. "No. Ba-el."

"I could swear that's what I'm saying."

"No, B-A-E-L. Bael."

Jillian would admit that, at this point, she was needling him just a little bit. She had an excellent ear for accents, but very little patience or politeness left in her.

"Sorry about that. I guess it will take me some time to adjust to the accents."

Bael sniffed, "Well, it will take us just as long to get used to yours."

Jillian watched the sheriff's angular face carefully. Clearly, he was amongst the people who were "not all that thrilled" with

Jillian's presence in town. And given the Boone family's apparent stranglehold on the town's economy, that pricked at Jillian's distrust.

No, she was a scientist. She wouldn't let preconceived notions or her discomfort in having someone attempt to stare through her skew her opinions.

"Well, I'm here to stay, Sheriff, at least for a while, so you'll have plenty of opportunity." She smirked at him.

Bael jerked his shoulders. "I just don't see the point in it, is all."

Jillian's brows drew together. "Your town represents one of the few settlements where supernatural creatures from nearly all cultures live and work together in relative peace, and have for generations. The League expects humanity to stumble on 'the secret' of the otherworldly any day now. The Loch Ness monster can't hide from Google maps forever. And when one domino falls, so will another and then another, until everyone knows that it's all real. Werewolves, fairies, shifters, spirits, mermaids, witches, all of their fairy tale nightmares come true. Don't you think it would be better if they had information on how other communities overcame their differences instead of running around in a blind panic and well, act out the whole 'War of the Worlds' phenomenon all over again."

Despite her impassioned speech, Bael was not moved. "I'm just sayin' that no good has ever come from people havin' the answers handed to them."

Zed rushed back out of his office, the papers flapping sloppily as he moved. "All done 'cept for the last one, which has to be signed in front of a witness. Sheriff?"

Bael sighed, "Hold on."

The sheriff very carefully reviewed each page...to the point where Jillian became concerned about his reading comprehension.

Zed seemed endlessly amused by Bael's insolence. "Bael hates it when I boss him around. He's hated it ever since we were kids. But I just remind him that his job description includes "other duties as assigned" tacked right there at the end, with an asterisk, and then he has to do it. Because the asterisk says, "'assigned at the Mayor's discretion.'"

Bael's eyes flashed angry gold again. "Mighty big words from the guy who needed flash cards to remember his swearin' in speech."

Zed's grin should not have been as proud as it was. "I put the 'swear' in 'swearin' in.'"

Jillian cleared her throat. "Sheriff, that's a pretty standard cooperation agreement between the League and the town of Mystic Bayou. Because of your unique population, you are a perfect case study for assimilation tactics. You guarantee me access to any archives or census information I need and attempt to smooth the way for me with the locals. I agree to be as unobtrusive as possible and show you all of my research before I leave town. Mayor Berend was pretty specific about that."

"Maybe where you're from, people give their name without a care, but I want to know what I'm signin'," Bael drawled, placidly flipping through the paperwork.

"He's got this whole thing about not givin' his *true name*," Zed whispered dramatically. "The whole family's that way. Their first names are all nicknames. He refuses to tell me and I'm the closest thing he's got to a best friend!"

"No, you're not." Bael shook his head, blithely reading through the contract.

Zed grinned. "I've been guessin' for years though. I'm pretty sure his true name is somethin' like *Marion*. It's OK, buddy. Marion can be a boys' name, too."

Jillian looked to Bael, who silently shook his head.

It took several more minutes, but Bael finally signed the last page of the contract. A quick motion caught Jillian's eye, and she barely restrained a gasp as Zed sliced his palm open with a wicked sharp claw on his right hand. In a business-like manner, he pressed his mayoral seal onto his palm and then the paper, leaving a livid red crest next to the signature line.

Jillian shook her head. "Oh, that wasn't…necessary."

Zed frowned at her as he signed his name with a plain old Bic pen.

"Now, the local ladies' guild wanted to throw you a proper crawfish boil to welcome you to town," Zed told her.

Jillian gulped, audibly. "That's very generous of them."

Bael rolled his eyes a bit. "Don't get excited. People around here throw a party every time somebody loses a damn tooth."

Zed shot Bael a warning look, the first truly dark expression she'd seen on his face. The predator's threat sent a cold shiver down her spine. If Jillian had those icy eyes glaring at her that way, she might have added soiled pants to her list of hygiene issues. Bael simply jerked his shoulders.

In a pointedly pleasant tone, Zed said, "I thought that might be a little overwhelmin' for you straight out the gate. I figured you'd rather get settled in and get some sleep, get your legs under you, before you have to make your first impressions. We'll schedule your official welcome sometime this week."

"That was very thoughtful of you," she told him. "Thank you."

Zed grinned at her, putting his passive (no-longer-bleeding) hand on her shoulder. "You need anything, you just let me know."

Bael growled ever so slightly. Jillian frowned at him, and turned back to Zed. "Directions to my hotel would be appreciated."

Zed gave her shoulder a friendly squeeze. "Oh, we've got you set up with a real nice place."

"I didn't see a hotel on my way into town. I don't suppose there's a Holiday Inn one street over, that I just didn't see?" she asked.

Bael scoffed and Zed glared at him, then ratcheted up his smile a few degrees before saying, "Like I said, we've got a real nice rental place for you. It's got a lot of…charm."

Jillian found his pause before the word 'charm' to be highly suspicious. "Okay, I guess working out of a house will be more pleasant than working out of a hotel. Can you give me directions?"

Zed was half-way to a nod when he said, "Yes, but I can't help you get there right now. My *maman*'s expecting me at her place to fix her freezer. I keep tellin' her that she's over-whelming the twice-cursed thing, stuffin' two whole deer carcasses in there. But then she glares at me and reminds me winter's always around the corner and we need to think about puttin' on hibernation weight. And then, I shut up because there's nothin' scarier than a Berend woman when she thinks you're not listenin'."

Jillian tilted her head and stared at him. "It's May."

Zed shrugged. "Winter's always just around the corner to *Maman*. But the Sheriff here can lead the way to your place. He's one of your nearest neighbors."

Jillian shook her head. "I don't want to be a bother. If you just give me directions, I'm sure I can find it."

Zed snorted. "Not likely. The roads 'round here twist and turn and only half them have the right signs, because the fair folk think it's funny to switch 'em around. I can only find my place because I've lived here my whole life. But the Sheriff will be happy to give ya the full police escort, won't ya?"

Bael only glared at Zed.

"Other duties as assigned, Bael," Zed reminded him.

Bael exhaled deeply and for a second, Jillian swore she could see smoke rings billowing out of his nostrils. "Follow my car."

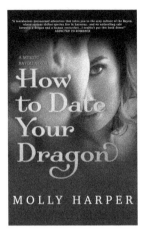

Click here to order How to Date Your Dragon on your retailer of choice!

The Care and Feeding of Stray Vampires

Driving Mr. Dead

Undead Sublet (A story in The Undead in My Bed anthology)

A Witch's Handbook of Kisses and Curses

I'm Dreaming of an Undead Christmas

The Dangers of Dating a Rebound Vampire

The Single Undead Moms Club

Fangs for the Memories

Where the Wild Things Bite

Big Vamp on Campus

Accidental Sire

Peace, Blood and Understanding

Nice Werewolves Don't Bite Vampires

The "Naked Werewolf" Series (paranormal romance)

How to Flirt with a Naked Werewolf

The Art of Seducing a Naked Werewolf

How to Run with a Naked Werewolf

The "Bluegrass" Series (contemporary romance)

My Bluegrass Baby

Rhythm and Bluegrass

Snow Falling on Bluegrass

Standalone Titles

And One Last Thing

Better Homes and Hauntings

ABOUT THE AUTHOR

Molly Harper worked for six years as a reporter and humor columnist for The Paducah Sun. Her reporting duties included covering courts, school board meetings, quilt shows, and once, the arrest of a Florida man who faked his suicide by shark attack and spent the next few months tossing pies at a local pizzeria.

Molly has published over thirty books. She writes women's fiction, paranormal romance, romantic comedies, and young adult fantasy. She lives in Michigan with her husband and children.

Please visit her website for updates, news and freebies!
https://www.mollyharper.com/

Twitter: @mollyharperauth

Facebook: https://www.facebook.com/Molly-Harper-Author-138734162865557/

Printed in the USA
CPSIA information can be obtained
at www.ICGtesting.com
LVHW061547260824
789254LV00006B/186

9 781641 972079